Slashed By You

Chicago Steel
Book 5

Jessica Buss

Dedication

To those who want more for themselves. Reach for your dreams. Make them happen.

Chapter 1

Josh

September 2017

alking into the locker room of my new team, the Chicago Steel, I feel the familiar rush of excitement flood through my veins. The emotion in the air causes me to hold my breath. I am so thrilled to be here, on this team. Leaving Arizona wasn't easy, but it was necessary. I suck a deep breath into my lungs and my chest seizes. At the same time, my baby-blue eyes begin to water. *What the hell? Am I crying?* Wiping at my teary eyes, I realize they're also burning. My nose picks up the pungent odor of bleach that permeates the room. "Guess that's better than sweaty hockey gear." I laugh under my breath. Walking farther into the space, I see all the names of my new teammates, and it makes me smile.

Spinning around, I notice the cubbies are all grouped by position. When my eyes land on mine, I see it's already been filled with my gear. Stepping closer, I run my hand over my new jersey. *I'm a member of the Chicago fucking Steel.* Pride fills my chest. Voices travel down the hallway and my nerves slam into me just like a forward trying to get past me in front of the net. I hadn't realized how nervous I was until this moment. My palms sweat and my shoulders tighten. Lowering myself onto the bench in front of me, I roll my head back and forth, trying to loosen the tension crawling up my neck. The voices get closer, and I force a smile to my lips just as the locker room door swings open, putting me face-to-face with some of my new teammates.

"You're Josh Logan," Ludkov, one of the more well-known defensemen, says as he sizes me up. As a professional athlete playing the same position, I get it. There are rumors he's planning to retire in the next few years. He's probably questioning if I'm here to take his slot.

Standing up, I run my hand through my white-blond hair. I realize I'm desperate to make a good impression on my new team. "Last I checked," I answer with a laugh. He smiles, then steps away. Another few of the guys give me chin lifts or fist bumps as a greeting. As I start dressing, my mind wanders to my career. So far, I've been fortunate to put up decent numbers, building a reputation as a solid defenseman. In researching the Steel prior to my transfer, I studied tape to better understand what I could expect. Earning your spot on a starting line depended on the chemistry and effectiveness you developed with your teammates. I hoped that by identifying my teammates' strengths, I'd better understand whom I'd best play with. It was a risk, and I could be completely wrong, but I'm hopeful my investment will be worthwhile. So far, the player I'm most excited to skate with is Connor Jefferies. His speed and puck handling are unmatched, and his reputation in the league is untarnished. As far as they were concerned, he could do no wrong, and everything he did was impressive. As a center, he made things happen. It didn't matter if they seemed impossible or improbable. From what I'd seen, his overall skills are remarkable, and I can't wait to experience it live.

The build-up to today was excruciating. Coming to a new team was an adjustment, and I expected some growing pains, but I didn't expect to be so tightly wound. Leaving my old team, the Arizona Jaguars, was tough. Mostly, I liked my old team, even if our record was shit.

Sitting down, I consider it all. Arizona was in a rebuilding period. In the last year, they'd been working on team dynamics and chemistry. Before I left, the organization had experienced some shake-ups. Most of us had survived, coming back stronger than ever, but the team lost a major component—the head coach. Management had hired a younger, greener coach who'd yet to prove his worth to replace him. In his first year, Coach Steve had been all over the place. His lack of experience left us confused and without direction.

It's a wonder we managed any wins. It felt like a giant clusterfuck. Basically, it proved to be the perfect time to get out. Even if I'd been willing to give the new coach a chance to get his feet under him, my grandfather's passing was the final push I needed to leave. But leaving was bittersweet.

My knee bounces harder as I try to tamp down those memories, but the fight with my father that came after the funeral always seems to worm its way into my head; his voice incessant, aggressive, and accusing.

When William Issac Logan Sr. died, the need to leave became absolutely necessary. The environment surrounding his death, and his inheritance, had become toxic. From the moment I received a call from my mother that my grandfather had passed, everything decent about my father had vanished. He'd always been entitled, but after reading his father's will, he became angry and demanding. And a narcissistic asshole. Every conversation we had was always the same. He thought he was being cheated. It was exhausting trying to communicate with him. His acidic accusations about how I stole his birthright were non-stop.

"You don't even deserve it. I'm the next in line. It's mine," he said.

One day it was too much. Unable to ignore him, and

tired of our interactions, I finally responded, giving him what he wanted—a fight. Growling, I spit, "I didn't ask for it. If you've got a problem with grandfather's will, talk to him about it. Otherwise, shut the fuck up and leave me alone."

Normally, I'd just grunt and mutter something under my breath that my father wouldn't pay attention to. But finally, I'd had enough. My father wasn't the victim he claimed to be. Grandfather was a smart man. He'd learned that it would be a disservice to Logan Electric customers and its employees if he left my father in charge. True, I knew nothing about running the company, but my grandfather knew I would treat it with the same care he had. I was a born leader, and I cared about people.

After my harsh words to my father, I stormed out of the house and sat on the aging deck swing my parents had had since I was a child. No longer pristinely painted, I ran my fingers along the weathered and peeling wood and thought. What is it about people behaving their absolute worst after a loved one dies? When we should have been supporting each other through the heartache, my father began acting irate and unreasonable. I still didn't know what the will stated. I'd only picked up bits and pieces when my father was ranting. But I knew I needed to find out. Especially if Grandfather intended me to take over. That was an enormous responsibility, and I wasn't sure I was ready for it. Questions flooded my *mind as I considered what running Logan Electric meant.*

A few days later, when I'd cooled off, I visited my parents for a family dinner. However, despite my mother's pleas, my father was in a drunken tirade, spouting off. Through his ramblings, I learned more of what the will included. Apparently, what he was inheriting was not to the liking of William Logan, Jr.

I'd had to sit there and listen while he'd snarled my name several times, and each time I heard it, I cringed. I'd need a lawyer to help me understand all the legal jargon in the will. But one thing I knew for sure was that it had turned my father from a grieving son into an angry dick.

My grandparents were stable members of the community. Grandfather met my grandma, Darla, after starting Logan Electric. At that same time, he also established himself as one of the most respected men in the industry.

Darla was only a few years younger, twenty-four to his twenty-eight. Unlike most women her age, she'd pursued a different path. Instead of marrying young like most of her peers, she'd sought higher education, earning a degree in business. Once she graduated, they married and joined forces, becoming a powerhouse in the field. When they were established and the business was stable, they decided to start a family. And after years of struggle, they finally got pregnant with their miracle baby—my father.

Being the only child, William Jr. assumed he would inherit everything his parents had worked so hard to build. But he, like many children who were raised with money, never showed the desire to take over Logan Electric. And so grandfather made other arrangements. Unbeknownst to me, I'd been selected. Because of that, my father was in a tizzy. Doing everything he could think of to unseat me. But as the lawyers explained, grandfather's will was ironclad, and I would be the face of the company.

Scary as that knowledge was, I was grateful that it included a clause that afforded me some much-needed time. Grandfather stipulated I couldn't take over as CEO until I was thirty-five. So being that I was only twenty-one, I didn't have to make any drastic changes yet. Until I'm of age, I'm off the hook, and a proxy, selected by the board, will serve as the head of Logan Electric.

Sitting in the locker room, staring at the Steel logo at my feet, I question whether I made the right choice. Stepping away from the family drama has left my stomach in knots, instead of the relief I expected. Each piece of information revealed by the attorneys about my grandfather's estate made me sick to my stomach. It was all in limbo, and until the proxy was selected and my father stopped causing a ruckus, it would only get worse. Questions constantly flooded my mind, and the answers eluded me.

To those close to me, my leaving Arizona for Chicago made little sense. But it was a necessary choice for self-preservation. Without it, I wouldn't have a chance at a semi-normal life. As a professional athlete, you're used to the media, but those in Chicago know nothing about how I became a billionaire overnight. And staying in Arizona would have continued to make my life hell. And I hope all the lies, fake stories, and soap opera moments they turned my life into will stay on that side of the country.

I continue dressing in my gear as a few more guys come in. I feel someone approach from behind. Turning, I recognize him immediately. "Grady. How are you?" I say confidently as I extend my hand to him.

Shaking it, he answers, "I'm great, man. It's good to have you on the team, Josh."

Grady Roberts, another impressive defenseman, is a force not just on the ice. Let's just say he has intimidation down. At 6'5" and 250 lbs., he's huge. He greets me with a smile, but every picture I've ever seen of him shows a deep scowl on his face. His bright blue eyes are piercing, giving him a tough edge. If that's not enough, he has a buzz cut that reminds me of an Army Ranger and screams, *mess with me, I dare you.*

Grady has played the majority of his career for the Steel. He's logged six years, half of that as the captain. From what I've heard, he's promised a few more years.

Until then, I'm planning to learn everything I can from him. My goal is to be captain one day, and I hope it'll be with the Steel organization too.

Once Grady moves on, most of my other new teammates come by and introduce themselves. Overall, they seem like a decent group of guys. I already know their skills on the ice, and I'm excited about this fresh start.

The last few weeks of practice and training camp have been grueling, leaving me achy and sore. I should be physically and mentally exhausted. Instead, I feel energized, moody, and more than ready to blow off some steam. Hoots and catcalls fill the air as we enter the club. Our rock-star entrance only drives up the adrenaline coursing through my body. *Did they know we were coming?*

The air is thick, like the club released a pheromone directly through the air conditioner, attracting every available woman nearby. Within moments of entering the VIP section, we're surrounded. I've had my fair share of puck bunny conquests over the years, and I'm getting tired of it. Their games don't have the same thrill they once did. For me, it isn't about the easy score anymore. Now I'm looking for something that requires a bit more effort.

Kicking back with a beer on the black leather

couch, I watch the show before me. Lights dance and music thumps as bodies grind up against each other. Watching our rookies is the best. They are goldfish in a sea of piranhas, and they have no chance of survival. These women are no joke. And it's fucking hilarious. All I need is some popcorn to enjoy this live-action soap opera in front of me.

Looking to my left, I see Ludkov also enjoying the show, and we exchange a smirk. Being new to the team, I don't know my teammates that well. I don't know what I'll see tonight. It's anyone's guess. In Arizona, I knew which of my teammates were faithful, flirty, or filthy. Here, I watch with rapt attention. Sure, I have my assumptions, but I've learned that people don't always do what you expect of them. When I see Abe and Steve, two teammates with wives at home, getting friendly with some ladies, my stomach drops. *Come on, don't be those guys. Respect your wives.*

Not wanting to see their blatant adulterous trysts, I turn back toward the rookies, who I know are single. Even if I didn't know them, our rookies would be easy to spot because their eyes are as big as saucers. Their tongues are practically wagging. And their smiles... *Fuck.* They grow wider the more the women rub up against them. For these guys, they've just figured out this place is the adult version of Chuck E. Cheese. It's like they've never seen a scantily dressed woman willing to do anything your heart desires. The only thing it'll cost you is a little limelight.

Thankful I'm not part of the chaos, I kick my legs out in front of me, making myself more comfortable. Out of the corner of my eye, I see a brunette on a slow approach. She's a looker, for sure. It's hard to miss the royal blue dress she's wearing because it's wrapped tightly around her, showing off her best assets. When she gets to me, she lowers herself down, almost into my lap. *Presumptuous, much?* Not interested, I scoot myself over and she follows, again trying to glue herself to my side like we're a thing. We aren't. I've never seen this woman before. And, yes, I get she is beautiful, but there's something about her that sits wrong with me. I'm all for a confident, independent woman who knows what she wants. But when she crosses into arrogance, I'm totally turned off. To me, that seems more desperate than attractive. It's not all about a woman's looks for me. I want something more.

Again, I try to add some distance between us, but she doesn't take the hint. Instead, she starts touching me. *Really?* Annoyed, I make a huffing sound.

"Are you a grouchy boy? Do you need someone to make you feel all better?" Her syrupy-sweet baby voice makes my skin crawl.

"No," I growl, using my tone as a warning. And, apparently, she isn't as dense as I imagined because she gets up without another word and leaves. Most likely she'll approach another player who's more amenable to her games.

Relaxing back into the weirdly comfortable leather

couch, which you're more likely to see in a low-budget porno than in one's living room, I take a pull off my cold beer. I'm here to unwind, nothing more. On some nights, I'd be in the thick of it. Front and center in the horde of ladies. But tonight, I'm not looking to get sucked off or have a quick fuck. No, tonight I'm here just to be. Take it all in. Learn the scene.

Grady approaches with a beer in hand and joins me. He's taken me under his wing since I joined the team. I've become the captain's protégé. Finally, he breaks the silence with his deep baritone voice. "I'm planning to head back to the hotel. You staying here?" Looking around, I don't see anyone who remotely interests me, so I give him a chin raise to let him know I'm down. We drain the last of our beers before heading out.

Chapter 2

Josh

They went and hired a new coach. *Oh joy!* Management is ecstatic. Me? Not so much. *Been there, done that in Arizona.* Rumor has it he's as surly and bad-tempered as his predecessor, Jim Doogan. *Fucking fantastic.* When I came to the Steel two years ago, I had high expectations regarding the coaching and level of play. It didn't take long to figure out the coaching was total shit. Coach Doogan, was both old and grumpy. In serious need of retirement. The only thing I learned from him in the past two years was that he yells more swear words than plays. If it's true about our new coach, I'm not sure how much more I can take. This next season is going to be tough.

Before he arrives, management holds a team meeting to inform us of all they expect from us. We're told that Tristan Murphy, our barely thirty-year-old coach, has spent the past five years as the head coach for an AHL team in Aurora, Illinois. His team, the Aurora Anacondas, is quite impressive, winning the Calder Cup the previous two years. *Maybe this won't be as bad as I think?*

Definitely confident with their hiring decision, management touts that Tristan had also played in the NHL for the Boston Storm until suffering a career-ending injury. He'd been drafted straight from high school, and during his five years in the NHL, he made impressive marks in the hockey world.

W eeks later, when Coach Tristan's finally introduced to the team, I'm not the only player skeptical of him. Throughout the league, you'll hear rumors about coaches, players, and the drama that surrounds them. And everything I've heard makes me question whether he's what our team needs. The thing I fear the most is his attitude. Gossip says that even on his best days, Coach Tristan is cranky. And after Coach Doogan, I'm not sure how much more I can take. I want a coach who is forward-thinking and knows how to develop the strengths of each player and can use that knowledge to benefit the team.

After he arrives, the first thing I learn is that he isn't to be doubted. He wastes no time shaking up the organization from the coaching and support staff to the players. Granted, he doesn't have the authority to get rid of players or staff, but he came into the program intending to do everything necessary to make us the team to beat. From restructuring plays to focusing on the basics, as a team, we work harder than ever before.

With Grady gone, it's just like I assumed it would be; we are lacking leadership. I step up and try to fill the position by showing up early to practices, meetings, and community events. I work hard and maintain a can-do attitude. My dedication and consistent encouragement don't go unnoticed, and I'm named the captain at the beginning of the season. The title feels incredible, and I'm determined to be the best one yet. Grady taught me a lot, but with Coach Tristan in charge, I plan for our team to become an unstoppable force. Because we spend a lot of time together, I learn Tristan can still be an asshole. But the more we work together, the more I recognize his mood swings. And I've learned when it's best to stay clear.

G oing back to Arizona for the holidays was a mistake and is something I will avoid in the future. I can't even refer to it as home anymore. Home is somewhere warm and inviting, somewhere you feel safe and comforted. Arizona is where my father lives, steeped in endless anger and feelings of betrayal. Two years have come and gone since my grandfather's will changed everything, and my father still can't let it go. Because of his hostility, I see no reason to stay. Which is precisely how I end up agreeing to attend an extravagant New Year's affair.

On New Year's Eve at ten on the dot, Jac, my teammate, calls to let me know the chauffeured car we secured for the evening is parked in my driveway. I live outside the city in a quiet residential neighborhood in Glen Ellyn. Walking through my Scandinavian-inspired farmhouse, I'm ready for a night out. Pocketing my keys and phone, I slip out the Chicago Steel-blue front door and head out for an evening I know I won't forget.

"Hey, Jac," I call out while climbing into the car.

He meets me with a smirk. "Hey, man."

Phillip, our driver for the evening, looks sharp in his three-piece suit as he whisks us through the Chicago suburbs, grabbing teammates for our night on the town.

"Move over!" Troy growls as he climbs into the car, pushing Mikey into the middle seat.

"Rick, is that your leg touching mine?" Mikey seethes.

"Yes, it is. The boys need room to breathe. Stop fucking whining!" Rick barks back.

"Dudes, you're going to have to make it work. We'll be there in a little while. Right, Phillip?" I ask from the comfort of my large heated passenger seat. I grin at my good fortune.

"On the way back, I call—" Rick starts before all the rest of the guys chime in with "shotgun." I just laugh. Tonight, my plans include finding a lady to hook up with. If I'm lucky, I won't be needing a ride home from Phillip. Calling shotgun is the least of my concerns. These assholes can argue all they want.

After stuffing the SUV like a Thanksgiving turkey with six whiny, bulky, hockey players, we're ready for an evening out. When Phillip pulls up to an unfamiliar building, I look over at him, questioning, "Where are we?"

"It's a members-only club called Onyx, sir," Phillip answers.

"Members only," shouts Mikey as he pumps his fist. "I know what that means." Turning around, I see he's wearing an enormous grin.

"Yeah, what?" I ask.

Rick elbows Mikey. "It isn't a sex club like you're hoping, Mikey."

Mikey's eyes go wide. "It isn't?"

Rick laughs and shakes his head. "No, man, it's just uber-exclusive and there's normally a membership fee."

"Then how'd we score an invitation?" Parker questions from the third row. He looks to Jac, who's remained mum so far.

Jac smiles while we all stare at him, waiting for an answer. "Lincoln Luciano invited us. He and a few of his buddies rented out the entire VIP section of the club tonight to throw an epic New Year's party."

Mikey clears his throat. "Luciano, like the crime family?"

Jac lifts his hand in the air, stopping us all from talking. "I'm not sure he's related to them. All I know is he's a very successful businessman who splits his time between Chicago, New York, and Miami. He's filthy rich and likes to party. Oh, and he loves hockey, especially the Steel," Jac answers confidently, not showing any concern about the suspected mafia connection of our party host.

Is this a good idea?

We exit the vehicle and follow Jac toward an unmarked door. *Has he been here before?*

Jac knocks on the door, and it slowly opens. An enormous bodyguard steps out.

"Dude," Rick mutters under his breath.

"Hello, big guy." Mikey snickers. I elbow him in the ribs in case Mr. Big, or that's what I've decided to call him, doesn't find him funny. I'm intimidated by his stature, and that's saying something because I'm far from short. None of our group is.

"Password," the behemoth says.

Jac looks around and whispers, "Party time, excellent." *Really?* He must be correct because Mr. Big smirks and allows us entry. Looking at the building as we enter it, I notice a small black and silver placard. If I hadn't been looking, I would have certainly missed it.

Stepping inside the nondescript club, complete darkness surrounds us.

"Did I go blind? Mom warned that would happen one day," Mikey shouts.

"What are you talking about, Mikey?" Jac grunts from the front of the group.

"My mom said if I jerked off too much, I'd make myself blind," he admits.

I roll my eyes and grumble, "What backwoods bullshit teaching is that? No, you can't go blind from jerking off too much. Let me guess, you spanked it before we picked you up."

Mikey huffs and then answers, "Yeah, I did. Didn't you? I didn't want to blow my load if some hot chick was grinding up on me."

"He has a point," Jac counters. I can imagine we're all nodding our heads, but because of the darkness, I can't see shit. Minutes in and my eyes still haven't adjusted.

Rick snorts, then says, "Your vision is fine. The club blacked out everything. None of us can see."

I hear a deep breath next to me and I assume it's Mikey, feeling relieved.

Navigating is problematic. No one wants to be the asshole running into another teammate or the wall. A loud thumping reverberates around us and I can tell we're getting closer. Passing through another doorway, the club comes into focus. Once my eyes finally adjust to the mood lighting, I see we're in a turn-of-the-century factory building. Looking up, I notice all the exposed pipework. It, too, is painted black.

Jac continues leading us deeper into the club. *He's definitely been here before.* We arrive at a hostess stand at the bottom of a grand staircase. The perky young blond working asks who we are. "The Steel men," Jac answers with a wink. She blushes and flutters her eyelashes before leading us to the VIP section. Jac walks in with a swagger, and instantly, women drape themselves all over him. The shit-eating grin spread across his face tells us all the plans he has for the rest of the evening. The fucker is planning to get lucky. Several times. Well, happy New Year to him. He's ringing it in right.

"Guys. You're here," a husky man in a tailored pinstripe suit shouts, his words slightly slurring. I've never seen him before, but he seems to recognize us. *This must be Lincoln.* How long has he been here partying?

Rick nudges me. "Hey, Cap. Does he sound all right to you?" *Oh good. It isn't just me.*

Unsure, I shrug my shoulders, replying, "I don't know."

With no shame, Mikey walks up to the man I'm still assuming is Lincoln. He looks him dead in the eye, lowers his voice, and asks, "You, Lincoln?" The man grunts, giving confirmation. "Okay. Are you all right, man?"

Lincoln swallows hard, then blinks his eyes, and nods. "Yeah, man. Just doing some pre-partying until you all arrived." He pulls the girls on either side of him closer, adding, "With these hotties." Lincoln then looks around and commands, "Don't let me party alone. Everyone grab a drink and a couple of women; it's time to get the fun started." Mikey turns back toward Rick and me and shrugs. We move to the bar and I order a beer.

I turn away from the bar and scan the club. I don't have a plan for tonight, and truthfully, I don't really need one. Being a well-built professional hockey player has its advantages. The women come to me and all I have to do is pick the one I want. Fortunately for us, they packed this club with women who would kill for a piece of us. That's not arrogance, just facts. I'm going to score tonight.

Glancing around the VIP room, I notice a black couch that looks more artistic than comfortable. As I walk over to it, I let my eyes wander over all the ladies, and a petite blonde catches my attention. It's been a while since I've had any release that hasn't involved my left hand. I will the mystery beauty to look at me. It doesn't take long until her eyes lock with mine, and I give her a nod. When she smiles, my heart picks up its pace. Patting the couch next to me, I'm asking her to join me. Her hand flies to her chest, and my gaze is drawn to her breasts. They're large for her small frame, and they're perky and inviting. *Are they real?* I don't really care. All I'm looking for is a hookup, and that starts with an introduction. Again, I pat the couch, and she rises on her sexy high heels and saunters over to me.

My eyes can't move fast enough as they trace her entire body. She's beautiful and has an hourglass shape that I'd love to run my hands and tongue over for hours. When she finally lowers down next to me, her unique perfume registers. It's both spicy and seductive, not flowery or feminine, like many women. Is she as feisty as her scent suggests? If so, that could prove incredible during sex.

Taking a chance, I set my hand on her knee, then run it slowly up toward her thigh. The soft skin under my touch is heavenly. When I near the short hem of her dress, she sucks in a large gulp of air. *Good.* I'm not the only one affected.

Leaning in, I whisper against her ear, "Hey, beautiful. What's your name?"

This woman who holds all my attention is dressed like sin incarnate in a short, tight, sparkly black dress that accentuates all her assets. Her high, full breasts, tight ass, trim waist, long blond hair, and bright blue eyes captivate me.

"I'm Kayla," she whispers back.

Smiling widely, I say, "Kayla, I'm Josh. It's nice to

meet you. Want to get a drink?" At her nod, I motion to the server standing nearby.

After she orders a lemon drop, she asks, "What do you do, Josh?" Then she flutters her lashes at me

Is she serious? Giving her the benefit of the doubt, I answer, "I play for the Chicago Steel."

Kayla gasps dramatically, making me uneasy. "You're a professional hockey player? I've never been to a game. Do you think maybe you could help me get a ticket?"

Immediately, her request sets me on edge. Over the years, I've met my share of opportunistic people just looking for a handout. *Is that her angle?* Sitting back and watching her while the server delivers her drink, I chastise myself. *You were looking at her like a quick fuck. Can you really judge her for trying to get something out of this meeting too?*

Taking a refreshing swig of my beer, I wonder if I should just move on. But then Kayla says something that makes me reconsider if I've judged her too harshly.

"Wait, Josh. I just realize that sounded bad. Shit. I'm not asking for a free ticket. I can afford one. Being new to Chicago and still learning my way around, I don't know where to go to get one. Do I go to the arena or can I get one online?" Her words are rushed, and it shows she's flustered. It's a bit of a relief.

Reaching out to grab one of her hands, I try to calm her. "No worries, I got you. You can go online to the

Steel website." Relieved, she flashes me a radiant smile. Her perfectly straight white teeth sparkle at me from underneath her expertly painted red lips. *Damn, she's sexy.* Thoughts of the rest of my night crowd my brain and I know I want her starring in it. Just when I'm about to broach that subject, something she said registers. She just moved here. "Where did you move from?" I ask, nervous about her response. *Please don't say Arizona.*

She giggles. "Born and raised in New York."

"What made you move to Chicago?"

Instead of answering me, she deflects with a question of her own. "Have you always lived in Chicago?"

Maybe she isn't interested in getting to know each other past a certain point. That's okay with me. I don't do repeats, so I likely won't see her after tonight.

"I grew up in Arizona and moved to Chicago a few years ago to play for the Steel."

"I love Arizona. It's so warm." She hums, then an uncomfortable silence hovers between us.

Looking toward the dance floor, I nod my head toward it. "Want to dance?" Kayla squeals and gives me a big grin. Jumping to her feet on her sky-high stilettos, she pulls me to mine and I follow her through the VIP section and over to where everyone is dancing. She starts moving, and I spin her, then pull her back to my front. Kayla grinds up against my dick. And it doesn't take long for me to go from half-mast to hard as steel. As soon as Kayla feels it, her dancing becomes even more erotic. Because of her movements, her short dress rises, exposing a lot of her smooth, tanned skin. While dancing, it feels like she's channeling a pole dancer and I'm her own personal pole. It's beyond sexy, watching her twist, gyrate and slide up and down me. With women, I've never looked beyond physical chemistry for a hookup. And tonight is no different. Apparently, what we have is just what it'll take to be explosive together. Maybe if it's good, I'll even consider a repeat. That's if things between us are as hot as I imagine they'll be.

When the song ends, I pull Kayla tight to my groin so there's no misunderstanding my intentions when I lick up her ear and say, "Want to get out of here?"

Her answer is to turn her mouth to me, lick her lips, and moan, "Yes."

Wasting no time, I weave us through all the patrons, through the darkened hallway, and to the club's entrance. Pulling up my Uber app, I order a car. It's nearby, so in the few minutes it takes to arrive, I pull up hotels in the area, booking a room at the first five-star option I see.

A notification pops up on my phone to let me know the Uber has arrived. "Let's go." Taking Kayla's hand, I lead her out to the waiting car. After we get in, I tell the driver where we're headed. Then I sit back and enjoy the short ride with a sexy blond who can't seem to keep her hands off me.

Kayla leans into me, setting her hand on my thigh, extremely close to my cock, and drops her voice. "We aren't going to your house?" She doesn't even try to hide her disappointment, but it's something I never do.

Firmly, I answer, "Kayla, I have hookups. I don't do relationships and I take no one home." She pouts, looking at me, and bats her lashes. *Sweetheart, don't even try.* That won't work on me. Annoyed, I frown at her, hoping she'll take the hint. Kayla loses the pout and I ask, "If you're still interested, I already paid for the room. If not, you can stay there tonight and I'll go home, alone. But I'd rather see where the night takes us. I'm betting from the chemistry we have, tonight will be phenomenal." The Uber arrives before I have her answer. Kayla climbs out and pulls me with her. Guess that's a yes. *Smart girl.*

As soon as the room door closes us in, I'm pushing Kayla toward the wall, desperate for her. Because she's so petite, I lift her up to better access her mouth. She tightly wraps her legs around me and grinds her hot center into my hard cock. *Damn.* She's not holding back. *I like it.* Thrusting my hips into her, I let her know I'm all in and ready.

Releasing her lips, I pull back far enough to see her face. A lust-drunk smile stretches across her face as if she's already come, but I'm pretty sure she hasn't. Her hips are still grinding fervently against my hard-as-steel cock, and it feels fucking amazing. Then I notice her eyes are rolled back in her head. *She has to be close.* Thrusting my hips forward, giving her more pressure, causes her to release another moan. After a few quick rotations, her mouth drops open, forming a perfect O. *That's sexy as fuck.*

Once she comes down from her high, her body slumps against mine. I nudge up her head and she gives me a dreamy stare.

"Hi," Kayla says on a sigh.

"Hi," I answer with a smirk. "How are you?"

Without missing a beat, she licks her lips and confidently answers, "Ready for round two." *It's hot that she knows what she wants.*

Making sure she's still wrapped around my waist, I move over to the king-sized bed. I toe off my shoes before I set her down. Then I strip off my clothes, unashamed and eager for what's next. Then I'm standing before her, buck-ass naked. Kayla kicks off her heels and shimmies out of her dress, leaving her in a scandalous set of barely-there black lace bra and panties.

Crawling up on the bed, she lies back and I hover above her. She giggles. Running her hands over my biceps, she croons, "You must be really strong, Josh."

Leaning down, only inches from her lips, I run my tongue along the seam of hers and mutter, "I am," then I claim a kiss. While kissing, she shimmies out of her undergarments. When I break the kiss to look at her, she's a vision.

Needing more, I dive back in for another taste. Kayla's kisses are mind-numbingly good, leaving me feeling not only winded, but off-kilter. It's like she's cast a spell on me. She pulls me in tight and I settle between her legs, very aware that I'm naked and only inches from her heated center. She kisses me again and while I'm lost in the haze of lust; I feel her nudge her hips forward. It's like she's trying to align us. Confused, I know I haven't put a condom on. I pull back roughly and ask, "What are you doing?"

Upon hearing the accusation in my voice, she makes another pouty face. I push up, backing off of her, and scowl. When we met, I'd gotten a weird vibe off her for asking for that ticket. Now this. Whilst my dick is happy to lead this parade, my mind is shouting at me to be wary of this chick.

"Kayla, I don't have a condom on, and I don't ever fuck without one. So, if you're ready, let me know and I'll wrap up," I growl.

"I'm clean, Josh, and I just had my period last week, so we don't need a condom," she answers in a syrupy, sweet voice that sets off warning bells. No chance in hell I'm going bareback in some random.

"It's a condom or nothing. Your choice," I gruffly explain, not caring either way. At this point, I can either fuck or not. My hand works just fine if she's going to continue pushing me. Nothing is worth this hassle.

Kayla rolls her eyes, grabs her dress, which is still on the bed, pulls a condom out of a hidden pocket, and hands it to me. Not wasting any more time, I rip it open, roll it over my long, hard shaft, and move back over her. There's a nagging in the back of my mind saying *don't do this*. But I tell myself to shut the fuck up. I deserve a good fuck. So, I stay.

Seeing that we're both eager and ready to get on with it, I line myself up and drive home in one thrust, bottoming out completely. "So good," I say on a moan. Giving our bodies a second to adjust, I savor the feel of Kayla's muscles squeezing me tight. Pulling out slowly and thrusting back in harder gains her attention and her blue eyes flick open, focusing on me.

She smiles and rasps, "Harder, Josh." *Don't have to tell me twice.*

Each thrust into her moves her farther up the bed. "Harder," she demands, and I grunt. *She wants it harder?* When I feel her muscles tighten around me, I pull out and flip her over. Tugging her hips up toward me, she sneaks a seductive look over her shoulder. Anchoring my hand around her hip, I forcefully drive back in. With this new angle, I can go even deeper than before, and the feeling is exquisite. Knowing I'm close and that Kayla is too, I reach around and find her clit. With sure, swift flicks, I send her over the edge. When she tightens around me, I give in to my release. Plummeting over the edge, I join her in ecstasy. Collapsing over her, draping my body like a blanket, we ride the high together.

"Damn," I pant as I try to catch my breath.

Once I've calmed down, I climb off her. Entering the bathroom, I take care of the condom and clean myself up. Kayla's cuddled down in the blankets when I return. Seeing me, her eyes light up with hope, and it makes my entire body shudder. Think of it as self-preservation. My body confirms that I need to get out of there, asap. Just knowing her after-sex reaction has spooked me only guarantees how much of a dick I can be. But so far, I've never stayed the night with a woman, and I never plan to. Because of my family's wealth, the inheritance I've received, and what I earn in the NHL, I'll always question others' motives toward me. I don't trust many. Trust is hard, and to this day, I've never been able to give it to any woman except my grandmother. I've never allowed myself to get that close to the opposite sex. No woman has even come close to tempting me to relinquish the tight hold I have on it. That part of my life's locked down, hidden away.

The idea of being used or taken advantage of is something my grandfather always drilled home. He'd tell me, *"Opportunistic people are everywhere, looking for a chink in your armor. Wanting to force their way into your life, no matter the cost."* The thought of that is maddening. It's caused me to question everything and everyone. I've never truly known if people's intentions are honest and trustworthy or fake and deceptive. Having someone only want me for my money or because I'm a professional hockey player is upsetting. Well, mostly. I guess I have used my job for my benefit. Not to sound too egotistical, but by using my name, I can get laid as often as I want.

Reaching down, I grab my clothes off the floor and begin getting dressed. Kayla's hopeful expression falls, but I shrug it off. I told her I don't do relationships. Over the years, I've learned I don't want or need a relationship to be happy. Hockey is my life, and it's all I need.

When the last of my clothes are on, I lean over the bed, kiss Kayla on the cheek, and say, "Thanks, that was fun." She lets out a high-pitched squawk that sends a shiver down my spine, reminding me of nails on a chalkboard. Immediately, her arms fly across her chest, crossing against her still-naked breasts, thrusting them higher. Her pouting is childish and annoying as fuck. Another reason to get out now.

Knowing my staying any longer won't help the situation, I head toward the door.

"You're really leaving?" she squeals like a banshee.

Calmly, I nod and answer, "Yes. A hookup was all this was ever going to be. I thought you understood that."

Again, she pouts, but then her lips turn into a snarl. It's alarming and scary as fuck. I've never had this reaction from a hookup before. Some women look sad, but mostly they're as eager for me to leave as I am to go. Confused by her reaction, I mutter, "I thought you understood."

"Understood," she growls. "I understood I was going to have sex with you, but I didn't understand that you would run from the room afterward like your ass was on fire." She launches a pillow at me with the accuracy of a starting pitcher on a softball team. I'm impressed. But then she opens her mouth and hollers out, "You are a class-A dick, Josh." *Time to go.*

Not wanting to deal with her drama anymore, I reply with, "Yep, I guess I am." Shutting the door and walking away is the smartest move I'll ever make. Her raging tantrum carries through the thick door and into the hallway. Hopefully, she doesn't do too much damage since the room is on my credit card. It's not like I can't afford to pay for any repairs, but I'd rather not. I don't need her or an opportunistic hotel employee starting rumors about me. I walk away calmly. My father doesn't need any ammunition against me. But until then, I'll do my best to fly under the radar, avoiding conflict and unnecessary drama.

Chapter 3

Josh

A month and a half later, when the team is back in Chi-Town for an upcoming series against Florida, I get a surprise. As I walk out of the arena after our Thursday morning practice, I notice a scuffle in the parking lot. It draws my attention, and I see it involves a petite woman and our security guard, Stan. It's not uncommon for fans to make drop-in appearances following our practice. But usually, the security guards don't have to worry about them getting out of control.

Just as I'm about to unlock my Tesla, I hear my name. Spinning around, I lock eyes with the girl I hooked up with on New Year's Eve. She made a lasting impression. In fact, I haven't been out since. Something about the way she reacted that night made me a bit gun-shy for future hookups. Attracting a crazy puck bunny was not my intention, and considering what I'm looking at, I hope I haven't.

Wanting to avoid making a scene for the rest of my teammates to hoot and holler about, I jog over to where Stan stands with the scorned woman. A scowling face with wide eyes stares at me, giving me chills. Her loud voice is disjointed and her movements are fidgety. It's not normal. She alternates between stomping and pacing. Basically, she looks crazed and ready to maim. *Shit!* What was her name again? Slowing my steps, I search the recesses of my brain. I know it starts with a K. I'm sure of that. Kim, Katie, Krista, Kaylie... Kayla. Her name is Kayla.

"Kayla. Hi," I say on approach, and Stan's head whips around as if a demon spirit possesses him. Mortified, I avoid eye contact with him.

Frowning, her eyes in thin slits, her response is snarly. "You do remember."

Slightly scared, I gape at her. There she stands, apparently a force to be reckoned with. Petite, like I remember, huddled in a long winter coat with a bright scarf tied around her neck. Her cheeks are rosy, her nose is pink, and her eyes look wet, which I assume is from the harsh wind Chicago's known for. Taking in the rest of her appearance, I shudder. Kayla's arms are folded firmly across her chest. My mom does the same thing. It is her *you know what you did* stance. To be honest, it's as fucking terrifying on Kayla as it is on

Mom. Even though I don't know her well—or at all—I'm still nervous.

Stan steps back to let us have a conversation. Like a good guard, he remains close enough that he can intervene if necessary. Scratching my head, wondering why she is here, I draw a blank. "Kayla, it's been a while since I saw you last. Why are you here?" Instantly, she scoffs at me, as if she's displeased with me and my question. Then she looks around, taking in all the people still milling around the arena. I look too. It's mostly players and some reporters waiting to get a plug for the upcoming games.

Kayla steps closer, and in my peripheral view, I see Stan shift his stance too. Always at the ready. He knows how to spot a threat, and something about Kayla has set him off. His body remains rigid, which is uncommon for him. Normally, he's pretty relaxed and at ease. But today, right now, he stands there, deathly quiet, wearing an intimidating scowl across his face. It doesn't even seem to faze Kayla and her mission to get me alone.

"We need to talk," she informs me, and it takes everything in me not to reply with a snarky remark. *There's no way in hell she's telling me what to do.*

Making sure I don't roll my eyes, I ask, "Oh yeah? What do we need to talk about?"

Without missing a beat, she raises her voice, getting the attention of the nearby reporters, and says, "I'm pregnant and it's yours." My mind scrambles to find meaning in what she's just said. I go to say something, but it's as if the air has been sucked from my lungs. Panic sets in and everything feels sluggish. *I can't get a breath.*

Stuttering, I whisper. "W-what? H-how? We used a condom and only hooked up once. How the fuck could this have happened?" *You had sex, moron. Pregnancy is still a risk.* Shut up, brain.

Standing there, frozen in place, my mouth hangs open. I feel Stan step next to me. "Josh, maybe you want to take this conversation somewhere more private. Prying eyes are on you." Nodding my understanding, I look at Kayla and ask, "Can we get out of here and go somewhere to talk about this?"

Before answering, Kayla looks around. Would she rather have our conversation witnessed by the swarm of reporters whose job it is to report the highlights and shortcomings of the team? Yes, I bet she would. "Please," I beg.

When she finally responds, it's with an off-putting smile that makes me nervous. "I guess that's fine. Where should we go? Your place?" Flashbacks to the night we hooked up remind me she wanted to go back to my place then too. My house is my sanctuary. I don't invite strangers over. Is that what she is? A stranger? I guess I can't call her that anymore, not if she's having my baby. I'll have to let her in eventually. It's not like we'd meet up at local gas stations to do child handoffs.

Nervous, I step closer, so I'm not overheard. "How about Cool Beans? It's a few blocks over."

Her lips twitch like she is about to snarl, but at the last second, she pulls them into a tight smile and nods. Obviously, she isn't happy about my suggestion, but I'm not ready to let just anyone into my space. *She's not just anyone anymore. She's the mother of your unborn child.*

Stepping back, I look at Stan, who wears a pained look on his face. Giving him a chin lift, he understands what I'm trying to do. He'd been close enough to hear our entire conversation. Stan lifts the barrier and lets Kayla through.

We walk to Cool Beans and, after ordering our drinks, we make our way to a somewhat private table at the back of the near-empty coffee shop. My stomach churns as we settle into our wooden chairs, and my mind races with questions.

Since she's going to be the mother of my baby, I should try to get to know her, right? It's a good place to start. "So. What is it you do for work?"

Sitting up tall, she takes off her coat, revealing an extremely low-cut top. Her boobs are practically falling out of it. Leaning forward, she flashes me her excessive cleavage and tells me she's an influencer on social media. *What the fuck does that mean?* "That sounds interesting. Do you like it?"

Primping her hair before she flips it over her shoulder, she answers, "I really do. It's the best job."

Still confused, I ask for more. "What's your favorite part about it?" Maybe her answer will help me understand what she actually does.

Giggling, she bats her eyes at me. "Josh, you're silly." *Okay.* Remaining quiet, I wait for her to explain.

"I get paid to post online about all my favorite beauty products and clothing lines," she gushes, obviously impressed with herself.

Dumbfounded by her explanation, my words leave my mouth before my brain is onboard. "Really? That's what you do for a living? You tell other people what to wear?"

A horrified gasp fills the air between us. Knowing I've said something wrong, I panic. *Did the temperature just shoot up in here?* It's suddenly stifling. I'm sitting in the depths of hell, roasting alive. "Josh... Kayla," the barista calls out. *Lucky break for me.*

"Uh, I'll grab them," I offer before jumping up from my chair like it's on fire. Glance back over my shoulder, Kayla looks murderous. Her arms are crossed firmly against her heaving chest. And her scowl? It could frighten even the scariest monster. As I head toward the pickup counter, I feel her heated stare burn into the back of me. Taking extra time to add cream and sugar to my coffee, I hope she'll calm down before I turn back. *Holy shit.* Apparently, she's got a hair trigger. She's scary. I guess in the future, I'll have to remember to tread carefully. Blowing out a couple of breaths, I head back to our table. Hopefully, the second half of our conversation goes better than the first.

Nervously smiling on my approach, I see Kayla isn't as agitated, and I try to relax my body. Sitting down, I apologize. "I'm sorry about my comments. They weren't meant to sound critical or judgmental. I just really didn't understand what your job entailed. Honestly, I didn't think before I spoke." Rolling my shoulders, I try my best to prepare myself for her reaction. I'm not sure what to expect. The moment passes and the silence between us is uncomfortable.

"It's okay, Josh. I understand. I'm sorry I was so reactive. It must be all the pregnancy hormones. Or it's because there are plenty of trolls on social media who do their best at making fun of and being critical of influencers like me." She stares at me, looking like she's holding back a few tears. Reaching over, I pat her hand. She grasps at it, forcing our fingers to interweave. Holding her hand makes me incredibly uncomfortable, but I'm afraid of her reaction if I pull away. With all she's said, doubt still clouds my mind.

"Kayla, I don't mean to be an asshole, but are you one hundred percent sure the baby is mine?"

Kayla draws back, ripping her hand from mine, and snarls, "What are you saying, Josh? Are you calling me a slut? Do you think I got pregnant on purpose?" Before I can even jump in with damage control, she hits me again. "What kind of man doesn't want to take care of his responsibilities?" My head drops. "I'm sorry.

I wasn't trying to upset you or imply anything. You just caught me off guard and I'm still reeling. And to answer your question, I won't ignore my responsibilities."

As the afternoon winds down, our conversation becomes more pleasant, less antagonistic. But we've yet to make a concrete plan for the future. I didn't expect we'd hammer all the details out now, but I'd like to have a tentative idea since the baby is due in October. Needing to know and at her mercy, I ask, "How do you see this playing out, Kayla?"

Looking up at me through her lashes, she launches into a well-prepared, and obviously practiced, speech. "I know we aren't dating, but our hookup left us with a permanent reminder. I'm Catholic, so I don't believe in abortion. I think we should do this together."

Shocked and overwhelmed, I wring my hands. "Together?" My question comes out as a squeak, like I've sucked too much helium. *I wish I could float away like a balloon right now.* This isn't really happening to me, right?

"Yes, together," Kayla repeats in a firm, confident tone. There's no doubt she's serious. Then she gives me a cheery smile and giggles. I'm confused. *What part of this is exciting or funny? Why isn't Kayla freaking out and sobbing?* This is fucking terrifying.

Needing clarification, I pointedly question, "What does 'together' mean to you?"

Kayla bats her lashes at me, and I'm instantly filled

with dread. *She's going to say it.* My stomach sours and I feel like I'm about to be sick. I swipe my hand against my clammy forehead and it covers my fingers in perspiration. *Where's the bathroom? I'm going to throw up. Please. Please. Please don't say what I think you're going to.*

Assured, Kayla answers, "We really need to be together for our child. But I don't mean just co-parenting. We both need to be a hundred percent invested. Don't you think?"

Her answer puts me on the defensive, and I growl my response. "I'll be there a hundred percent for my kid, but I want to know what your idea of 'together' means."

She squeezes the hand I've forgotten she's holding again. *How did I not notice?* My mind's preoccupied, scattered. I can't seem to focus on anything.

"Josh... Josh... Josh." Someone keeps saying my name, but it sounds far away. Another squeeze of my hand brings me back. Looking up, Kayla is staring at me, annoyed. Forcing a smile that probably resembles a grimace, I encourage her to answer. "Well, I think we need to date and eventually move in together. Do you know how difficult it would be shuffling a baby between two houses all the time?"

Date? Move in together? *Excuse me?* All of her answers irritate me. I don't want any of what she's suggesting. A mass the size of Alaska lodges in my throat. I'm so stunned, I realize I've forced my body to remain glued to my chair, even though I desperately want to flee. From her. From this. Maybe this is a nightmare and I just need to wake up to make it stop. I pinch myself. "Ouch," I mutter. *Not a dream.*

"Live together?" I rasp. Kayla smiles widely and nods excitedly. What the fuck am I going to do? What if we move in together and we end up hating each other? I've never lived with anyone by choice, and now I'm looking at playing house? With someone I don't even know? This has to be a joke. Or a prank, perhaps. Where's the hidden camera? Who's punking me?

Looking around in a panic, I'm hopeful I'll spot a camera, or Rocco, the team's jokester, hiding behind a chair, poised and ready to jump out and tell me it's all a joke. But there is nothing. My mind is frantic with paralyzing thoughts. Sweat trickles down my back, and my heart thuds in my chest.

"Josh, are you okay? You don't look so good," Kayla prods while looking at me with concern. Nodding and swallowing hard, I answer in a strained voice, "Yeah, I'm fine. It's just a lot to take in and wrap my mind around."

"It'll be fun. You'll see," she exclaims. *Fun?* This isn't a sleepover with your best friend.

Clearing my throat, I murmur, "Kayla, this situation we find ourselves in is tricky. I'll always support you and the baby, but I need to take things slow. I'm not prepared to jump into living with someone I barely know. We should spend some time together first and see where it goes. Hell, you might decide I'm a grumpy asshole and the last person you want to live with. Or we might decide that we like each other and our next step is living together. Who knows? But because of the baby, I want to be there for you as much as I can financially, emotionally, and physically. Being a hockey player who's gone a lot of the year, I hope you'll include me in the entire pregnancy. I want to be a part of both of your lives. And in a few months, we can reevaluate our situation. Does that sound okay?"

Kayla's sad eyes beg me to reconsider, but I'm steadfast in my decision. I want to date my baby momma before we take anything further. Exchanging numbers and confirming an upcoming first date, we walk back to the arena to a nearly empty parking lot. Pointing out my car, I say, "I'm there. Where are you parked?"

Kayla pulls her long winter jacket tighter to her slender waist, and I can't help but fixate on her stomach. *My child.* The realization of that hits me harder than I thought, and I pull her into a hug, suddenly desiring to be close. But despite the closeness I'm craving, I recognize it isn't sexual. Instead, it feels protective. *Makes sense as she's carrying my child.*

Instead of hugging back, Kayla clings to me like a capuchin monkey. I don't understand why. Is she afraid I'll leave and not return? Overwhelmed for the hundredth time today, I realize I need space. I tip her head up to me and ask, "Where are you parked? Let me walk you to your car."

"Okay," she softly replies before she nuzzles her head back into my chest. Pulling back, her head falls away from me and I see another pout on her lips. Internalizing my frustration, I question what I've gotten myself involved in. It's not like when we hooked up I ever considered a future with Kayla. But it looks like that's now what I have to do. At least for the next eighteen years, we'll be connected.

Chapter 4

Josh

The next weeks fly by. When I'm in town, Kayla and I try to squeeze in as many dates as possible. Since it's still new, we're doing our best to navigate this situation. I'll often grab dinner, and she'll come over to my place. We've both tried to get to know each other better, but we don't have much in common. She keeps insisting that we just need to start officially dating, but I'm not sure how that will make everything less awkward or uncomfortable between us.

To make matters worse, Kayla keeps pushing me. According to her, we'll be fine if we go public. I disagree fully. At this point, I'm not ready to advertise our relationship or whatever the hell we are. I fully understand that once she's showing, we'll have to make some sort of statement, but until then, I'm keeping quiet. And she wants to start having sex. Sex is harder for me to explain. For now, it's off the table. It may sound heartless, but in my mind, Kayla was a one and done. And now she's carrying my child. My brain is taking a while to catch up. To be honest, it's a complete mindfuck.

While I'm traveling, which is most of the time, we have limited communication. It's nothing like I imagined a couple being. And I guess that's what we are—a couple—but I don't really know. It's the start of March and in a few weeks, I'm scheduled to be home for two weeks in a row. Kayla has scheduled her first OB appointment during that time because she'll be twelve weeks along.

A few weeks after she told me she was pregnant, I downloaded some "what to expect" books and I'm reading them in my downtime. I haven't told anyone what's going on because I can't seem to say it out loud. My teammates are some of my closest friends and I'm not ready to share this with them. The books have been my own only support and, so far, they've been very informative. As far as I understand, at this upcoming appointment, the doctor will confirm her pregnancy and the official due date. Kayla will have blood drawn and possibly undergo an ultrasound. Seeing my little baby will be surreal, and the confirmation I need.

Because of our situation, I'm struggling to fully accept the truth of it. Blame my past and that I don't trust easily or the fact I used a condom, but without seeing a positive pregnancy test, I can't fully accept it.

As I've gotten to know Kayla better, I really want to believe her, and this appointment will solidify everything for me.

The weeks before her appointment drug by painfully slow. Finally, the day arrived and I was filled with anxiety. Tomorrow was the big day. When the team bus finally pulls into the arena parking lot, I'm exhausted after our late flight from Ottawa. We'd been there to play a series against the Wolves, and we split it, as I expected. Before the team can disembark, I give a quick pep talk.

"Make it fast, Cap, please," Conner begs. He has a new baby at home, and from what I've heard, they're a lot of work. Despite that, every day at practice, he remains positive, regardless of his exhaustion. He's working his ass off to be everything for everybody. I need to remember that. He's an outstanding role model.

Giving him a head nod, I keep my message short and simple. "Guys, I'm really proud of the hockey we played this weekend. Let's not lose the momentum we're building. Tomorrow morning, we have skate, tapes, and weights. See you at ten. Thank you, Coach, for those extra hours. Use them wisely." Each of my teammates gives me a fist bump before exiting the bus.

When I pull up to my house half an hour later, I'm

surprised to see Kayla's Navigator. We have plans for tomorrow night, but I wasn't expecting to see her today. Worry stabs at my heart. I jump out of my Tesla and jog over to the driver's side of her SUV. She isn't in there. My worry morphs into panic. Should I call the cops? Where is she? Looking up at my deck, I wonder if she's on the steps. No, but I notice something else. My lights are on. *That's weird.* Moving swiftly to my front door, I check it. It's locked and doesn't look like it's been tampered with. Since I was out of town, I know I didn't leave the lights on. The only other person who has a key is Maria, my housecleaner, and she's more conscientious than that. *Who's in my house?*

Unlocking the front door, I quietly tiptoe inside, hoping I don't find a thief or worse. My heart is pounding in my chest and sweat runs down my back. I shout, "I've called the cops and they're on their way. You need to show yourself and leave immediately if you want to avoid any trouble." Why the fuck, when I had the interior designer in here, did I not have my house wired with a security system?

"Josh, is that you?" a sleepy voice calls out from upstairs. Trying to place the voice, I know it's familiar. Then I remember. Kayla's car is in the driveway. It has to be her. But how did she get inside? I never gave her a key.

"Kayla?" I ask, confusion thick in my words.

Stepping down the stairs is Kayla, and she's dressed only in one of my Steel shirts, showcasing her naked thighs. Usually, I'd be happy to see her, but now I'm concerned. "Kayla, why are you here? In my house? Dressed in just my shirt?"

Saying nothing, Kayla continues her descent down the stairs like it's completely normal for her to be here. As she nears, I notice her eyes are puffy and red. *Has she been crying? And what happened to her hair?* Her normally well-styled blond hair looks like it's being used for a bird's nest. Every day her appearance is striking. However, today it's not in a good way. Fear churns through my body. *What is going on?* I've never seen Kayla looking like this. She's all about designer clothes, perfect hair, and flawless makeup. She'd never let anyone see her like this. Not if she could help it.

As she steps closer, I realize she's crying, and I pull her into my arms. "What's wrong, Kayla? Please, tell me." Minutes go by and the only answer I get is her sniffling and whimpering against my chest. Leaning down, I pick her up and carry her over to my sofa, grabbing a box of tissues off the counter. Kayla's petite body clings to me. *Something is definitely wrong.* "Here you go," I softly say while offering her a few tissues. Once she's cleaned herself up a bit, she pushes off my chest, looking distraught.

"Kayla, what's wrong?" I ask again, worry plaguing my voice.

She doesn't answer, just sniffles. This is my first time being in a situation like this, and I feel completely helpless. Instead of saying anything, I just hug her tightly and rest my head on hers. *Is this about the baby?* Just the thought of that makes me shudder. Lifting my head draws her attention, and she looks up at me with sad blue eyes. Grasping my words, I force down my fears and rasp, "Does this have anything to do with the baby? Is the b-baby... Is the baby okay?"

Just thinking about anything happening to my baby shreds me. Waiting for an answer, my heart thumps wildly in my chest and tears well in my eyes. *Am I being silly getting this upset?* It's hard for me to understand my feelings. *How do I care about something I haven't even met?* But I do. I'd barely gotten used to the idea of having a child, and now I'm unsure what is happening. In hardly any time at all, I've accepted I'm going to be a father. Even though it wasn't something I planned for, I'm stoked. Kayla doesn't know, but I'm planning to ask her to move in with me. I've done some major thinking, and Kayla's right. Our baby needs one hundred percent of us, and the only way we can do this is together.

"Kayla, sweetheart, please tell me what's wrong. You're killing me."

Burying her head into my chest, she gives a muffled response. Only catching part of it, I recognize, the word *mad*. Why would I be mad?

Nudging her head up, I calmly tell her, "The only way I'll be mad at you is if you lied to me or cheated on me." Her blue eyes, luminous and sad, flicker to mine and away again, some flash of emotion held within that

I don't get time to decipher. "Did you do either of those things?" I ask while staring at her, my eyes assessing for anything suspicious. I hate that I do this, but I've always struggled to trust. Nothing registers as Kayla shakes her head no. "So, what am I going to be mad about? When we talked yesterday, you seemed fine. What's happened since then?"

Kayla tries to bury her head again, but I don't let her. Using her chin, I lift her face to mine, forcing her to tell me.

"Josh, I'm so sorry," she apologizes with a whimper.

"Sorry for what, sweetheart?"

"The baby... I lost the baby. Yesterday, I was bleeding and cramping after our call, and I miscarried. I am so sorry." Her words register, but it's like they bounce off of me, refusing to be absorbed. My body is completely numb and I can't figure out why. I wipe my hands across my face and they come back wet, which confuses me more.

Kayla shifts in my lap and retrieves a tissue. My vision blurs and my chest feels like it's being constricted. My stomach rolls and quakes, and I'm certain that at any moment I'm going to throw up. But this isn't just about me. Looking at Kayla, I want to make sure she's all right. "What can I do for you?" I step closer as my mind whirls with ways I can take care of her. "Can I run you a bath? Do anything for you? Are you in any pain?" Pain lances through my chest every time I think about the baby. Chastising myself, I remember that I'm not the only one grieving. My eyes connect with Kayla's and I consider all that she might be feeling. "Do you need me to just hold you?" A smile appears on her lips, but it's all wrong. It's too happy. Why isn't she as torn up about this as I am?

For me, the grief I'm experiencing courses through my body, affecting every part of me. There is no way to recover from this kind of loss. An unspoken dream, hope, and wish. Forever a masterpiece that will remain unfinished or titled. So why does she look unbothered? Maybe she's in shock?

I wrap my arms around her tightly. As I hold her, my mind remembers the last few weeks. I'd finally come to terms with the fact I was going to be a father. I was at peace with it. But now that's gone. I feel a tear fall down my cheek. That doesn't matter anymore, because it will never be. Our baby is no more. Losing my grandfather didn't hurt as badly as this does. It feels like my heart's been ripped from my chest, and all I feel is empty.

I don't know how long I sit there—minutes, hours, days? Time has stopped, and I know when it finally resumes, it'll never be the same. I'll forever be missing a part of myself. One that can never be replaced.

Warm hands on my forearm let me know that I'm still alive even though my baby isn't. All along, I hoped it would be a boy so I could teach him to skate and play hockey. I would be the father mine never was. But that dream's been shattered, just like my heart.

"Josh, I have a glass of water for you." The voice registers as Kayla's, but the lack of emotion in it has me confused. *Didn't she just tell me she miscarried our baby yesterday? Wasn't I just holding her on my lap as she cried? Why does she now seem unaffected?*

Forcing myself to focus, I take in her appearance. She's still dressed in only my shirt. I notice it looks like there is nothing underneath. *That's odd.*

"Let's get you upstairs and into a shower. The hot water will make you feel better." Not following her rationale, but understanding I can't stay on my couch forever. Feeling numb, I push to my feet. Heading upstairs, when I get to my room, I stop. It looks different. Unlike days ago, multicolored throw pillows and a fancy new comforter I've never seen before now cover my king-sized bed. Kayla leads me into the en suite bath, and while she steps into the large shower to turn it on, I notice it too looks different. It's more decorative than when I left. The towels all match and the countertop is covered with lotions and candles. *WTF?*

"Let's get you ready for a shower, big guy." Kayla steps to me and grabs the hem of my shirt. Like a toddler, I lift my arms, and while she stands on her tiptoes, she tugs it off. Next go my pants. She kneels down in front of me and slowly unzips my jeans, sliding them down my legs. Stepping clear, I kick them aside. Still on her knees, she looks up at me through her lashes, and everything goes sideways. *Am I seeing this?* Kayla licks her lips and stares at my covered cock. My stomach rolls when she begins to eagerly pull down my boxer briefs. *What am I missing?* To her dismay, my very flaccid cock hangs there, looking as weepy as I feel. On normal days, a desirable woman on her knees before me would get me hard in seconds, but today is not a normal day. As far as I'm concerned, my cock might as well be broken. That bastard got me into this mess. The dumb fuck broke my heart.

Grunting something unintelligible, I trudge past Kayla and step into the hot, steamy shower spray. Standing there with my head submerged under the water, my heart aches.

It startles me when I feel something brush against my back. Small hands wrap around my biceps and before I know it, Kayla's large, fake breasts push into my back and her hip bones rub up against my ass. *What is she doing?*

Whipping around quickly catches her off guard, but she recovers quickly by throwing her arms around my neck and pulling our bodies tightly together. *This feels wrong.* We had sex once, the night she got pregnant, and that was the last time I'd been with anyone. Even though I'm grief stricken and probably in need of some talk therapy, my cock decides that he's suddenly all in for some touch therapy. *Huh. What do you know... maybe he isn't broken.* Kayla notices and reaches for me, stroking my growing length from root to tip. She has a firm hold and is stroking at the perfect pace. My mind is no longer thinking about anything other than my now rock-hard cock.

"Do you need some relief, Josh? I know you're hurting. So am I. And the only thing that will make my pain go away is to be close to you. Because you... you are the only one who understands what I've lost." Nodding my agreement, I go willingly when she pulls me into a kiss. Unlike the gentleness I expected, Kayla's aggressive, nipping and biting at my lower lip. Pulling back to get a breath, she moans and says, "Take away my pain, Josh. Help me feel something good." Her words trigger something deep within me, channeling not only my intense pain but my anger at what I've lost. Harnessing that, I push Kayla up against the wall. When she hits it, her eyes go wide in surprise. Then she smiles, but it isn't sweet. Shaking my head, I push it away. Bending down, I pick her up and wrap her legs around my waist. Pressing her back to the wall, I don't give her any warning before I push into her, thrusting hard until I bottom out.

When I register the pressure of her muscles squeezing me, I savor the shocked gasps falling from her lips. Removing myself almost completely earns me a whimper, and I reward it by shoving back in with more force. Setting a feverish pace, I push her legs up and change the depth of my thrust. The telltale signs of an orgasm begin within her body and I keep my rapid pace. *Holy fuck.* She screams as her muscles squeeze my cock hard and then she slumps against the wall.

Knowing she's had hers, I decide it's my turn to feel good. Sliding a hand between us, I flick her clit and she releases another moan that sets my blood on fire. After she succumbs to another orgasm, I feel a familiar tug in my balls. Immediately, I pull out and set her down. I stroke my cock until my orgasm tears through me, spills from my body, and washes down the drain.

Kayla stands against the shower wall with a look of regret on her face. *Oh shit.* I tug my hands through my damp hair. We shouldn't have done that. Would having sex after a miscarriage hurt her? And I wasn't even wearing a fucking condom. What if I'd gotten her pregnant again? Worry swims in my head. *Is that even possible?* It doesn't matter. I wasn't thinking.

Reaching out, I ask, "Are you okay? I know I was pretty rough. Did I hurt you?"

Kayla shakes her head, hiding her emotions from me. Not buying that she's okay, I try another approach. "Listen, Kayla, I'm sorry for what just happened. I should have been more thoughtful about what your body's going through. Do you need to go to the hospital and get checked out?" *Did I make things worse?* Dread fills my gut. I don't know anything about miscarriages and how fast a woman's body recovered.

I turn off the water, waiting for her answer. She looks distant. It's like she's here, but not really. She finally answers me by shaking her head no. Believing she knows her body best, I decide to give her space. Drying off, I head back out to my bedroom and over to my walk-in closet, and stop. Hanging up, neatly orga-nized, is an excessive amount of what I can only assume is Kayla's clothing. *What the fuck?* The more I look around my closet, the madder I get. And then I remember everything Kayla's been through in the last day, and my anger goes from a red-hot boil to a simmer. *There's probably an explanation.* It looks like she just moved in without even any discussion. That knowl-edge sits like a boulder in my stomach. *When did all this happen?* After the news I just received about the baby, the grief shower fuck, and coming off the two-weekend series, I'm exhausted and all I want is my bed. Snagging a pair of clean boxer briefs from my dresser, I pull them up before I move to what I think is still my bed. Shoving pillows out of the way, I pull back the comforter and find that not even my sheets are the same. *WTF?* I growl but decide I'll deal with it tomorrow.

But I don't. And before I know it, months have passed, and the season is over. I barely survived it. Ever since Kayla told me she lost the baby, things have been off for me. That horrible night, I became numb, and it hasn't changed. The best way to describe it is I've been on auto-pilot, doing the minimum just to survive. Drifting through life. And Kayla has remained in the periphery. She's resumed her life. She's going out, shopping. shooting lives for social media, laughing, and having fun. Apparently, at some point, she moved into my house. And we still haven't had any conversation about it. She loves the WAG status it comes with, and I realize having her around makes it less lonely. But it's all for show. We sleep in the same bed, but ever since that night—ever since I grief fucked her and then refused to come inside her—I haven't touched her. And don't think she hasn't tried.

Kayla has become my platonic buffer for everything. My plus one, making social obligations less awkward. She loves to get dressed up and go to events the Steel's either hosting or involved with. Over the past months, my teammates have started calling Kayla a WAG, which she loves. She is the closest thing I have to a girlfriend—without the benefit of sex. But only she and I know that. If my teammates found out, it would guarantee unwanted conversations. So, I let the lie continue and allow people to make all the assumptions they want. She could sleep with the entire team and I wouldn't care. As long as she leaves me alone.

<hr>

Carrying our lie becomes too easy, and now, after two years, we are pros at it. I notice that some of my teammates don't really like Kayla, but she's not that big of a problem. *Really?* Yes, she's opinionated and high maintenance, but if you let her have her way, she's not too terrible. At least, that's what I do to keep the peace in my life. There is no shame in my game. We aren't serious, or at least I'm not. Yes, she lives with me, but I'm gone most of the year and it's nice to come home to a clean house.

I can hardly believe it's been two years since we lost the baby and she moved in with me. Thankfully, most of the time we've gotten along fine. I know Kayla is more than capable of drama, so I do my best to avoid it. I've had one too many conversations with her about what people say about her on social media to know she's kind of scary. And I don't want that directed at me.

During our time together, we've had a couple of tense moments between us. Every time, it's how she disregarded my privacy to post something on social media about me. I have always been a private guy, and I prefer to stay off everyone's radar, but it seems sometimes Kayla can't help herself. That or she doesn't care that it bothers me. One too many times, one of my teammates shows up to practice ranting about something Kayla has said about the team or the guys individually. And at the beginning of our relationship, the guys assumed she got her opinions from me. Since then, I've had to do some major back-peddling and explaining that's not the case, just to maintain my relationships.

Over the past two years, that we've been "together," the Steel won the Stanley Cup once and playoffs for this year are already underway. And just like always, Kayla is in the family box, cheering us on and going live for all her followers. It's because of this, she causes the most trouble with my friends. If she's not infringing on people's space and trying to get the perfect picture, then she isn't happy. She acts like she's better than everyone else. At least that's what Samantha tells Lucas, and he tells me. It would cause too much drama to break up, so I just ignore her and tell everyone to do the same. I know it's the chicken-shit way of dealing with it, but I don't have the energy to end things right now. *Maybe in the off-season?*

The other issue that always causes controversy for us is what she says about us as a couple. She likes to talk up the relationship, pretending it's something it isn't. We both know she's full of shit. I don't make any of the romantic gestures she gives me credit for, and I certainly don't call her pet names like K-bear. Yes, she's at big events, always my plus one, always dressed perfectly as we walk the red carpet. For only those evenings, I allow her to hang on my arm and appear like we couldn't be happier. But it's all a farce. She knows that's the price for staying with me and having me covering the bills of her lavish lifestyle.

A few months before the playoffs, and needing a break from life, I mention taking a vacation. I mean for it to be a trip by myself, but Kayla takes the idea and runs with it. Not only does she invite herself on it, but she books us an expensive vacation in the Bahamas. *I know I'm in deep, but I don't know how to get out.* Not having time to think about it, I focus all my energy on the Cup. It must work, because we win, for the second year in a row.

Chapter 5

Josh

It's summer, and you know what that means. Steel parties. Samantha and Lucas started the trend last year by having a Fourth of July party. And whether or not they like it, their house has become party central for our team during the offseason. These get-togethers are always fun and stress free. After much nagging, I agree to take Kayla with me, but make her promise not to stream the entire thing.

We arrive fashionably late, because I have Kayla with me and I want to avoid any unnecessary drama. Lucas answers the door, smiling. "Hey, Cap. Glad you could make it." Then he turns to Kayla. His smile fades and his voice dulls. "Kayla." Unaware he's dissed her, she shoves her way inside.

"This way?" she asks while heading toward the backyard. I don't know why she's asking. She's been here before. Maybe it's for the live stream she's apparently already begun. Grinding my teeth in frustration, I say, "Sorry."

Once she's out of earshot, Lucas looks at me pointedly and asks, "Is she for real?"

I shrug. "Parts of her, I think." Lucas laughs.

"Definitely not her boobs or lips." Smirking, I keep my mouth shut, but he nailed it. "Everyone's out back," he informs me while heading into the kitchen.

I nod to him and then head outside. As soon as I'm past the door, I hear hoots and hollers coming from the pool. Ace and Rocco are splashing in there with Jasmine, Rocco's best friend, and Nicole, a friend of Jasmine's. Both ladies are welcome additions to the Steel family. They fit in perfectly, unlike Kayla. Glancing around the backyard, I wonder where she is. It's easy to spot her. She's relaxing on a lounge chair in her string bikini, talking to her followers. Over the last two years, she's built quite a following, and anytime she can go live, she does. Hence her poolside behavior. The guys notice, and Rocco splashes hard next to her, getting her wet,

"What are you doing?" she squeals, sounding like a possessed witch.

Rocco smirks. "Kayla, in case you didn't know, you're at a pool party, wearing a bikini, and sitting on a deck chair in the splash zone. What did you think was going to happen?"

Flipping her phone around, she focuses on Rocco,

and in a shrill tone, she complains, "You got me wet and ruined my live stream."

Unbothered, Rocco just shrugs, grunts, and swims away. Meanwhile, Kayla scrunches her nose up, fumes, and stares daggers at his retreating back. *Shit. This isn't going to be good.* Needing a distraction, I notice that the food table is all setup. Stepping up beside her, I hand Kayla my towel. "Here you go."

"Thank you, Josh." As she dries off what little of her actually got wet, she mutters under her breath, "Some people are just so rude." Pretending I didn't hear her and her not-so-subtle dig, I point to the food and ask. "Are you hungry?"

"I am. My power smoothie didn't last as long as I planned." Standing up, she rubs her body against mine. *Really? That wasn't obvious.* "Let's take a selfie." Her suggestion comes with puppy dog eyes. Even though I want to say no because I know it'll end up on social media, I don't, choosing to avoid the tantrum she'd likely have.

"Fine," I grumble. She pulls me closer and lines up the picture. One picture turns into a mini photo shoot where I'm basically her accessory. *Can't wait to see how this turns out.*

By the time we finally make it over to the food, most everyone has grabbed a plate and moved over to the tables and chairs. We find two empty chairs at the end of the table and settle in. Of course, while loading up our plates, Kayla mentioned several times that everything contained either gluten or wasn't vegan. It took everything within me not to come back with a snarky response. But I just held my tongue, trying to keep my eye rolling to when I was facing away from her. Looking over now, she loaded her plate with fruit and salad. *Looks like she found something.* While sitting and enjoying my food, I ask myself, *is she always this tiring to be around?* Before I can answer myself, Christian shouts out, "Sam, this food is incredible!"

"Thanks. I got a catering recommendation from one of our client's wives and it turned out great," she replies.

Biting into my dessert, the flavors explode on my tongue. *Amazing.* "Where'd you get these cupcakes? They are the best thing I've ever eaten," I say after devouring one.

"Even better than Kayla?" Rocco whispers loudly to Ace.

Ace sputters and Jasmine slaps Rocco's arm. Then she gives him a half-hearted glare and she whispers, "Don't mess with crazy."

Samantha clears her throat. "Kenzie, the owner and baker of CakeStop, is incredible, and everything she makes is heavenly. She's already been hired to cater the desserts for the Steel Your Heart gala next year. You should all definitely stop by her shop and give her your business."

"Thanks, Samantha. I think I'll do that," I say.

"Joshie, baby, you could have her make my birthday cake this year," Kayla suggests in a baby voice.

Scratching my head, I respond, "Maybe? I didn't think you really ate cake, Kayla." *Didn't she just make a fuss about gluten?*

"Or cock," Ace whispers loudly, then bows his head to control his hysterical laughter. *Shit. How does he know?* Looking at him, I see his shoulders bobbing up and down. *Is the shithead laughing so hard he's wheezing?* Looking at the rest of my teammates, I notice they're also trying to maintain their composure. They are all well aware of Kayla's dramatic tendencies, but I thought I'd kept our lack of intimacy locked down. Right now, I wonder if I slipped up and confessed it to one of my teammates and don't remember. Why else would he be saying these things? Just then, Ace looks up with a smirk, and recognition hits. He's trying to set Kayla off. They're poking the bear. *Why?* Letting out a deep breath, I pray she keeps her cool.

Apparently, Kayla doesn't appreciate their teasing, because she slams her napkin down and screeches something unrecognizable. My balls cower in fear as she stomps away from the table.

"Thanks a lot, asshole," I mutter before heading after her.

On the way, Mika grabs my arm and asks, "Why do you put up with her drama?"

All I can do is shrug my shoulders, answering, "It's complicated, man."

In moments, I find her pacing in the side yard, still screeching. I do my best to calm her down, but it's no use.

"Kayla, do you want to stay or go?"

She scowls at me, making my decision to stay that much easier. "I'm staying, but I can order an Uber for you if you're leaving."

"You're staying here? After the way they treated me?" Her accusations are fully loaded, ready to destroy.

"I am. It's a team function, and they were just teasing. You can't take them seriously," I explain.

Kayla pouts in silence the entire time until the Uber arrives ten minutes later. Then, without another word, she gets in and is gone. *Shit.* "The fallout from this is going to be fun," I grumble to myself as I make my way back into the backyard. My friends and teammates are sitting around the table, quietly watching me.

Rocco breaks the tension when he asks, "Ace, how much do we owe you for the show?"

Nervous laughter travels around the table as I shake my head and grumble, "You're all assholes."

"Are you staying or leaving?" Lucas asks.

Grabbing my abandoned beer, I drain it before answering, "Definitely staying."

The next few hours breeze by with no drama, only

fun. Coach Tristan eventually shows up and makes a brief appearance.

When I get home, I'm not sure what to expect. "Kayla," I call while approaching our bedroom. Looking in, I see she's asleep, and I know I dodged a bullet.

Trying to be as quiet as a church mouse, I get ready for bed and slip under the covers undetected. The next morning when I wake up, Kayla is already up. Staying out of her way, I avoid her for most of the day. Later in the afternoon, as I'm watching the Cubs game, she strolls in, looking happier than I've seen her in weeks. *What is happening?*

"Hi. What are your plans for dinner?" she asks.

"I was going to throw a steak on the grill. Anything you want?" I offer, even though I know her answer will be no.

She smiles. "That's sweet of you to offer. But I think I'm going to make a salad."

Seeing that she's in a good mood, my body relaxes. "Great. We can talk about what we want to do while we're in the Bahamas."

"I already booked a fishing and snorkeling trip for us." Another smile and she adds, "I hope that's okay."

Giving her a genuine smile, I reply, "Thank you. I can't wait."

The trip to the Bahamas was just what I needed. While there, I relaxed and shook off the stress I'd been under the past few years.

Returning to Chicago, I jump back into training with renewed vigor, and before I know it, the new season is only days away. Heading into my sixth year with the Steel, I know I need to rebuild and repair some relationships I ignored the previous season because I was a mess. Losing the baby had destroyed me, and for the rest of the season, I'd just gone through the motions. As the captain, I know I need to do better. Thankfully, the guys and Coach Tristan haven't lost their faith in me, despite my shortcomings. Truth is, my heart's shattered. Instead of sharing that, I kept it all to myself.

During some downtime in the Bahamas while Kayla was off streaming whatever she deemed important, I worked through my feelings. Although I'm still sad about losing the baby, I understand it wasn't the right time or with the right person for me to start a family. After finally saying goodbye to that painful chapter of my life, I'm ready to move forward and live the life I want. I know I have changes to make. I also know some would be harder than others.

November arrives, hitting hard and I'm already exhausted. After our third away series, I'm ready to be home. Management moves up our flight from Dallas, and I arrive home four hours before I expected. It's still nighttime, but eight was better than midnight, especially when Coach ordered a scrimmage for the next morning at seven. A few lights are on, and I wonder if Kayla is home.

"Kayla, are you home?" I call out as I enter from the garage. Lights and music are coming from the back deck, so she might be in the hot tub. When I'm gone, she has girlfriends over to keep her company. Just as I'm about to open the patio door and say hello, I hear my name through an open kitchen window. Curious, I move closer to hear what's being said.

"Kayla, you are so lucky. This house is gorgeous," a woman I don't recognize gushes.

I see Kayla beaming. "Well, he *is* my boyfriend. Where else would I live? He wants me all the time."

I scoff to myself. Her explanation is complete bullshit. One, she isn't really my girlfriend. I actually don't know what I'd label us. *Roommates, maybe? But then why do you sleep in the same bed?* I don't fucking know. Maybe she's become like a weird safety blanket for me. And what is she talking about? I want her? *No.* The last time we were *together* was almost three years ago when we grief fucked after she lost the baby. Shivers run down my spine. Just the thought of our baby tears me up inside. Feeling guilty for eavesdropping, I'm about to step away when Kayla's friend says something that stops me dead in my tracks and turns my blood cold.

"Who are you kidding? This is me you're talking

to, and I know you've only slept together twice. The only reason you're here is because of your fake pregnancy story. Josh is a good guy and you're using him. If he were interested in you, you'd be having sex all the time, not just when you're scheming."

Did she just say fake pregnancy? My stomach drops and it feels like I can't breathe. Clutching the kitchen counter, I bend over and suck in a few deep breaths.

There was no baby, no pregnancy, no miscarriage. Shock morphs into anger. I ball my fists at my side, my body shaking with rage. *She's been using me. How could she?*

Needing an explanation, I move to the patio door and slide it open.

"Ladies," I say as calmly as I can as I move near the hot tub. Kayla has a smile plastered to her face, and I force myself not to glare. Her friend, whom I now see clearly, I recognize as Ally, her best friend from New York. *She must be visiting. Such a shame I can't make her visit more enjoyable.*

"Josh, what are you doing home already?" Kayla asks, sounding worried.

It's impossible not to notice Ally is extremely tense. Her back is ramrod straight, and she isn't making eye contact. "Hey, Ally. Are you visiting long?" Looking around, I see that they have wine glasses and snacks on a table to the side of the hot tub. "Am I interrupting anything?"

Kayla sits up taller, showcasing her cleavage, and

bats her eyes at me. "Just girl talk." I try my best to ignore her and not roll my eyes.

"If that's all it is, you won't mind if I join you. I'm sore from the game, and a good soak sounds great." I look at Ally, and she's frozen, while Kayla continues her charade. Walking back into the kitchen, I stop when I'm out of sight, and I listen.

"Do you think he heard us?" Ally questions nervously.

Kayla scoffs. "There is no way Josh is on to me. He was one hundred percent convinced I was pregnant and had a terrible miscarriage. And before long, he'll see we are meant to be and make things official between us. We've been together for so long. How could he not believe we're perfect for each other?"

Ally answers, "You better hope so, because if he ever finds out what you've done, it won't be pretty."

"He'll never find out. No one besides us knows, so unless you tell him..."

Let's just see about that. I grind my teeth together as I head for the stairs. I'm going to change into my shorts and then catch Kayla in her lies. Before the evening ends, she'll be out of my life for good.

Stepping back onto the patio, I hide all emotions. "Need anything before I get in," I offer them while still dry. Kayla and Ally both shake their heads. "Great." I set my towel on a deck chair I've moved nearby and then make my way up the steps. Kayla's hungry eyes roam over my bare abdomen. The feel of her eyes on my skin crawl and I feel queasy.

Lowering myself in front of a jet, I let it massage my weary muscles. Tipping my head back to rest on the ledge, I close my eyes. "That feels so good." I groan. I feel Kayla move next to me, brushing her fake boobs on my arm. *Really?*

"Do you know what else feels good?" she whispers in my ear. Shivers rocket through my body and I feel bile climb up my throat.

"Winning the Stanley Cup," I offer sarcastically.

"Josh," she whines.

When she places her hand on my bicep, I hold back a snarl. Reaching up, I pluck it off and drop it into the water. "We aren't doing that again," I warn her in a stern voice.

"Why not? We're so good together. Don't you want me?"

I open my eyes and look at her point blank. "Do you really want to have this conversation in front of Ally?"

She flips her hair and looks over her shoulder at her best friend to gauge her reaction. Apparently, she doesn't get one and shrugs her shoulders. I glance around her and notice Ally looks incredibly uncomfortable, as if she's trying to disappear.

"Okay, Kayla. You want this conversation, you got it. No, I don't want you. Twice was more than enough."

Shocked, Kayla puts her hand on her surgically enhanced chest and gasps. "What? Why?"

Shaking my head, I mutter, "You asked." Then I make sure I'm making eye contact. "We have only ever been a hookup, nothing more. And then I find out you lied."

Both ladies' eyes go wide, and they share a panicked look.

"Lied… about what?" she squeaks.

"From what I've heard… so, so many things."

Before she can even defend against my claim, I launch into what I know before the truth rips me to shreds. "There never was a baby, was there?" I'm not really looking for a response. I already heard the truth. She just doesn't know it. I just don't know the why. Panic registers across her face. Climbing out of the hot tub, because I can't stand to be close to her, I snarl, "Since there was never a pregnancy, your miscarriage was also fake and just a continuation of your original lie. Correct?"

Ally gasps and Kayla sputters. "Josh. L-let me explain." Her whining just makes me angrier. *How the fuck is she going to explain this?* Glaring at her, I say nothing, wanting to see how she'll try to dig her way out. But she doesn't say anything, because she can't. She is a lying, conniving bitch, and I want her out of my life. *Now.*

Kayla tries to climb from the hot tub to reach me, but I step away and growl, "Don't come near me. You have five minutes to get yourself out of my house. I never want to see or hear from you again. You can make arrangements with my personal assistant to get the rest of your things."

"But, Josh, we're perfect together. You can't kick me out. I have nowhere to go. I love you. Can't you see that?" she whines, only making me angrier.

I whip around to face her. "Love me? Is this how you treat someone you love? Lucky me. Guess what? I don't love you. I loathe you. If you aren't gone in four minutes, I will call the cops and have you removed. With force if necessary."

Ally steps up behind Kayla. "Let's go, Kayla. It's time."

Kayla drops to her knees and sobs uncontrollably. I roll my eyes and go back into my house, unaffected by her dramatics. Even in the distance, I hear Ally's warning. "I told you that you were going to get caught. It serves you right. Now, get up. You're making a scene and acting ridiculous."

Before the five minutes are up, I hear Ally dragging Kayla through the house and out the front door. A minute later, she returns and grabs her bag from the entryway and Kayla's purse. She makes eye contact with me and mutters, "Sorry, Josh. That was a shitty thing she did to you." When she leaves, I go to my fridge, grab a beer, and sit on my couch, stunned by the last half hour of my life.

What do I do now?

Chapter 6

Kenzie

Having your own bakery is a lot of work. Late nights, early mornings, burns, a sore back, and aching muscles are all part of it. But I love it. It's been my dream as far back as I can remember, and I'm determined to make it successful. Having my bakery allows me to try new recipes and experiment at making them better. The best thing about it is making people smile when they taste what you've poured your heart and soul into.

Last year, when I met Stephanie, she mentioned the idea of my getting involved in Steel Your Heart. It's a gala sponsored by the non-profit she works for, Embrace You, and the Chicago Steel. All proceeds raised go to help those fighting breast cancer. When she first pitched me the idea of supplying all the desserts for the event, I scoffed at her, thinking she was silly. My bakery is small, and even though I'm proud of what I make, I was hesitant about committing to such an enormous event. *What if I failed?*

For months following our initial meeting, she'd stop by the bakery and talk me through all my fears. Once I was comfortable with the expectations, our business arrangement turned into a friendship. Before I knew it, she was helping me plan the menu. Stephanie is the big sister I never had, but always wanted.

About two weeks before the gala, Stephanie comes into the bakery, flustered. "Kenzie, we have to talk. I forgot to tell you something about the gala." My heart thumps in my chest and my stomach sinks. *What is she going to say?* Worry fills my mind. Is she going to tell me we need another two hundred desserts? Did she forget to tell me I was supposed to avoid an allergy like almonds? Concern seeps into every corner of my body, and my breathing speeds up, making me feel light-headed. I settle my hands on the countertop next to the display case I'm emptying. Each night, I bring any leftovers to the homeless shelter a few streets over. It's never anything huge, but they seem to appreciate it.

Stephanie stands in front of me, chewing on her bottom lip, making me even more anxious.

"Spit it out," I beg. She wrings her hands together before she speaks. *The suspense is killing me.*

After clearing her throat, she dives right in. "Kenzie, you know this is a gala, right?" I nod. "I know you figured you'd be behind the scenes all night, hiding out in the kitchen. But we actually need you out front so we can introduce you to everyone there. You'll need to dress up like everyone else attending."

I gasp. I don't have the money for a fancy dress. What am I going to do?

Panic grips me tightly. Stephanie must see the worry on my face and reaches for my hand. "Don't worry. We're the same size, and I know I have something you can borrow."

"Are you sure?" I tentatively ask, hoping she doesn't recant her offer.

Smiling widely, she says, "Yes, you can totally borrow something."

Relieved, I go back to boxing up the leftovers. "Thank you." I'm not above asking for help when I need it, especially when I know I'm in over my head. And I'm just that with this gala.

I feel like Cinderella when I enter the Museum of Art History in the bubble gum pink dress I borrowed from Stephanie. The shimmery material of the form-fitting dress I'm wrapped in reminds me of the majestic sunrise pictures I saw in *National Geographic* as a kid. Depending on how the light hits it, I sparkle. I'm wearing my blond hair down and my makeup is simple because I use all my creativity on my cakes.

They decorated the museum with silver, pink, and

snow white. Right away, I know that the Steel Your Heart gala is the fanciest thing I have ever been to. The round tables are covered in pressed white tablecloths and housed in the center of each is a dazzling pink bouquet. Silver-tipped white china dishes are at each place setting. Blush pink crystal glassware joins it. Everything from the chair covers to the rest of the table swag is in various shades of pink, matching the centerpiece.

Checking the dessert table, I see everything from the pink champagne truffles, death by chocolate cupcakes, fruit tarts, and sea salt chocolate chunk cookies made the transport from my shop this afternoon. In total, I have over ten different desserts that will hopefully satisfy everyone's sweet tooth.

When Stephanie was planning this event, she insisted that I be the one supplying all the desserts for the evening. Honestly, this entire experience has been so humbling. *A literal dream come true.* Stephanie informed me I needed to bring business cards for Cake-Stop so I could hand them out when people raved about the desserts. I'm doubtful anybody will want one, but I still packed them. Standing behind the table, I feel nervous and out of my element. I'm a shy baker offering myself up to some of the richest and most influential people in Chicago. *I have nothing to worry about, right?*

"Kenzie, come here," Stephanie whispers at me from the other side of my display. Scurrying over, my gaze falls upon a very handsome, very familiar man. "Tristan," I gush.

"Hey, Kenzie, you look fantastic." I blush at the compliment, despite knowing it's as platonic as a brother gives his sister. I've seen the way Tristan looks at Stephanie. And it isn't one-sided. I know from conversations with her they had a difficult past, but she still cares deeply for him.

Looking around the room, my breath catches when I see all the people filtering in. Tristan nudges me and asks, "Are you ready for this?" When I look at him, his face morphs from a carefree smile to concern. "Hey, you got this. You have nothing to worry about. I think Steph and I have tasted everything you bake and can attest that you are a certifiable baking genius."

Again, I'm flattered, but he isn't kidding about one part. I had him and Stephanie try everything I was making for tonight. I wanted to make sure everyone would like it. "Thanks, Tristan. So, this event is co-hosted by Embrace You and the Steel? Will the entire team be here? I don't think I've ever met a professional athlete before. I've heard they're big eaters. Will they eat all my desserts... or save some for everyone else?" *Stop rambling.*

He laughs. "Your desserts are safe."

"Why? Aren't they good enough?"

Giving me a stern look, he says, "Kenzie, they are delicious, but most of the players are on special diets where desserts or sugar are limited. Most of them will avoid the temptation, even though I've raved about you for months and they had your cupcakes at Samantha and Lucas's party." He leans in closer and whispers, "In fact, Josh, our captain, had several there, and he is the strictest eater I know."

"Oh. Wow. I guess that's a great compliment," I say with a smile.

Offering one in return, he tells me again, "You got this. Now, I have to go say hello to a bunch of people, but I'll see you later. Let me know if any of my players are problematic."

Sucking in a breath, I whisper, "Will they be? I'm not sure I can take on a professional hockey player."

Laughing, Tristan wraps me in a side hug. "They won't be any trouble, I promise. Now, go show everyone what an amazing baker you are."

"Thanks, Tristan. See you later." Stepping back to the table, I make sure everything looks perfect before I stand and wait.

About an hour into the evening, after dinner plates have been cleared, Stephanie makes an announcement about the desserts and CakeStop, and my heart goes berserk in my chest. My body sweats and my hands grow clammy. *You got this. I think.* Anxiety washes over me, and I question how I will respond if someone asks about any of my desserts or the bakery. "Suck it up, Kenzie," I chastise myself. Then, out of the corner of my eye, I see the most beautiful man I've ever seen. He's tall, over six feet, and the way he fills out his tux has me salivating. He's expertly styled his white-blond hair. I can't see the color of his eyes from where I'm at, but they are full of emotion. He fiddles with his cuff-links and bow tie, and it's obvious he's more comfortable in casual clothes. I understand that completely. At one point, the man next to him leans in and says something, and the most melodic laugh carries across the room. And the smile that covers his gorgeous lips is one that makes my heart skip a beat. I could stare at him all night. From his perfect cheekbones to his rugged chin, I have never seen such perfection on a human face.

Swallowing hard, I try to avert my stare from him, but no matter what, I always find myself drawn back. *Shit.* He's heading my way. Looking over, I see Stephanie at the next table, telling people about the desserts, me, and my bakery. *This is really happening.* Controlling the urge to break into a happy dance, I look at the ceiling and quietly cheer, "Yes!"

Chapter 7

Josh

Following dinner, I feel my eyes getting heavy. I need to wake up. Just shifting my weight has me groaning. I had a brutal leg day today, and right now, they are screaming. As I'm stuck at this event, the only thing I can do to ease my discomfort is to get up and move around. Really, I need to get home and spend some TLC on my muscles with my Theragun after an ice bath.

Joining some of my teammates, I notice Coach glaring at someone across the room. I follow his eyes and see a man talking to a familiar woman. It's Stephanie, Coach's friend. *Wink, wink.* Then I notice the absolutely stunning woman standing next to her at the dessert table. Wrapped in a shimmery gown, she glows like she has a halo above her head. Her smile takes my breath away and the twinkle in her eyes makes me smile.

Desperate to know about her, I ask, "That's Stephanie, but who's the goddess next to her?" Lucas and Mika snicker, and I glare at them.

Coach breaks his focus and answers, "That's Kenzie, she's the baker who made all the desserts for tonight."

My mouth falls open, and I stutter, "S-she's the one who made the cupcakes for the Fourth of July?" They were absolutely sinful. I think I ate four of them. My eyes trace over all the desserts displayed. "And she made all the desserts for tonight?" I pat my stomach. "You know how I love my sweets. I think I'll go introduce myself and grab a business card if she has one." Lucas and Mika snicker again, and I whip my head to them. "You know, in case I have a dessert emergency."

Mika groans while Lucas mutters, "pathetic," under his breath.

"Go for it," Coach answers distractedly, and I feel my heart pound in my chest. *I have to meet her.* Heading that way, I see Stephanie step away to another table. *Guess she can't introduce us.* Sweat breaks out under my tux. As I get closer, I'm dumbstruck by how breathtaking she is. Wrapped in a pink dress that hugs every one of her decadent curves, I'm transfixed. I lick my lips. *She looks like a gift, one I'd like to unwrap.* I haven't responded like this to a woman. Ever. *What is it about her?*

Out of the corner of my eye, I see my teammates

moving closer. *What are they doing?* Probably spying on me. Looking back, I mutter, "Assholes."

As I approach the table, I give her my best smile, the one that's charmed many women in the past. "Hi," I say, purposefully dropping my voice.

"Hi," she shyly answers.

"Did I hear right? You made all these desserts?" I ask, blown away by the variety in front of me.

"I did. Can I get you something?" she offers.

"What's your favorite?" I ask, hoping she'll keep talking.

I watch as her ocean-blue eyes look over all the desserts. When she's done, she replies, "My favorite isn't here."

Looking again at the table, I wonder how that's possible. "There are so many options here. What's missing?"

"A plain old chocolate chip cookie," she replies with a laugh. There's no denying it. This goddess intrigues me in so many ways.

I laugh. "Those are the best, especially when they're still warm and gooey."

She nods her agreement, but then her eyes flick to all the desserts in front of her. "Is there anything you'd like to try?"

Pointing to a cupcake that reminds me of the ones I demolished at Lucas's, I say, "That cupcake looks amazing. What flavor is it?"

An electric smile appears across her face. "It's death by chocolate, and it's the number one seller at my bakery."

The name confirms it's the same, and I know it'll be divine. "You don't say? Then I have to try it."

As she hands me the delicious-looking cupcake, our hands brush. It's the briefest of touches. A whisper of skin on skin, my callused fingertips sparking off her smooth, alabaster hand, but it's a spark that flickers and ignites, shooting up my arm. The surprise and pleasant tingle of it causes me to almost drop the cupcake. *Did she feel that, or am I imagining things?* I look at her for confirmation, but nothing registers in her expression. Meanwhile, my body is on fire. All neurons are firing and craving more of her touch. I haven't had nearly enough. My heart races in my chest, making me feel lightheaded. My mouth feels dry and I'm suddenly parched. *Calm down, Josh.* Taking a drink of water, I swallow past the nerves wreaking havoc in my body. The woman I know only as Kenzie the baker stares at me, waiting for me to take my first bite. A panicked look stretches across her face, and I wonder why.

"Are you going to try it?" she asks, a tinge of nervousness in her voice.

I nod and bite into the cupcake, then groan. "That. Is. Amazing." The decadent flavor explodes in my mouth, and right now, I couldn't be happier. *Really?* Okay, maybe if this delicious creature in front of me was letting me lick this rich and creamy icing off her nipples, I would definitely be happier. But, since we haven't even been introduced, I'm going to settle for second best. This cupcake is named appropriately because it may be the death of me or the cause of serious blue balls—those little fuckers I've been sporting since I spotted her.

Lost in my thoughts of her, I barely hear her say, "thank you." I just smile.

"Well, now that I've tasted your incredible baking, and it changed my life, I feel like I need to introduce myself." I offer her my hand and say, "I'm Josh Logan, the captain of the Chicago Steel. And you are?"

Upon hearing my name, a frown covers her face, and she steps back. *What is going on?* I usually don't have that sort of reaction from women. Then she says, "I'm Kenzie. Can I get you anything else, Josh?" Is she dismissing me? Her tone is emotionless, and it's clear she's uncomfortable. I can't wrap my head around what just happened. I feel like I have whiplash. I guess it's best to answer her and leave. Apparently, whatever I felt between us, I imagined. *But why do I feel so drawn to her?* Everything was going fine until she heard my name. *Weird.* I don't understand. I'm a pretty good guy, but her reaction makes me question what she thinks she knows about me.

Not wanting to leave, but feeling unwelcome, I say, "No, thanks. But that cupcake was amazing." I step back. "It was good to meet you, Kenzie." Grabbing one of her business cards, I add, "I'll definitely be stopping by." Then I give her a smile and a wink before returning to my teammates, a.k.a. the spectators of my fumbled attempt at flirting.

"What just happened?" Mika asks when I rejoin the group.

Not wanting to feed into their antics, I answer, "What do you mean? I just met the woman of my dreams."

Lucas laughs. "Yeah, and she wants nothing to do with you. Good luck with that, buddy."

I scowl at him. "What are you talking about? We had chemistry."

Mika joins the fun, rolling his eyes. "No wonder he was with Kayla for so long. If he thinks that was chemistry, he's destined to be a stalker or only date psychos." *They don't know about Kayla and what really went down during those years we were together.* I'm not ready to tell anyone the truth of all that happened. So, I shove the last bite of the delicious cupcake in my mouth, effectively silencing myself. Frowning, I replay the conversation Kenzie and I had. Then it hits me.

Clearing my voice so they'll all listen, I say, "Maybe she doesn't date athletes?"

Lucas laughs again. "Who would pass up a chance to date a professional hockey player?"

All the guys shrug and go back to their conversations, but I'm left wondering if that's what it is.

Looking back at Kenzie, I can't deny the attraction I feel to her. Finding out why she pulled away is something I have to know. I just hope it isn't too painful. *Maybe she knows about Kayla?* How would she, though? We've been over for months. Because social media changes so rapidly, I figure I'm no longer appearing on anything Kayla's posted recently, but I honestly don't know. I'm still so angry with her. I've avoided her or anything having to do with her after I kicked her out. Stepping away from the boys, I pull out my phone and pull up TikTok. I have social media accounts, but my assistant monitors them for me. And she hasn't mentioned anything.

Only moments after loading her page, my face appears. I see that I'm the object of dozens of her posts over the last few months. Slipping my AirPods into my ear, I select the first video. My heart drops and my gut churns as she tears me apart. Everything's choreographed to music and special effects. *What has she done?* Her words register deep and then I realize she's describing herself during our relationship. *Relationship.* I hate that word; it tastes like pungent ash on my tongue. Yes, I guess we were in a relationship for years, but it was never romantic. Looking back, I would have done so many things differently, but fears paralyzed me.

At first, we were having a baby, and the tremendous responsibility that was, weighed on me. Then she lost the baby, and I was fearful of how to handle her and her emotions, let alone deal with my own. By the time I'd addressed mine, so much time had passed and I didn't know what to do. I'd just given up. I felt destined for the life I was stuck living.

Had Kenzie seen this? Opening Instagram and Facebook, I find similar messages. Apparently, Kayla used all her platforms to smear my name and reputation through the mud. And now it's affecting my life. I have to stop her. But how? Freedom of speech is a real thing. You could do or say pretty much anything you wanted to across social media. And for the most part, it's tolerated, shared, and liked by millions of people you don't know. People who aren't privy to the truth, just the *version* being spread. I don't want to get into a legal battle with her. She'd already stolen years from me.

Angered, I pocket my phone, knowing I can't do anything about it tonight. Tomorrow, I'll call my assistant and see about getting some good press out about me. We're going to change the narrative being shared. We just have to be careful about how we do it. I don't want to lower myself to Kayla's level, but I'm going to make it known I'm not any of those things she's calling me.

It's tough not to wonder what Kenzie's reaction to me would have been if she hadn't seen all that's been spread about me. It frustrates the fuck out of me that six months later, Kayla is still screwing with my happiness.

Despite her uneasy reaction to me, I stopped by CakeStop's dessert table throughout the night with the excuse of grabbing something for one of my teammates. Each time, I avoid Kenzie so that I don't make things uncomfortable. I just can't seem to avoid the pull I feel toward her.

Chapter 8

Kenzie

Stephanie is a genius. Ever since the Steel Your Heart gala, the bakery phone hasn't stopped ringing and the foot traffic into the shop has been insane. It's only been a month and I've already had to hire two additional employees, one for upfront and one to help me bake.

It's Saturday afternoon and we've finally slowed down. The shop is only open for another hour, and because we're closed tomorrow, I'm in the back, cleaning. Toby, my new cashier, peeks his head through our swinging double doors. In the short time he's worked for me, our friendship has blossomed. At almost six feet, his skinny frame towers over me. He is the perfect vibe for the shop. A complete hipster from his tight, ripped jeans to his ever-present beanie. At twenty-one, Toby knows who he is. He's definitely handsome, with the perfect five o'clock shadow and thick-framed glasses.

"Hey, Kenzie. You have a very handsome visitor up front." He smirks, then disappears. Instantly, Josh Logan flashes into my mind, and I reprimand myself. *He's a bad boy and not someone you need to be interested in.*

Wiping my hands on my apron and pulling off my hair net, I step out front and my eyes fall on the incredibly handsome man casually talking to Toby. My stomach drops. *Why did it have to be him?* My palms sweat and my blood pressure jumps as I make my way over to them.

Our gazes connect, and my heart flutters. *This isn't good.*

"Hi, Kenzie. Told you I'd stop by," Josh says in a deep, sexy voice. *Damn him.* Why does he have to be so attractive? Standing there in a pair of well-worn jeans and a dark blue Henley, my pulse hammers at the sight of him. His effortless look is doing things to me that have my mouth parched and my knees weak. How is that possible? This man is an ass. Or at least that's what I've seen splattered all across social media.

About a month before the gala, I'd been wasting time on TikTok and had come across the page of an influencer who's hit it big in the city. In the last few years, the number of her followers has skyrocketed, and she's gone viral. *Lucky.* Apparently, besides being a doppelgänger for model Hailey Baldwin, she used to live with and date Josh Logan. Yes, the same one who's now standing in my bakery. *I couldn't compete with that. Even if I wanted to.*

"Josh," I say. He gives me a panty-dropping smile that makes my knees weak.

Toby turns toward me and whispers, "Kenzie, say something else."

Nervous, I stumble through another mashup of words. "Uh... hi... I mean, how are you?" Mortified by my lack of social skills, I want to slink into the back and hide for at least an hour after the shop closes.

A customer steps up behind Josh, and when he tries to get out of the way, he's recognized. "Josh Logan," the woman gasps. Turning to greet the fan, I realize this is the perfect chance to escape. I'm just about to bolt when Toby steps in my way.

"Where do you think you're going?" He smirks at me, and I try my best to glare, but because I suck at it, I'm sure it's more sweet than sour.

"I need to finish cleaning the back and inventory the walk-in to make sure I have enough eggs, butter, and milk for next week. Why?"

Stepping closer, he lowers his voice. "I already did the inventory for next week. We're great. Why are you running from him? He definitely seems interested. And in case you didn't notice, he's hella hot."

Folding my arms across my chest, I reply, "I appreciate you taking care of the inventory. Thank you. I'm not running, and he's definitely not interested."

Toby clucks at me. "Really, Kenzie? The entire time you've been trying to escape while he's distracted with a fan, he's kept his eyes on you."

"What?" I choke out. Looking around Toby, sure enough, Josh is focused on me despite the conversation he's having with a gushing fan. They take a selfie and then he excuses himself, heading toward me with the sexiest smile dusting his lips. *Swoon.* Shut up, brain.

"So... what have you been up to since the gala?" he asks, seemingly genuinely interested. *Is he, though?*

"I've been busy here. Business has kind of exploded since then," I tell him while looking around my quaint shop. It isn't much, but it's all mine, and I've put everything into it. It's built on blood, sweat, and tears, and I couldn't be prouder of myself.

Again with the smile. *This man is killing me.* "That's great. I'm so happy for you."

"Thanks. Did you stop in to pick up something?"

Josh shakes his head, and I'm confused. "Then what did you need?" I question.

Stepping closer, he lowers his voice so our conversation remains between us. "Honestly, Kenzie, I came by to ask you out for coffee."

"You did?" *Is this really happening?* Maybe Toby was right; maybe Josh is interested. But what about all the things I saw on social media? Every platform I'd visited seemed to have its focus on him. His name was mud. And making it worse is he hasn't defended himself. Nothing is on his social media accounts attempting to disprove Kayla's claims. *Why doesn't he defend himself? What are people supposed to believe?* It's so confusing. I've learned that when people are seeking attention, they'll say or do just about anything to keep everyone's focus. *So, what's the truth?*

Shifting my feet, I don't know what to say. I don't really date. And if I did, it wouldn't be a professional athlete who is way out of my league, even if half of what's on social media is true.

"It's just coffee. No pressure," he assures, but I'm still hesitant.

Looking into his eyes, I explain, "I don't really have time to date. I'm pretty much married to this place. When I'm not here, I'm sleeping." My words are true, but it isn't what he wants to hear.

He hangs his head. "At least it isn't because I'm a professional athlete or the lies being spread about me." He shrugs his shoulders and steps back, ready to leave.

How did he know? "I'm sorry, Josh," I admit.

"For what?" He steps closer, clearly confused about my apology.

"I saw all that stuff about you... and it is the main reason I said no."

Looking dejected, he mutters "fuck" under his breath. Hanging his head again, he shifts his stance and asks, "The main reason?"

I just nod, unsure of what to say.

He looks up, his eyes clear and pleading. "It's all lies, Kenzie. I wish I could explain it easily, but it involves a whole long story that I hate to relive if you've already decided about me."

Worried I made a rush judgement, I wringing my hands together. *What if he's telling the truth, and it's all lies?*

Josh pulls his cell phone from his pocket and angrily types a message to someone while he grumbles, "I can't believe Kayla is still fucking with my life." Then he raises his eyes to mine. "All of it is lies, and I'm going to prove it to you." Then he forces a smile, making me want to believe him.

I hate confrontation, and that's what this feels like. I'm judging Josh unfairly and being called on it, and now I'm full of nervous energy, twisting and pulling at my fingers. Josh watches my every move, reaching out to take my left hand in his grasp. His much larger hand nestling mine, the thumb of his other hand tracing circles around the center of my palm. His hands are huge, his fingertips rough, the nails neat and trim, but it's the sizzle and crackle of lightning that shoots all over my body, that makes me stand up straight. *What the hell was that?*

I take my first real deep breath since Josh walked into my bakery. "Did you feel that?"

Josh, still holding my hand, squeezes, then shakes his head no. "Kenzie, how do you feel about grabbing coffee?"

"I wasn't kidding when I said I practically live

here. My only day off is Sunday, and that day is just mine. I sleep in, run errands, and do chores."

He gives me a tender smile that registers heat in the middle of my chest. "You're busy, I get that. How about I come to you? What time does the bakery open?"

My mouth drops open. *He's joking, right?* Let's see. "I get here by three a.m. to get things started. The shop opens at seven." He nods, and I bet he's reconsidering his offer. *His interest was short-lived.*

"You have a coffee machine, right?" he asks, already knowing the answer. I just smile.

"Can I use it?" he asks, and I flinch. *There's no way he knows how to use a commercial espresso machine.* "I know what that look means. I worked in a coffee shop when I was in high school. I could blow your mind with my latte art." His sexy smirk makes my heart flutter. *Blow my mind?*

"R-really?" I stutter. "You want to wake up incredibly early, make me a fancy coffee drink, and talk, all while I make an excessive number of baked items?" *Why?*

He smiles widely. "Yes."

"Why?" I finally question. *Is he pranking me? He can't be serious.*

Tugging his free hand through his hair, he looks frustrated. He lets a breath out, makes eye contact, and admits, "Because you seem like someone I want to get to know." *Is he for real?* I mean, that's a good line, and he's definitely making me rethink my opinion of him. But I'm no one. Why would he want to get to know me? He could have any woman he wanted. Josh squeezes my hand again, bringing me back to our conversation. "Is that a yes?"

"I guess so," I answer hesitantly.

He tilts his head at me. *He is so handsome.* My stomach flutters like a hundred butterflies have taken flight.

"Yes, I'll have coffee with you." He smiles. "But I understand it's early, and if you don't show, I won't be surprised." His smile falls. *Will he come?* Wishing I could silence the internal dialogue telling me I'm not good enough, I grit my teeth. *Guess we'll see.*

He steps closer, so we're toe-to-toe, and places a kiss on the hand he's been holding. He runs a finger down the side of my face, tucking in a stray hair behind my ear before he lowers his husky voice and says, "When I say I'm going to do something. I'm going to do it. You'll see." Then he winks, and it hits me right in the knees, making me sway.

Watching him walk away, I'm stunned at what had just happened. "Wow," I whisper to myself.

Toby steps up next to me. "Did you just agree to a coffee date with Josh Logan, the hottest professional hockey player out there?"

Blushing, I dip my head. "I did." *Wait, did he just say the hottest guy in the NHL?* "Did I make a mistake? Should I have said no?" Panic sets in and my mind floods with all the reasons I should have said no.

Toby puts his hands on my shoulders. "Kenzie. Stop analyzing this. Just let it be what it is."

My eyes popping wide, I screech, "What is it?"

He laughs at me, and I give him a puny-sounding growl. "It's a coffee date. Nothing more. Slow your roll, cinnamon."

I croak out a laugh at his weak dad joke and shake my head. "You're right. It's just a coffee date at my bakery."

Chapter 9

Josh

After the gala, my assistant, Tara, and I launched an attack on social media. For every post where Kayla spread lies about me, we posted positive ones, talking up all the good things I'm involved in. And a month later we're finally seeing results. The tides are changing. It also helps that I had Tara call Kayla and threaten her with a defamation lawsuit. I'm not sure I even have a case, but just the thought of that should scare Kayla enough to back off. Once I'm moving back into the positive ground on social media, I'm able to relax a little.

Kenzie has been on my mind 24/7 since I met her, and although I'm nervous. With both anxicty and excitement pumping through my veins, it's time for my coffee date with Kenzie at her bakery.

Standing outside the store, I realize how kitschy it is—faded red brick with a bright blue door. It's definitely unique. When I was here the other day I hadn't much noticed it. My focus had been on Kenzie and getting her to say yes to a date, which explains why I'm here at the literal butt crack of dawn. Four in the morning is early no matter what, but I want to show her how serious I am about getting to know her.

Knocking on the front door, I pace until I see a head pop into the window. A surprised look covers her beautiful flour-dusted face, and I can't help but smile. She is fucking adorable, and she has no idea. Pulling open the door, she whispers, "Josh. You're here."

Leaning in, I kiss her on the cheek and reply, "I am. Good morning, Kenzie."

Opening the door wider, she let me in. Looking around, I take in all the colors. It's bright, alive, and happy. "I don't want to get you behind schedule. Show me to your coffee beans and I'll get started on a cup of coffee for you."

Kenzie looks at me like she's still stunned. "Really?"

I put my hands on my hips. "I wasn't kidding. I'm a master at latte art. Now, pick your poison and let me get started."

"Okay. I'll take a mocha, please."

After showing me where everything is, she saunters off to the kitchen. Preparing the perfect drink takes a skilled touch, especially the art on top. Thankfully, it's just like riding a bike, and after my first attempt, I'm able to give Kenzie something I'm proud of. I stick my head through the swinging doors and holler, "Ready for the best mocha you'll ever have?"

She laughs while she loads baking sheets with cookie dough. "Ready as I'll ever be," her sweet voice calls back, calming my anxious heart. *I want to impress her.* Walking slowly into the kitchen, I carefully balance the mocha, keeping the art pristine.

Kenzie finishes loading her last cookie sheet, wipes her hands on her apron, and moves toward me. "That smells amazing." Handing her the cup, I see a deep smile grace her lips when she sees the heart on top. Her sparkling blue eyes flick to mine, causing warmth to course through my body.

Moving closer, I ask, "Are you going to try it?"

"It's so pretty. This is my first latte art. Thank you." Then she lifts the mug to her lips and takes a sip. She closes her eyes and moans. "This is so good." At her compliment, I swear my heart grows three times its size and I feel like I'm ten feet tall. *Who'd have guessed?* And all over a cup of coffee.

Once she's caffeinated, she sets her cup down, washes her hands, and returns to another batch of cookies. Watching her, I notice how organized and orderly she is. It baffles my brain. She reminds me of a robot as she moves through the kitchen, loading the various cookie sheets. Apparently baking is next, and she has it down to a science. The trays go into the oven and the timer's set.

"Bread is next," she says as she gathers ingredients.

After watching her load them into a giant mixer, I decide Kenzie is magic. She takes simple ingredients and turns them into heavenly treats. *It's not magic. It's baking.* Maybe. But she is an artist, and everything in this kitchen is her medium. It's mesmerizing. I know I'm intruding on her quiet time, and until now I've been content to watch her work. Our silence is comfortable and soothing. But I want to get to know everything about her.

Silence surrounds us as she removes the dough from the mixer and separates it into the perfect size for loaves of bread. Interrupting the quiet, I ask, "Have you always loved to bake?"

Looking up from the dough she's kneading, she smiles. *Breathtaking.* She doesn't have any makeup on or fancy clothes, but she's radiant. "Yes, I've always loved to bake. Some of my best memories are in the kitchen with my mother and grandmother, making the recipes that have been in our family for generations."

"Do you still bake with them?" I ask, curious about her family.

Her smile waivers. "Not as much as I'd like. My grandmother passed a few years ago, and my parents live in Seattle and I don't get to visit very often."

Moving my chair closer, I say, "I'm really sorry to hear that. Do you not get home very often because of the bakery? Do they come here?"

Kenzie lowers her head, and dread fills my gut. *What did I say?* She moves to the oven to pull tray after tray of hot chocolate chip cookies from it before placing them on a wheeled cooling rack. The air smells heavenly and makes my mouth water.

When she finally answers, I hear the pain in her voice. "It's complicated." Wanting to move on, she asks, "Do you bake?"

Letting out an awkward laugh, I ask, "Does making toast qualify?" Kenzie laughs too, and it's the best sound I've ever heard. "You have a great laugh."

Her cheeks turn red and she focuses on the bread dough, measuring it again before she tucks it into a bread pan. *Fucking adorable.*

"So far, you've made cookies and bread. What's next on the agenda?"

After placing the bread aside, she pulls out a giant mixing bowl and all her ingredients. "I'm making cupcakes. Do you want to help? I have an extra apron."

Standing up, I go to the sink and wash my hands, then make my way over to her. "Are you sure about this? I don't want to mess anything up."

She nudges me with her hip. "I'm going to be here the whole time. It won't be possible for you to mess up. Plus, baking isn't too challenging."

"Says the baker," I mutter under my breath, which earns me another laugh from her. *Holy shit.* This woman. Before I can get lost in my thoughts, she hands me eggs. "You want me to crack them?" I ask nervously.

"Yeah," she answers, then she pauses. "You have cracked eggs before, right?"

Clearing my throat, I admit, "It's been a while. Because my diet is so rigid and my schedule is what it is, I have a personal chef who makes all my meals. Every two weeks, he stocks my fridge and freezer with perfectly balanced meals that adhere to my nutrition-ist's specifications."

Kenzie looks over at me. "Wow. That's intense." She looks at the bowl in front of us. "So, then, you don't really eat the things I bake?"

"No, not really. I try my best to stay away from sweets. But if you promise not to tell, I have a minor confession."

Her eyes light up as she waits. I clear my throat. "Despite my strict diet... I may have had four of the cupcakes you made for Lucas and Samantha's party. And at the gala, I may have sampled a few items."

"You did?" she gushes with a bright smile. *I did that.* I made her smile.

Returning her smile, I pat my stomach and admit. "I sure did, and they were all delicious. My favorite is the death by a chocolate cupcake."

She laughs. "Well, you're in luck, mister, because that's what we are making right now."

Chapter 10

Kenzie

Josh is full of surprises. He actually showed up bright and early this morning and made me the best mocha I've ever had. The longer we talk, the more I discover about him. I realize quickly that there's more to Josh than I first believed. Being a professional athlete isn't who he is, but what he does. He's sweet, funny, considerate, and looks at me like I'm something special.

Once all the baking's finished, we have a half an hour before the bakery opens. "Thanks for your help this morning, Josh. It was nice to have the company."

"I've had a great time. Although this is a dangerous place to be when you're trying to stick to a strict diet. Everything smells and looks amazing." He laughs.

Smiling, I lean toward the display case. "How would you feel about getting a sweet treat as your payment for helping this morning?" I offer, eyeing the death by chocolate cupcakes we made. I know he loves them.

His eyes dance and then flick to my mouth. A gigantic smile spreads across his face, causing butterflies to flutter in my stomach. *What's he thinking?* Then he licks his lips, and my brain misfires. "What do you have in mind?" he asks in a low timbre that shakes me to the core.

"I was thinking of a death by chocolate cupcake," I answer. Looking at him, I see his smile dip. "Why do I think you had something else in mind?"

A pained expression appears on his face, and my heart drops. Josh shakes his head no and says, "That would be great. Do you have milk too?" Then he forces a smile.

"Sure, I'll go get some." I head toward my walk-in fridge, needing a moment to process what happened. *Did I say something wrong? Why does he look upset? We were having a great time. What happened?* Worry fills my mind as I pour two glasses of milk. Returning to the front of the bakery, I see Josh has already pulled two cupcakes out and set them at a table. He's smiling again, and that calms my anxious heart. I realize I didn't enjoy seeing him upset.

Not long after we finish our cupcakes, Toby shows up, ready to open the bakery.

"Morning, Kenz," he hollers as he unlocks the door, brings in the newspapers, and turns on the OPEN sign. When he turns around and sees me casually sitting at a table with Josh, his mouth falls open. "Sorry, I didn't expect you to have company. I know I'm early. I can go hide out in the back until we have a customer." He shuffles to the back and through the swinging doors, disappearing completely. Josh laughs and I roll my eyes and shake my head.

Josh pushes back his chair and stands. "Guess I better be going." He stacks our cups and plates and walks them over to the tub we have designated for dirty dishes, then he rejoins me. "I had a fantastic time hanging out with you, and I'd love to do it again."

Suddenly nervous, I tug on my apron. "You would?"

He smiles. "I would. I'm headed out of town for a few games. Can I have your number so we can text or talk to set up another coffee date?"

He wants my number and to spend time with me. My teenage self does a happy dance while I try to maintain my composure. "Sure, that sounds great. Do you have your phone?" He pulls it from his pocket, unlocks it, and hands it to me. I try to control the shaking in my hands while I enter my information.

"Thanks," he says when I hand it back.

"I sent myself a message so I'll have your number too," I confess.

"Good," he replies with a smirk.

Josh pulls off his apron and hands it to me. "I better go. I need to get to practice in an hour."

What? I'm shocked. "You have practice this morning?" He laughs and nods, then pulls me into a hug. *This is the best hug I've ever had.* Wrapping his muscular arms around me, he squeezes tight before he kisses the top of my head. "Thanks again for this morning, Kenzie. I'll text or call you soon." And then he's gone.

A few minutes later, I hear Toby holler from the other side of the swinging doors. "Is it safe to come out?" I laugh.

"Yes, Toby, he's gone."

"Good," he says while pushing into the storefront. "I was getting bored in the back and I need to get the coffee machine ready before any customers show up."

I turn to him with a smile on my face. "Coffee machine should be up and ready to go."

Toby shrieks. "What did you do? You don't ever touch Jazlyn."

"Why did you name the coffee machine? And for your information, I didn't touch Jazlyn. Josh did when he made me the best mocha I've ever had." I head past him and into the back to start on another batch of muffins.

"What?" he squeals as he follows behind. I just smile. Then I hear the ring of the bell above the door and I laugh out, knowing we have customers and he can't come back and interrogate me.

Later that afternoon, as I'm prepping for the next day, I feel my phone buzz in my back pocket. It's Josh.

JOSH

Hey, Kenzie. How was your day?

ME

It was great. Started out amazing and
got better as the day went on. How
about you?

JOSH

Mine started out incredible, but
practice was tough. We're gearing up
for the next round of Stanley Cup
playoff games.

ME

I know nothing about hockey. I've at
least heard of the Stanley Cup,
though.

JOSH

No worries. The playoff games are
after the regular season has ended.
They begin in April and end in June.
With a winner of the prestigious
trophy.

ME

Wow. Well, good luck to the Steel.
I've never even seen a game.

JOSH

Really? You mean you haven't seen a
live game? That's not uncommon.
Tickets aren't the cheapest.

ME

Even if they were affordable, with the
hours I work, I can't even catch a
game on TV.

JOSH

That's right. You're usually sleeping
when we play. It's too bad. I'd love to
have you in the stands cheering
me on.

ME

Who says I'd be cheering you on?
<winking emoji>

JOSH

Ouch. I think you hurt my pride.
<crying emoji>

ME

I've never been around professional
athletes, but I'm assuming they all
have some to spare. Or come by the
bakery and I'll dry your tears and
make it better with a cookie.

JOSH

Now that's something I can get
behind. I'll stop by when I'm back.

ME

Sounds great. I'll see you then.

JOSH

It's a date.

Did he mean that? A date with Josh Logan? Yeah, I'm not ready for that. Sure, he's nice, funny, and sexy as sin, but I can't imagine he'd want anything with me besides friendship. This morning was amazing, but I can't expect anything to come of it. I don't want to get my heart too invested. The uncertainty of it all has me feeling fidgety. I pocket my phone and force myself to focus on what I need to get done before I leave for the day. Unfortunately, the quiet of the bakery makes that task difficult, as I again think about Josh and my uncertain feelings for him. I need to figure this out. The sooner the better.

Going home that afternoon after closing the bakery, my mind once again drifts back to my date with Josh. I don't really have a dating history. When I was in high school, no one asked me out. My best friend was Amanda, and we were incredibly shy. We were really close until college. She left Chicago to go to school in Florida. She wanted to be a marine biologist, and I stayed home and attended culinary school.

Since I was young, I always wanted to bake and have my own bakery using the recipes from my grandma. And I'm making that happen. Over the last few years with school and starting my bakery, there hasn't been time for friends or boyfriends. It probably would have been easier if I had moved to Seattle to be closer to my parents. But when I was in school, I'd made some valuable Chicago contacts that took me under their wing, and I didn't feel right about leaving. Even though my shop is still small, I have big plans. In a few years, I hope to open a second location, which means I'll have even less time to be social.

Chapter 11

Josh

With only a month left in the season, our main goalie, Rusty Simmons, who suffers from severe arthritis in his joints, retires. Management suspected it was coming and had already started looking for another goalie earlier in the season. They looked high and low. They investigated all plausible options and finally struck gold when they found a goalie who was being underutilized in the league. New York has an exceptional starting goalie, and because of this, their backup, who was also a force in his own right, was stuck riding the pine.

In February, Jersey transferred to the Steel, reuniting with Lucas, his former teammate. They played together during Jersey's rookie year and became instant friends. Jersey fit seamlessly into the Steel organization. Not long after he arrived, Rusty's arthritis got worse, causing him to miss several games. Because of that, Jersey got ice time. With his impressive record, they promoted him to main goalie weeks before the playoffs began. He'd proved both in practice and during games he was superior to Swindle, our rookie backup. Because of his efforts, we managed a playoff spot.

Playoff games started in April, and after six games, we come out on top, winning the first bracket against the Los Angeles Raptors. Those were some tough games, and we barely made it to the next bracket.

This round we're playing the Las Vegas Stars, and it has me worried. They swept their bracket, maintaining the same intensity they had the entire season. Predictions that the Stars would win the Cup are rampant around the league and media, and I'm hoping we don't embarrass ourselves. I mean, I'm confident about our level of play, but in the last bracket, we lost one of our defensemen to a knee injury and he's out for the rest of the series. We also have a few other players who are nursing injuries and have been playing on borrowed time. Considering we've won the last two Cups, expectations are high, but I have doubts we'll pull it off. The pressure is mounting, and it's starting to feel like we're in a pressure cooker. All eyes are on us.

Showing up in Vegas, my nerves are shot. I know as the captain, it's my job to keep the energy up, and I'm going to try my best to do that. Before the first game, looking around the locker room, I see I'm not the only one who's anxious.

"Listen up," I shout after I stand up and slap my hands together, getting my teammates' attention. They all focus on me.

"We know this bracket will be a tough one to win. Vegas has had an outstanding season, winning everything with ease. But we aren't planning to make this easy for them, are we?"

A chorus of no's surrounds me, and I can feel the energy building. "Let's fucking do this! Show them why we've claimed the Cup the last two years."

Being the away team, you never know what to expect when you take the ice. As the defending champions for the past two years skating in enemy territory, you expect some heckling. But these Vegas fans take it to a whole new level. At every turn, we are booed and yelled at, and let me tell you, it's hard to maintain your energy and positivity when in an environment that hostile. Not only are the fans aggressive, but the players are too. Coach Tristan addresses that in the locker room between the second and third periods.

"Guys, I know this has become a clusterfuck. The Stars are being chippy and making poor plays. Since the refs aren't calling them on it, and we have no guarantee they will, we need to take advantage of the vulnerabilities they're revealing." Coach looks around the locker room, making eye contact with every single player before he continues. After giving us his new strategy to gain an advantage, he releases us. Sure enough, not even a minute into the new period, Rocco is cross-checked into the boards and he goes down. Their defenseman, Tyler Adams, is called for the hit and given a two-minute penalty. We take advantage of the penalty, and Ace scores the only goal for the game. It's a beauty. He has a breakaway and beats the goalie in a one-on-one through his five-hole.

Following our game, we meet with the press, then we head back to our hotel for the night. I want to text Kenzie and see how she is, but I know she's already asleep because she has to get up in a few hours to bake. It boggles my mind how she gets up at three every morning. *She's just passionate.* I guess it's like all the things I do for hockey. She'd probably find some of what I do for my love of the game unique. I know some of my teammates do. Things like drinking a glass of chocolate milk and eating a ripe banana right after a game. Or taping my stick a certain way, and listening to the same song on repeat on the way to the arena. Katy Perry's "California Gurls" is my jam right now. It might not make much sense, but it works for me.

When I finally reach my room, I'm wiped. I strip off my suit, brush my teeth, and crawl into bed. Waking up the next morning, I see I have two hours before I have to show up for a light practice. I head down to the conference room where they're hosting a team breakfast and I see Coach and some of my team-mates are up. "Morning guys," I say.

"Morning, Cap," Mika and Lucas holler from their table. They've spread themselves out, monopolizing an eight-person table. With the way they're sitting, it would only comfortably fit four. Guess it's a good thing not everyone is up yet.

I head to the line to place my order of an egg white, ham, onion, mushroom, pepper, and cheese omelet. I grab oatmeal and sprinkle brown sugar on it. Before I head over to a table, I load up a bowl of fresh fruit. Coffee and water are on the table. Sitting away from the guys, I pull out my phone, hoping Kenzie might be free to text.

ME

Good morning.

Sitting there, waiting for her reply, I wonder why I'm so drawn to her. Girlfriends aren't really my thing, so it baffles me I'm actively pursuing her. It's beyond her beauty. She's different from most of the women I interact with, other than maybe Samantha, Shiloh, Monica, or Stephanie. Kenzie doesn't spend time with me because she's after something else. In the short time we've hung out together, I've already discovered she's down-to-earth, genuine, and so fucking real. Because of that, I want to spend more time with her, getting to know her better. She intrigues me. Before I can give it too much thought, my phone dings. Looking down, my heart skips a beat and a smile spreads across my face.

KENZIE

Morning. How are you?

ME

I'm good but tired.

KENZIE

What's that like? <laughing emoji>

ME

Sorry, forgot who I was talking to. You must always be tired.

KENZIE

It's really not that bad if you stick to a schedule. I know that in order to be productive, I need to get at least seven hours of sleep. In order to do that, I have to be in bed by eight. Man, I sound so old.

ME

You don't look a day over twenty-one.

KENZIE

Is that your way of asking how old I am?

ME

Maybe? Are you one of those women who hates to say her age?

KENZIE

No.

ME

Then I'll go first. I'm twenty-seven.

KENZIE

I'm twenty-three.

ME

Cool. What else do I need to know
about you?

KENZIE

You already know I'm a baker and I
have my shop. I don't have any
siblings, and I grew up here in
Chicago. My parents live in Seattle
because when I was in culinary
school, my dad's job transferred him
there. How about you?

ME

Let's see… You know I play hockey
professionally, but before I played for
the Steel, I played in Arizona, which is
where I was born and raised. I also
don't have any siblings. My parents
still live in Arizona, though I'm not
very close to them. I was really close
with my grandparents until they
passed away.

KENZIE

I am so sorry for your loss, Josh. Was
it recent?

ME

It's been a few years since my
grandfather died. My grandmother
was before that. I really don't like to
think about it. But, I miss them a lot.

KENZIE

Okay. I saw you won your game last
night. Congratulations. When is your
next?

ME

Thanks. It was a tough game. Our
next is here, and it's tomorrow night.
During the playoffs, we do two games
with a night in between, rotating the
two cities. So, after this next one,
we'll return home for two. It'll be nice
to be at home, in my bed.

KENZIE

Hotel beds aren't comfortable?

ME

Not really. Over the last almost ten
years of playing in the NHL, I've yet to
find one that's really comfortable. Do
you like hotel beds?

KENZIE

Can't say I've slept on too many. I
haven't traveled much.

ME

If you could go anywhere, where
would it be?

KENZIE

That's tough. I can't really answer
that.

ME

Why not? You don't have a dream
vacation?

KENZIE

Not really. Because there are so many
places I haven't been to, my list is
incredibly long. And since I have
CakeStop, I don't see myself free to
travel for a while.

ME

Yeah, I guess I understand. I really
didn't think about that.

KENZIE

So, where's your dream vacation?

ME

I've never been to Alaska. They say
it's the land of the midnight sun.

KENZIE

My parents went there for their
thirtieth wedding anniversary. The
pictures they showed me were
incredible. I'd like to go there one
day too.

ME

Maybe we can go together.

KENZIE

...

Minutes pass without a response from her, and
dread weighs heavily in my gut. *Shit, did I come on too
strong?* I like Kenzie. She isn't just gorgeous; she's
funny and kind too. In the short time I've known her,
I've already discovered she's someone I enjoy being
around. I want her as a friend, if not more. But that's

up to her. Did I ruin things with my vacation suggestion? It isn't like I'm going to drop everything tomorrow and schedule tickets, rentals, and lodging.

Another few minutes pass, and I need to get to the team bus to head to the arena for practice.

ME

Kenzie? Are you there? Sorry if what I
said made you upset. I have to go to
practice now. I would love to talk later
if you're free.

I wait another minute for any response, and when nothing comes through, my heart feels like it's being squeezed by a vise. I hope I haven't ruined things between us already.

Practice is light, as we have another playoff game tomorrow. Despite that, I struggle to get engaged. I'm distracted by the lack of response from Kenzie. About a third of the way through drills, Coach pulls me to the side.

"Josh, you seem off today. Is everything okay?"

Hanging my head, I struggle to make eye contact. "Yeah, I just have something on my mind," I admit.

"When I find it tough to focus, I ask myself a question. If the answer is no, then I force myself to move on temporarily. However, if the answer is yes, I have to accept that no matter what I do until I've dealt with whatever it is, I'm useless to myself or anyone else."

"What is the question you ask?"

Coach laughs. "It's simple... Can you do anything right now to make things better?"

Leaning on my stick, I let the question sink in. I know there isn't anything I can do. I just need to be patient. Maybe something came up and she had to put her phone down. What Coach said makes sense, and I prepare myself to wait for Kenzie's response. *She isn't ghosting me.* She's not like that.

Stamping down the desire to check my phone when practice ends, I march myself to the weight room and take out my uneasiness on the machines. After a workout that was supposed to include light cardio and weights, I'm exhausted. I pushed it harder than I should have. But with my mind racing and my anxiety making me edgy, I didn't really pay close attention to weight.

The team boards the bus and returns to the hotel for the night. My brain is whirling with uncertainty as I head to the conference room for the prepared buffet, but I'm not hungry. My worry stole my appetite. I force myself to grab grilled chicken, a baked potato, and broccoli. I know I need fuel so I'm ready for tomorrow. It'll be another tough game, and I can't afford to be distracted. Hopefully, Kenzie will text me back.

After shoveling down my plate of sawdust, I mean dinner, I head up to my room for the evening. I'm not very good company and I don't want to bring anyone else down.

Flopping onto my king-sized bed, I pull out my phone and I see a text message I must have missed during the afternoon.

KENZIE

Sorry, I got pulled away for a baking emergency. I'd love to go to Alaska, but with the shop, I'm not sure how I'd be able to. I hope practice goes well and you win your game tomorrow. See you when you get home.

I let out a deep breath and roll my shoulders to release the tension I'd been carrying all day. I'm relieved. Kenzie wasn't ghosting me. She was busy. I look at the clock and realize that she's already gone to bed, so I shoot off a quick text that she'll see in the morning. Smiling, I think of the perfect thing to say.

ME

I hope you slept well. Thank you for the good wishes for our game. I can't wait to see you when I get back.

The inclination to write more is strong, but I don't know exactly how I feel, and I don't want to scare her off by my jumbled emotions. I like Kenzie, but I feel in limbo, like I don't want to say it and jinx anything that could happen between us.

Now that I've heard from her, I'm able to calm myself enough to fall asleep.

Early the next morning, I head down to the hotel's gym and get in a run. We'll do a team skate after breakfast and then return to our hotel for a mid-day meal and nap. Tonight, we need to bring our A-game to get an advantage over Vegas for this series. I'm ready to get this game over and get back to Chicago to see Kenzie. Although I barely know her, I've missed her and I can't wait to spend more time with her.

Chapter 12

Kenzie

In just a few short weeks, Josh has wormed his way into my heart. I'm still leery, of course. I have so many questions. *Why me? Is this for real? Is this just a passing fancy?* All I know is I'm intrigued. Every time he's near, my heart thunders in my chest and a thousand butterflies take flight in my stomach. When he looks at me, my breath catches and I feel dizzy. When we touch, platonically, of course, my pulse skyrockets, and goose bumps cover my body. And the way he smells. It's not only hot and heady, but incredibly addictive. He is all man, and I find it irresistible with a capital I.

Since that first extended visit to CakeStop at four a.m., he's been back several times, and it always surprises me. Even though his season is over, it baffles me why he'd want to waste precious sleep time with me. The Steel lost the series against the Vegas Stars and are no longer vying for the Cup, so he has the next few months off. He doesn't come by every day, but he visits a few times a week, and not only does he make me the best mochas, but he helps make cupcakes and now cookies. I've discovered how detail-oriented Josh is. He always measures everything twice and follows the recipe perfectly. He's become an excellent assistant.

While readying the chocolate chip cookie balls on their cookie sheets, he asks, "Hey, Kenz, what do you think about adding something new to your repertoire?"

I stop pouring the flour into the mixer for our next batch of oatmeal, craisin, and white chocolate chip cookies and turn to him. "What are you thinking?"

"Ever had a brookie?"

Turning the mixer on, I head back over to the prep table. "No, I haven't but I've heard they are good."

He laughs and gives me a panty-dropping smile. "They're absolutely delicious."

Putting my hands on my hips, I tilt my head and say, "I thought you stayed away from desserts because of your diet."

Josh puts his hands up. "Easy there, sheriff. I tasted a small one at the hotel in Vegas when we were there for the playoffs." Then he winks, and I'm just like a moth to a flame, mesmerized.

Smiling at him as if he hung the stars, I agree. "I could try that. But since it's your idea, you have to help me."

He sets down the last cookie on the baking sheet and steps closer, reaching out to touch my arm. His fingers heat my skin. "I'm in," he declares. His words are simple, but they're heavy, as if they're loaded with unsaid meaning. *Maybe I'm hearing what I want to hear. Or seeing what I want to see.* Maybe none of it is real, just a figment of my lust-soaked brain? *Why does it feel so good to have him near? What does it mean that I want to be closer?* I don't understand what I'm feeling, but it's leaving me out of breath and worked up.

"Okay." My answer sounds breathy as it leaves my parched lips. I lick them and notice Josh watching me, focused on my lips. *Is he thinking about kissing me?* I'm not sure I'm ready for that. For him. But damn, that's all I want. No matter what my head says.

After a month of testing different batter options, we nail down the perfect brookie recipe. That day starts like any other. But shortly after we begin mixing the batters, it feels like the air in the kitchen becomes supercharged. It all starts when Josh reaches over the commercial mixer to add the semi-sweet chips to the cookie batter. No matter how hard I try, I can't drag my eyes away from the pull of his cargo pants across his muscular ass. Making myself focus on something else, Josh adds the rest of the ingredients to the mixers. When everything is combined, he brings the mixing bowl over to the workspace. And again, I find myself gawking. This time, it's the flex of his arms in his white cotton shirt. *Hello, gun show.*

"Is it hot in here?" I rasp while moving to the shop's back door. As I prop it open, I take in a few quick breaths, hoping to calm down my libido. Unfortunately, all it does is chill me and make my nipples pebble. Looks like it's the wrong day to have worn a thin sports bra under my tank top. Josh's wink when I return to the counter confirms he spotted my misbehaving headlights. The tension between us is new and exciting, kind of like our new baked concoction. When we finally unveil it, customers will hoot and holler, eager to try something new.

Within the first week, reviews are in and it's so well received, the brookie makes its way onto the permanent menu. Josh's idea is an enormous hit. Before I know it, summer is over and I'm gearing up for fall. I add pies to the menu and hire a part-time baker just for that. Josie, a retiree, comes in about four hours a day. In the mornings, I prep the dough and fillings so all she has to do is assemble and bake them. We've worked out a great system, and with all the steady business from the Steel Your Heart gala and word of mouth, the bakery is bursting at the seams with business.

Josh still comes by a few early mornings during the week, but I know when hockey begins next month, those visits will disappear. I really hope he doesn't. Over the past almost four months, we've become incredibly close. Nothing physical has happened between us other than hugging, and it's hard not to wonder why. He's become my best friend. We've shared all our secrets over baked goods. He even told me about his family and the drama surrounding his grandfather's estate.

"Hey, Josh. Can I ask you a question?"

He lifts his head from the loaf of bread he's working, instead focusing his attention on me. "Sure, you can ask me anything."

Nodding, I say, "I know it wasn't easy telling me about your family, but I'm curious about something else." My nerves are on full alert. *Should I be asking this?*

"Okay, what do you want to know?"

"Will you tell me what happened with Kayla?" I ask in a rush, then hold my breath.

He stops kneading the bread and looks up at the ceiling. *Did I make a mistake by asking him about her?*

Taking a moment, he breathes out slowly. "Kayla was a puck bunny that I hooked up with on New Year's Eve a few years ago. About six weeks later, she showed up outside practice, telling me she was pregnant. I didn't know what to do or say, so we went to a coffee shop to talk. I didn't want the news of her pregnancy getting out, so we kept it quiet. We started spending time together, getting to know each other. I figured it would be better to co-parent with her if we were on friendly terms."

I nod, and he continues. "As the weeks passed and the idea that I was going to become a father sank in, the more excited I became." He gives me a half-smile, and I smile back.

"The day before we were supposed to see the baby on ultrasound for some testing, she miscarried. I came home from an away series to find her at my house, distraught. It was the worst fucking day of my life. My heart broke that day, and it hasn't been the same since." He lets out a shaky breath, as if he's remembering all the pain he endured.

"I'm so sorry, Josh. I did not know," I say.

"We were thrust together in grief over our mutual loss. Before I knew it, she was living with me and we were dating. Only it wasn't real."

"I don't understand," I say.

"Yes, she lived with me. And in front of the cameras, we did all the things couples would do, but behind closed doors, we lived separate lives. She remained my plus one, and I financed her lavish life-style, all because we were tied together by a tragedy. But the story doesn't end there. For two years we lived as a couple until one night I came home early. I over-heard her talking to her best friend, admitting that she was never pregnant and therefore couldn't have had a miscarriage. That night, after I caught her in her lies, I kicked her out."

Enraged on Josh's behalf, I hiss under my breath, "I hate her."

"Yeah? You and me both, babe," he mutters.

It's true. Kayla is horrible, and if I ever meet her, I

don't know what I'll do. I'm literally shaking. I am so angry. What a conniving bitch. I didn't realize that when I first met Josh, it was her posts that clouded my opinion of him.

"This day is going to be hell," I say to the dough I'm working. It's Monday again, and I didn't sleep well last night. I tossed and turned, and I don't know why. I got up at two and got here about three.

A lazy beat is rapped on the bakery's back door. My heart thunders in my chest. *It's Josh.* Smiling, I wipe my hands on my apron and head to the door to let him in. "Good Morn—" I start. "Josh?" I don't see anyone, or I should say I *can't* see anyone through the gigantic bouquet in front of me. *It's beautiful.* Lifting on my toes, I try again. "Josh... are you there?" A deep laugh accompanies the bouncing, bright arrangement.

Josh lowers the flowers and answers, "Yeah, I'm here." I step back, letting him inside.

Confused, I ask, "Are you going somewhere after this? I mean, if you have something else to do this morning, you aren't obligated to come to the bakery at the ass crack of dawn." Josh looks at me with a stern expression. *That's new. I'm not sure I like it directed at me.*

"No, I'm not going anywhere after here. And there's no other place I'd rather be."

Pointing to the flowers, I say, "Okay. So what's with those?"

"Can't I just get a gorgeous girl some flowers and have it not be a big deal?"

Am I the gorgeous girl he's talking about? He's never said that before. *How does he feel about me? What is he saying?* Confused, I shake my head no.

"No? Why not?" he growls.

I turn away from him, unsure of how I'm feeling. I've been interested in Josh since the first time he showed up at my bakery. But it's been months, and he's never once hinted he feels anything more than friendly toward me. Everything has remained platonic, despite my heart and body screaming for more. Each time I see him, I have to lock my heart down and remind myself I'm lucky to have him at least as my best friend. But I know that will have to change when he eventually dates someone. Many people believe men and women can't be friends, and I don't want to impede his happiness if he finds the woman of his dreams. It doesn't matter that he's the man of mine.

Setting down the flowers, Josh turns me back toward him and pulls me close. It's heaven being wrapped in his arms, but I need to get over that and move on, because at some point, he'll find someone else and I'll lose him.

"Kenz, talk to me." I refuse to look up. I bury my

head in his chest and shake my head no as tears well up in my eyes. *I don't want to lose him.* In such a short time, he's become my best friend. "Please, Kenz. What's going on? I didn't think bringing you flowers would upset you."

I push back from his chest. "I just don't understand why you did. No one has ever bought me flowers before," I confess through sniffles.

Wiping a stray tear from my cheek, he says, "I wanted to buy you flowers because you're special to me and I wanted to ask you something." Panic sets in. What does he want to ask me? *Oh no.* What if he wants me to make a special cake or dessert for a woman he's interested in? *That'll kill me.*

Knowing I need answers before I further spin out of control, I push the conversation forward. "Thank you, Josh, for the flowers. They're beautiful. I love them." I look at the stunning bouquet and smile. Then I move my gaze back to him. "Now, what do you need to ask me?"

He shifts his weight like he's nervous, and my stomach churns. *I really hope I don't throw up.* "I'm not sure how to ask this. I mean, I've practiced it a hundred times in my head, but now I can't seem to get my thoughts out." I nod my understanding, unable to help him.

Standing there in silence, Josh reaches down and grabs my hand. It feels cold and clammy. *Is he okay?* I rub my thumb over the top of it, offering comfort. And finally, he speaks. "So, we've been friends for a few months, and I feel like we've gotten pretty close." I again nod my head, encouraging him to keep talking. "In fact, if I were to label us, I'd probably say you were my best friend." I look up to see his wide smile and it matches my own. But then my heart stutters. *Is that all he thinks of me?*

Josh clears his throat. "What I'm trying to say is... I like you more than friends, and I was hoping you'd go out on a date with me."

I think I've heard him incorrectly. *Did he just ask me out?* "What?" I gasp.

He pulls me in tight. "Kenz, go on a date with me, please?"

"Are you joking with me?" I mumble into his chest, afraid of his answer.

He nudges my head up and stares into my eyes, then says in a serious tone, "No. I'm not joking. I've wanted to ask you out since I met you at the gala, but you seemed hesitant to even talk to me; you kept me at a distance. So, I waited until I couldn't anymore and then I worked to earn your friendship, to build a firm foundation for our relationship. You are the best thing that's ever happened to me. I want nothing more than to take you out."

As if his words haven't stunned me, his next move does. Leaning down, he picks me up, wrapping my legs around his waist. He squeezes my ass while he lowers his lips to mine. As soon as they touch, I'm lost. In the moment. In *him*. Nothing has ever felt better. This isn't my first kiss, but it's already climbing the ranks to my best, and we've only just begun. Or I hope so.

Josh pulls me in tighter and I mewl into his mouth. He takes advantage and slips his tongue inside. Before I can think, his tongue is massaging mine, and then he's nipping at my lower lip. My heart races and my whole-body shivers. When he pulls back, I whimper. I'm disappointed until he lowers me slowly, sliding my body down his, and I feel his firm erection rub against me. *Oh my gosh.* Did I do that to him? I know he's lit my body on fire and it's begging for more, but wow.

"Josh," I pant as he drops his forehead to mine. His muscular arms wrap protectively around me and I've never felt safer or more desired. I can hear the pounding of his heart as I lay my head on his chest.

"Sorry, Kenz. I got a little carried away. I've been dying to kiss you for months, and once I saw an opening, I took it. Honestly, I wasn't planning that. I'm not trying to rush you." This man is adorable. Even his apology is tender and thoughtful.

"N-no, that's okay. You don't have to apologize. I-I really wanted to do that too," I sputter out, relieved. But where do we go from here? Now that he's kissed me, are we a couple? Does he want to be? If he doesn't, what does that mean? Can I handle it either way? I mean, he's him and I'm... well, I'm me. We certainly aren't the typical pairing.

Lost in thought, I feel Josh pull back. My heart

drops and my gut turns. Is this where he tells me it was a mistake? I don't think I could handle that. Worries and fears whiz through my mind.

"Kenz, can you look at me?" he asks as he tries to tip my chin up. I hadn't realized I dropped my head because I'd been so lost in my thoughts.

Afraid, I force my head up and look into his soft blue eyes. "Tell me what you're thinking," he demands. I shake my head no. There is no way I'm telling him about all the chaos taking up space in my head. He'll think I'm crazy or obsessed with him. And if I had to admit it... I kind of am. He's become very special to me.

"Feeling shy?" he asks, and I just nod because these lips of mine aren't opening. Otherwise, I'll probably spill everything I'm feeling and it will send him running from the bakery, never to be heard from again.

"Okay, I'll tell you what I'm thinking." He waits for a minute, seeing if I'll interject. *These lips are sealed.* I have to hear what he's going to say. When he speaks, I'm flabbergasted. "Kenz, I want to take you out. Date you. See where this goes." *Well, that sound's simple.* Much simpler than all the chaos bouncing around in my gray matter.

"Okay," I whisper.

Josh's mouth drops open in surprise. "Really?" *Why does he look shocked?*

"Why are you so surprised?" *Did he think I'd say no?*

Nervously, he laughs. "I wasn't sure you'd say yes."

Assuming he needs an ego boost, I pat his chest and then dramatically roll my eyes. "Okay, big guy. Who wouldn't want to go out with you?"

He clears his throat, drops his voice, and admits, "I couldn't tell if you were interested."

Realizing he's not looking for a compliment, I say, "Josh, you are sweet, funny, and gorgeous. And you're my best friend. Of course, I'm interested in you. I'm just out of your league, so I said nothing."

He pulls me into a tight hug, kisses my head, and tells me, "Kenz, you've got it all wrong. *You're* too good for *me*."

I gasp in disbelief and he hugs me tighter. "But you said yes, so I'm taking it." I laugh against his chest while sucking in his amber and leather cologne. *He smells so good. All. The. Damn. Time.*

He pulls back with a grin. "Now that that's out of the way, don't we have some baking to do?"

Throughout the rest of the morning, we bake, laugh, flirt, and exchange sweet kisses. When we're done prepping for the day, Josh pulls me into his arms and kisses me senseless. *Is this what I have to look forward to?* If so, I'm ready for it. This... us... feels so right.

Lost in each other, I'm oblivious to my surroundings. A gasp, followed by a high-pitched squeal, fills my ears. Then I hear a slow clap. I turn my head toward it and there stands Toby. "About time, you two." Josh just laughs.

"Guess that's my sign to go," he says, then softly kisses my lips and nose before he pulls away from me. "We'll talk later?" I just nod. Then he fist bumps Toby and leaves. Meanwhile, my body is still trying to catch up.

Slapping his hands together right in my face, Toby brings me to. I slowly blink until my focus is clear. "Huh?" I ask.

"What did I just witness?" he questions impatiently.

I'm not sure what to say, so I wipe my hands on my apron. "Umm... well... you see..." I stammer.

Toby's voice raises an octave. "I saw, all right." I want to giggle, but I'm not sure if he's excited or angry, so I tamp it down.

"Toby, it was a kiss," I say, hoping I sound calmer than I feel. Inside, I'm a wreck. Albeit a happy one. I still don't know how to wrap my mind around what just happened. What it all means. I haven't had many relationships, but this one seems so much more.

Toby crosses his arms. "That, missy"—he pauses for dramatic effect—"wasn't just a kiss. I knew it felt electric in the air when I walked in, and now I know why. You two have major sparks." *I guess I'm not the only one who sensed that.*

I turn toward the prep table to start on some cupcakes. Because of all the talking and that kiss, I'm now way behind.

"Did he bring you those gorgeous flowers too?" I

grin, walking over to the brightly colored bouquet. Toby takes it all in, then says, "what a man," while fanning himself.

I roll my eyes because I know he's going to get worse before he moves on. "Toby," I sternly say. His head whips to me. "If you're going to continue grilling me, the least you can do is help." He groans. He's a hard worker and probably my best employee, but he hates helping me bake. He isn't so good at following a recipe, and that's pretty critical when you're a baker.

"Okay, Kenz. What do you need me to do?"

In the half-hour before the bakery opens, we've got a better handle on everything. *Thank goodness.*

Before heading back to the front, Toby looks at me and says, "I know all this is exciting, and it's hard not to be sucked into Josh's charm, but..." He stops talking, almost as if he's afraid to say what he's thinking. I look at him, hoping he'll continue, and a few moments later, he does. "Just please protect yourself. I only want to see you happy."

"Thanks, Toby."

Chapter 13

Josh

You might assume that once I got the nerve to ask Kenzie out, I'd be relieved. But there's where you're wrong. Normally, I'm a confident guy, but with her, I feel different. I'm nervous. And I'm never nervous. Maybe it's because I had to earn it. Or maybe it's because she's the first woman I've ever felt a real spark with. Perhaps it's because at first, she rejected me. But now I have a whole extra pressure weighing on me. I want this to be perfect. Just like that kiss we shared. That moment lives on constant repeat in my brain. It was incredible. Hands down, that was not only the hottest, but the best fucking kiss I've ever had. Pulling away from her was pure torture. But with Toby being a not-so-silent spectator, and knowing she still had a lot to do, I figured it was better to not cause any more distractions.

For our first official date, I take her to Mateo's, a

new restaurant for her, but the unofficial restaurant of the Steel. I arrive to pick her up with a bouquet of wildflowers gripped tightly in my hand. I don't know why I'm nervous, but I am.

Dressed in a comfortable pair of designer jeans, an untucked plaid button-up, and my Timberland boots, I know I look good. But it's nothing compared to Kenzie. When she meets me out front, she blows me away. Outfitted in a flowy, flower-printed dress, she reminds me of a forest fairy. Her light brown hair is pulled up into a high ponytail, revealing her sexy, slender neck. And when she blinks, I catch a hint of a shimmer, which makes her eyes sparkle when they focus on me. Hands down, she's the most gorgeous woman I've ever seen.

Because of her hours at the bakery, we agreed to an early dinner. At just after four, we're easily the youngest people in the establishment. After we're seated, the conversation flows easily between us. *What a relief.* Minutes later, our server appears, carrying our water and a basket stuffed with warm, crispy bread. He takes our orders—lasagna for me and a spinach manicotti for her. I'm really excited about the food; it's always delicious. And I'm excited to see what she thinks.

Opening the bread, I motion to it. "Would you like a slice?"

"Please, with butter," she replies. I smile as I butter the bread for her. Once she's enjoying it, I grab a slice for myself, butter it, and take a big bite. The crunch of the crust, the softness of the bread, and the incredible taste are why this restaurant is on the map.

"This is incredible," I say on a moan, and Kenzie laughs. "What?" Her reaction surprises me. *Had I been too loud?*

Reaching across the table, she swipes at the corner of my mouth. I turn to her, wanting her hand on my lips, eager for another taste of her. "You have butter on your face."

Oops. Reaching up with my napkin, I wipe it away. "Better?" I ask.

She nods and is about to say something when our server reappears with our meals. Garlic, tomato, and Italian spices waft through the air, making my mouth water.

"This looks delicious. I can't wait to try it." She lifts her fork to her mouth, and I savor watching her pink lips wrap around it. Kenzie closes her eyes and a soft hum comes from her throat. Slowly, she opens her eyes and gushes, "That is the best Italian food I've ever had."

I smile at her. "Looks like we just found our spot for future date nights." *Because I can guarantee there will be many more.*

Time passes too quickly, but we enjoy our meals and our conversation. Knowing that she has to still get up at the ass crack of dawn the next day, I get her home at eight thirty, like a gentleman.

Kenzie doesn't live in the best part of town, so I insist on walking her to her door. Her building's elevator doesn't work, so we trudge up the stairs to the third floor. I follow her down the dimly lit hallway to her apartment. *Why does she live here?*

"This is me," she says as she inserts her key into the lock. Opening the door, I see the small space inside is like the bakery—decorated with bright, happy colors. Even though I can tell it's a rundown building, it looks as if Kenzie has made her space all her own. "Want to come in?" she asks, and my body and mind go to war. I want to go inside, but I don't want to move things too fast. Do I want her? Hell yeah. But I want to show her that this is more than just physical for me.

So I politely refuse the invite. Even though we've been friends for weeks, talking most days about every-thing and nothing, we'd yet to go to each other's houses. Sure, I've been to the bakery a dozen times, but our living spaces seemed more intimate, and I'm not sure how Kenzie feels about me. Instead of accepting her offer to come in, I chance a kiss. One kiss leads to two, and before long, we're full-on making out at her door. And it's mind-blowingly hot. Thankfully, none of her neighbors are nosy because I lose all train of rational thought once I have her backed up against the door-frame. The way her body curves into mine feels unbe-lievably amazing, and there is no way she doesn't feel what she's doing to me.

The urge to pick her up and wrap her legs around

me is intense. Images of stroking my hands up her silky legs almost destroy me. My cock throbs angrily in my pants, and I force myself to step back.

"I need to go," I rasp in a voice I don't recognize. It's full of desire, want, and need. And it matches the heated look in her eyes.

"O-okay," Kenzie stutters. An emotion flashes across her face. *Was that pain?* Our chaotic hallway moments have left her beautifully disheveled, and I reach out to touch her once more. But before I have a chance, she's saying goodnight and slipping through her door.

"Goodnight, Kenzie," I mumble as the door shuts tight. I wait until I hear her flip the lock before I allow myself to respond to the night. Resting my forehead against the door, I take a few deep breaths to regulate my body. I've never had a reaction so explosive before. It's mind-boggling to imagine what it'd be like if we did something more than make out.

Because our date had been early, I find myself wired when I get home. My mind is full of chaos. I can't sit still. Should I call one of my guys and meet up for a beer? *No.* I don't want to deal with all the female attention we always get in hometown bars.

I pace my house, needing an outlet. My eyes land on a pair of running shoes by the door. Before I can talk myself out of it, I'm dressed in athletic shorts and a t-shirt and heading back out my front door. I slip my AirPods in and turn up some rock to drown out my thoughts of Kenzie. Thinking about her will only lead to me trying to run with an erection, and I have to say, nothing about that sounds enjoyable.

By the time I have two and a half miles under my belt, I'm feeling more normal. Making the turn for home, I think again about the evening and how enjoyable it had been. Not that I'm surprised. Taking Kenzie out was so different from any other woman, especially Kayla. It's hard not to draw a comparison, since that was the only other relationship I've had. And if it were up to me, Kenzie and I are definitely starting a relationship.

The transition into the season this year has been different. Normally I'd be psyched to play, but for some reason I'm dragging. Physically, I'm in great shape. But emotionally, that's another story. If I'm being honest, I'm struggling. The thought of being away from Kenzie is killing me. I know we'll text and I'll see her when I'm in town, but will that be enough? Ever since our first kiss, I've wanted to be near her. All. The. Time. It's not even the physical side of things. I crave her sweet, positive spirit. No matter how I feel, or how exhausted I may be, as soon as I'm near her, I'm re-energized.

Preseason flies by. Maybe that's because as soon as I'm done with practice, I drag my battered body over to the bakery. I'm hoping to spend as much time with Kenzie before the near-constant travel becomes my reality. With eighty-plus games a season, it feels like I'm always on the move. I want to enjoy every moment we can get before I have to leave.

"Are you coming over tonight?" Kenzie asks as she removes items from her displays, boxing them up. I learned early in our friendship that each evening she delivers the unsold baked items to a shelter a few blocks over. This woman has the biggest heart of anyone I've ever met. She'd give you the shirt off her back if you needed it.

I smile, grab a rag, and start wiping tables off. "I was planning to, if that's not a problem."

Her smile makes me feel like a million bucks. Her cheeks turn rosy as she admits, "I'd hoped so."

Moving closer, I reach for her hip and pull her into me. Dropping my voice, I ask, "You did? What did you want to do?" She bows her head, hiding herself from me. *Don't hide from me.*

Tipping her head up, I study her eyes. The sparkle in them makes my heart beat wildly. Without another word, I lower myself to her lips and kiss her. She raises on her toes and wraps her arms around my neck, tugging me closer. I dip and lift her. She comes willingly, wrapping her legs around my waist. I spin and she squeezes her thighs tightly around me. I can feel the heat coming off her center through her leggings, and it makes my cock throb in my shorts.

Pushing her up against a wall, I nudge my erection against her center and groan at the contact. Kenzie sucks in a sharp breath, and her body quivers in my arms. I tighten my hold and push my kiss deeper. Her hands, which have threaded through my hair, tug tightly as I grind against her. *That feels so fucking good.* She sharply pulls my hair, making me even harder. I nip at her lower lip and she arches her back, pressing her breasts into my chest. The feel of her tight, hardened nipples sets me on fire. I know I need to slow things down before I strip her down and lay her out on her worktable. My guess is the health department wouldn't think that was too sanitary.

I pull my lips from her. "Kenz," I pant.

"Yeah," she slurs, looking lust drunk. I lower her legs and step back from her, trying to cool my needy, overheated body.

"Let's finish up here and then we can head to your place. Okay?"

Kenzie, still riled up, murmurs, "Yeah, that sounds like a smart plan." *Smart plan?* The smart plan would not be to have me rutting into her like a crazed beast. At least not our first time together. Call me a pussy or not, but I want our first time to be special. I'm not picturing anything too corny, but I know I want it to be in a bed where I can take my time pleasuring her in all the ways I've fantasized about.

That evening, after we lock up at Cakestop and deliver the baked items, we go back to Kenzie's place.

As we enter her postage-stamp-sized apartment, I look around and realize that over the last few weeks I've spent a great deal of time here and I feel really comfortable. At the same time, it occurs to me that we haven't been to my place very often. Every time I go home now, I notice it doesn't feel as homey as Kenzie's place.

Kicking off my shoes next to hers, I follow her into her kitchen. Usually, we make dinner, but I'm not hungry for food. My body is still amped up over what happened at the bakery. I stand behind her as she looks in the fridge. Pulling her hair over her shoulder, I kiss her neck. Kenzie rolls her head to the side, giving me better access, and I trace my tongue up to her earlobe. I blow in it before I suck and nibble it.

"Josh," she moans as she relaxes into me. I hold her body against mine as I run my hands slowly up and down her body. Her goose-bump-covered skin lets me know she's as affected as I am.

Slowly, I turn her in my arms. Her eyes are dark and full of desire. I tip her chin up, then devour her lips like the starved man I am. I slip my hand under her shirt. "Is this okay?" I ask, mumbling against her lips while caressing her naked hip. She pulls away, surprising me by pulling off her shirt.

"Touch me, Josh," she begs as her hand goes to my chest and she rubs my pecs. Standing in front of me, nestled in a pink lacy bra, is the most perfect woman with the most amazing set of breasts I have ever seen. I hesitate for a moment before I talk myself into a quick touch. Running my finger over the globes, I notice how soft she is. Needing to have her skin against mine, I rip off my shirt and lower my mouth to her breasts for my first taste. After a few leisurely licks, I reach behind her and unsnap the closure of her bra. Tugging it down her arms, I toss it over her shoulder, and like a kid in a candy store, I lick my lips, staring at the sweet treat in front of me.

My eyes jolt up and meet hers. *Can I have a taste?* She reads my mind and answers me with a smile. Dipping my head, I place sweet kisses on her breast. I tease her areola with my tongue, making her shiver. When I bite her, she lets out the most beautiful sound I've ever heard. "Josh," she moans in a feverish pitch.

I dip and pick her up, and she wraps her legs around me, and I'm desperate to get inside her. "Do you want to take this to the bedroom?" I ask in a growl.

Kenzie presses her breasts to me and nods. "Down the hall," she pants.

I dive back in for another taste. The feel of her lips on mine makes my mind spin. When we reach a bedroom, I stride in like I know where I'm going, and set her on the bed. She scoots back, wiggles out of her pants, and lies back. Smiling, I climb on top of her, settling between her thighs. The heat coming off her is inconceivable. This is the furthest we've gone. I'm desperate to put my hands all over her, but I won't make any moves that might make her feel rushed or pressured. I don't just want her acquiescence; I want her mad for me, begging for my touch, my fingers, my cock.

I pull my lips from hers and rasp, "Babe, that feels so fucking good."

"Mmm," she moans while using her legs to pull me even tighter. Before I can pull back, she swivels her hips, adding an addictive stroke to the tempo our bodies are already creating. A few minutes later, her movements are rhythmless, a melody of uncontrollable judders, moans, and reverberations, as she grinds harder against me. "Yes," she declares as her orgasm overtakes her body. She arches her back right before her legs tighten around me. The squeeze is exquisite, and I can't wait to feel her tighten around my cock. Her hurried movements slow, and she relaxes around me. I push up and look at her face. Her normally expressive eyes are closed, and she wears a sated smile across her kiss-punished lips. She has a blush on her cheeks that makes her radiant. When her eyes finally blink open, she's the most relaxed I've ever seen. I lean down and rub my nose on her cheek, letting my eyelashes dance across her cheekbones. Kenzie mutters my name with a sweet sigh. No matter how badly I want to push the moment forward—and I certainly do —I suspect that what we just shared is monumental to our relationship and not something I should hurry past. Moving next to her, I pull her to my side and hold her. The warmth of her body lures mine into sleep, and before I know it, I hear an alarm.

Rubbing my eyes, I stretch my arms across the bed and bump into a half-asleep Kenzie. Using my fingers, I pry open my heavy eyelids and glance around the small room. "What time is it?" I ask.

"It's just after three. My alarm went off. I need to get ready to head to the bakery." Kenzie crawls over me and I grab her, pulling her in for a hug.

"Good morning," I say as I nuzzle her hair, kissing the soft spot behind her ear. Like putty, she becomes pliant in my warm hands. I want to snuggle with her all day. The cock-blocking alarm goes off again.

"Guess you have to get up." I groan while releasing my hold on her. She slowly climbs off the bed and I swat her butt.

"Eep!" she squeals before she dips in front of me to grab her clothes off the floor. Last night, she'd undressed down to her panties, and now that I have them only inches from my face, I want to pull them off with my teeth. Reaching out, I trace the panty lines as they taunt me. Kenzie wiggles her hips before standing up and sashaying to the bathroom. *Damn!* Her body is incredible. She has subtle curves that I'm desperate to familiarize myself with. Her skin is warm and soft. Her hips are supple, perfect for grabbing. My fingers flex, wanting to do just that. Her breasts are of the smaller size, but they're high and perky and just enough for my mouth.

Kicking my legs over the side of the bed, I know I should find my shirt so I can head home after I drop her at the bakery, but I don't want to. I want to crawl back into bed with Kenzie and snuggle. Did I really just think that? *What the fuck?* The boys are going to revoke my man card. I'm in deep already, and we've only gone on one date. I don't understand what that means, but what I know is—what this is, between us, is nothing like I've ever felt before.

Chapter 14

Kenzie

"Earth to Kenzie," Toby says loudly as he claps his hands next to my ear. Startled, my arms fly out and flour dust goes everywhere.

"What?" I question, panicked.

"Kenz, we've run out of your banana nut muffins. Do we have any more?" Like a robot, I nod my head. "Good." He sighs dramatically. "We're swamped up front and I've been hollering for you, but you never answered." He puts his hands on his slight hips. "Once the crowd finally settled down, I peeked back and found you like this." Toby's exaggerated movements draw my eyes to the messy countertop in front of me.

I grimace. Being type A, my kitchen is usually pristine, so the scene in front of me horrifies me. To prepare for fall, I've been making small batches of a new recipe—a ginger pear muffin with a strudel topping. I've been working out all the kinks before introducing it to my customers. So far, everyone who's tasted them has given rave reviews.

Looking up, I see Toby eyeball the batter in my bowl and lick his lips. "Are you making those pear muffins again? When will they be ready?" I laugh. Toby is as thin as could be, which you'd never guess from the way he consumes my bakery items. He uses his employee discount to the nth degree.

"Yes, Toby, this is my last test batch before we begin selling them next week."

"So, there will be some to taste test?" he asks, his voice raising a pitch with his excitement. I just smile as I go back to hand-mixing my batter.

Just as I start folding in my pears, I notice Toby still standing there. Pointing across the kitchen, I say, "The rest of the banana nut muffins are over there. Did you need something else?"

He grabs the muffins and walks over to me. "When I came back here, you were lost in thought. Is every-thing okay?"

Grabbing my muffin tin, I scoop batter into the liners I already set up. "Everything is great." I feel the edges of my smile tug up as I remember waking up this morning with Josh wrapped around me. His body was so warm and firm. Well, parts of him were firmer than others, if you get my drift. One in particular that I hadn't explored yet but had put me into the throes of passion last night was definitely making its presence known. Last night was perfect. We hadn't rushed into anything, but we'd enjoyed ourselves. Or at least I had. He hadn't gotten off, but he seemed more concerned that I was satisfied before I drifted off to sleep. Neither one of us had gotten a lot of rest, but it had been magical. Today, when I should have been drained and running on fumes, I feel invincible and energized. No other orgasm I've experienced had ever made me feel that way. What is it about the one Josh gave me? Why had his been different?

"Kenz." Toby groaned in exasperation. *Why did he sound so annoyed? Had he been trying to get my attention?*

"Huh?"

Toby crosses his arms against his chest. "I know something is up. You went from smiling like a deranged clown to utter confusion. Now, are you going to tell me what's going on?"

I don't know. I'm not sure if I want to tell Toby what's going on. It's all still so new. Maybe it didn't mean anything? For Josh anyway. For me, it was huge. In no time, I was already falling for the sweet, strong captain of the city's professional hockey team. But telling Toby means it really happened, and I'm not sure I'm ready to admit that. Other than Stephanie, whom I suspect is dating the Chicago Steel's coach, Toby is my closest friend and the one I share almost everything with.

"Come on, Kenz. Tell me what's going on in that pretty little head of yours." He side-eyes me, and my lips remain closed.

"If you won't tell me, I'm just going to guess until I force you to say something," he warns in a stern, take-no-prisoners tone. Again, I remain silent. *Let's see what he comes up with.* "Did you forget to wash your hands before you baked everything today?" I roll my eyes, because we both know I am borderline neurotic with hand washing. "I got it. You're planning to give me a large raise."

"Toby," I whine.

He claps his hands together. "Got you to talk. Now, what happened?"

Pushing the filled muffin tins to the center of the countertop, I look at him. "Aren't you supposed to be out front helping the customers, not back here harassing me?"

He scoffs. "I came back to get the muffins, and Erica is watching the front. Now, spill."

I lower my head, not wanting to make eye contact before I admit, "I'm not ready to talk about it." I hear his sharp intake of breath. "Stop pushing, okay? I'm your boss, and right now I need you to do your job and take those muffins out front."

Placing the strudel topping on the muffins before sliding them into the oven, I set the timer and go back to clean up my mess. While I'm scrubbing the counter, my mind drifts back to last night and I hesitate. *Was it too fast? Was he just using me and he'll walk away once he conquers me?* Uneasiness settles heavily in my gut. That isn't what's going on, right? I've never dated a professional athlete before, and I'd be remiss to say I hadn't heard a thing or two about famous people having relationship drama. Would that happen to us? Are we even in a relationship? Honestly, I don't know. We haven't had that talk, and even though I don't believe Josh would treat me poorly, the things his ex spread across the internet about him roar their proverbial heads, giving power to them.

The rest of the day flies by and we give samples of the new ginger pear muffins to customers for their feedback. Overwhelmingly, they're a big hit. One regular customer even preorders two dozen for their office for the upcoming week.

At three sharp, Josh walks into the kitchen. Even hunched over a cake with my focus completely on the piping I was doing, my body senses his presence. My heartbeat picks up and my skin tingles, as if someone is running a feather up and down my naked flesh. It tickles, but in a good way.

"Hiya, Kenzie." His deep, rich baritone does things to me.

Looking up, I see a sweet smile dusting his lips. "Hi," I say on a sigh. *I sound like a love-sick fool.*

Breaking the moment, Toby rushes in, thrusting a muffin at Josh. "You have to try these. They are divine.

Tell all your friends." Then he disappears back through the swinging doors.

Josh laughs. "He's quite the salesman." I smirk as he bites into the muffin. He doesn't say anything until two bites later, when his hand is empty. "Babe, that is amazing." I blush at the compliment.

He looks around the kitchen. "You already cleaned up?" I just nod while I finish the last details on the cake. Cleaning is my nervous habit. When I'm anxious about things, scrubbing helps distract me from my worries over Josh and me.

I carefully carry the cake over to the walk-in freezer and place it on a rack for the next day. Just as I'm exiting, Toby pops his head back through the doors. "Kenz, I called Mrs. Jackson to remind her about her cake pick up tomorrow. She'll be in around three."

"Thank you, Toby. I just finished it."

Toby looks at Josh, then at me. "Are you two heading out?"

"I need—" Before I can even finish my thought, Toby jumps in.

"The front's cleaned, the unsold items are boxed and ready for you, and the till is in the safe," he hurries to say.

Consider me impressed. Guess he's over whatever was up his ass earlier. "Thank you, Toby. I really appreciate it." He shrugs his shoulders.

"It was nothing." Then he pops back to the front and returns with two medium bakery boxes and hands them to Josh. "I'm assuming you're going to help deliver these." Josh smiles, accepts the boxes, and nods. Toby then strides over to me and wraps me in a big hug. Out of the corner of my eye, I see Josh stand taller and puff out his chest. And if looks could kill, Toby would be gone. *What's that about?* Blissfully unaware, Toby pulls back and says to me. "You know I'm here if you need me. Anytime."

"I know. Thank you." He hugs me again before he leaves with a wave of his hand. I look over at Josh and he still looks like he's upset and chewing rocks. "You okay?" I ask him.

Josh sets down the boxes and comes closer. "Are you and Toby involved?" His face is both serious and pained, like it hurt to even suggest that. I can't help it, but I laugh. Josh's face falls and my heart drops.

"I'm sorry I laughed... It's just Toby and I are definitely not involved. He's like the little brother I never had." I pull his hand into mine to reassure him. "There is nothing going on between us." He cocks his head sideways, as if questioning me.

"The way he looks at you, that hug, his promise to be there for you. *Anytime.*" He emphasizes that last part, and I smirk.

"Josh, Toby is not interested in me like that. Yes, we are close. He's one of my best friends. But honestly, he'd be more interested in you than me."

Josh's mouth drops open. "He's gay?"

I nod. "He is. Plus, I'm too hung up on this other

guy to even notice anyone else." He pulls his hand through his hair and I wrap my arms around him. Finally, he returns the hug and I'm being cocooned in his muscular arms. After a few moments, I tighten my arms and ask, "You ready to deliver some goodies?"

He grabs the boxes, and I lock up. Hand in hand, we walk a few streets over to the shelter I donate to. A few of the regulars wave hello.

Strolling back to my apartment, we're both quiet. I'm rehashing my day. Everything from waking up next to Josh, my afternoon of worry over his feelings for me, and the fact he seemed threatened by Toby's affection toward me. It's enough to keep my head spinning with uncertainty. This woman needs some clarification, like yesterday. We need to talk before I'm willing to take things any further.

For dinner, I preheat the oven and pull a take-and-bake pizza from my fridge. "I'm going to change. Make yourself comfortable," I tell Josh before heading back to my bedroom. Returning in a tank top and cotton shorts, I don't miss the way Josh's hungry eyes trace over my body. Everywhere his eyes travel, heat erupts, and in moments, I'm warm and toasty. I step closer and Josh pulls me into him.

He kisses my head, asking, "How was your day?"

I shrug in response.

He tips my head up, making eye contact. His baby blues are amazing. I could get lost staring into them.

He blinks, then asks, "Is everything okay?" He pauses. "What was Toby talking about at the bakery?"

A flash of this afternoon pierces my brain, and my insecurities and worries come flooding back. Overwhelmed by it all, I pull back. Josh looks at me with concern. "I just had a weird afternoon."

"What do you mean, weird? What happened?" he questions.

I wring my hands together, unsure how to bring it up.

He grabs my hands and cradles them in his much larger ones. "Please talk to me."

Forcing a smile, I admit, "I got lost in my head a lot today." His worry is evident on his face, and his eyes beg for more. "You see, when I don't understand something, I spend a great deal of time thinking about it, trying to make sense of it, my feelings, what it all means."

"Okay," he says hesitantly. *How do I explain this better?*

Leading him over to my well-worn cloth couch, I sit down and then pat the cushion next to me. With our knees touching, I begin my explanation. "So last night happened... and it got me thinking. A lot."

His eyes grow big and he sits up straighter. "Did I push you into doing something you weren't ready for?"

I shake my head. "Everything we did was great. Actually, it was amazing. It felt incredible to wake up in your arms. But then I started asking myself questions."

"What questions? Maybe I can help answer them."

I smile despite my uncertainty. "I hope so."

Josh offers a smile. "Lay them on me. I'll do my best."

Chapter 15

Josh

Kenzie is fucking adorable. When she said she had questions about last night, my heart sank. *Would she say it was a mistake and then ask how we could go back to being friends?* I don't think I could handle that. Since getting to know her, Kenzie has become one of my best friends. We talk about nothing and everything. And I want more, especially now that I've had a taste of her.

"What did last night mean? What are we exactly? Where are we going from here?" she asks nervously. Breathing out a sigh of relief that she isn't relegating us back into the friend zone, I consider her questions and how to answer them. Truth be told, I've had the same questions floating around my mind too.

"Just like you, I think last night was amazing, and no, I don't know what that means. It isn't a predictor of where we'll end up. But I know being with you felt right. It was perfect. And I want to keep exploring this, whatever it is, with you."

Kenzie's whole face lights up. Her eyes twinkle and her smile is wide and contagious. I feel myself mimicking her. *Does she feel the same?* "You do?" she questions in a whisper.

"I do. Kenz, you are my best friend, and you're the most beautiful woman in the world. Why wouldn't I want more?" Admitting my feelings is nerve-racking. As a professional athlete, I'm beyond confident in my skills and abilities. But to put my heart on the line after everything that happened with Kayla, I'm terrified, because Kenzie is the best thing that's ever happened to me. She is the most incredible woman I've ever met. I don't want this chance to slip away.

The timer on the pizza goes off, and I startle. Jumping to my feet, I grab our dinner out of the oven. Normally I'd be starving following an intense day of practice and weights, but my stomach is in knots because of our conversation. Kenzie steps up behind me and pulls out the pizza slicer. After our plates are loaded, we return to the couch to continue our conversation, and for the first time since we met at the gala, I'm uncomfortable. Kenzie must sense it because she sets her plate down and turns toward me.

"Josh, I don't have much experience here. Is what we're doing considered dating? Or if it isn't, would you like to be?" Her questions don't leave any room for misinterpretation. Once I answer them, she'll know how I feel.

Needing to feel close to her, I reach for her hand and weave our fingers together. "I don't have much experience with this either. Other than Kayla, I've never dated, and I'm not even sure that's what I'd call that shitshow." I grimace at the thought of Kayla and everything she'd done. "Kenz, I want to date you. And if that's what we've been doing, I want to keep doing it. I want you to be mine, and me to be yours." The smile she's radiating leaves me feeling breathless. My heart thunders in my chest. "So... you're my girlfriend," I rasp, the emotion of the moment hitting me harder than I expected. She beams a mega-watt smile at me before she crawls toward me and places a gentle kiss on my lips, electrifying me. She sits back and my body is humming. Needing another taste, I lean forward, pulling her back to me. When our lips touch, a burst of energy zig zags through me, driving my desire for her higher. I reach for her, wanting to pull her into my lap. Wrapping my hand around her hip, I nudge her forward, and she pulls her lips away.

She places her hand on my chest and whispers, "You make me so happy."

I smile. "I couldn't agree more." Her confession is a balm to my worried soul.

After her confession, we need something a tad lighter. We select a comedy and enjoy our pizza as we snuggle together on the couch. Tomorrow is Saturday, and that means I don't have early practice to get to. Kenzie still has to be up early for the bakery, so it doesn't surprise me when she falls asleep in my lap. When the end credits roll, I switch off the TV and carefully pick her up and carry her to her bed. Once I tuck her in, I find her phone and make sure it's on her charger, then I clean up the mess from our dinner. After that, I sneak back into her room and give her a kiss. I'm not trying to wake her, but when her eyes flutter open, I can't help but smile. This woman has my heart. Completely.

Reaching out, she hooks her hand around my neck, pulling me in, smooshing our lips together. "Don't leave," she begs against my lips. I deepen our kiss, and Kenzie throws back the covers, welcoming me in beside her. Who am I to argue?

I remove my shirt, kick off my shoes, and climb onto the bed. Just being next to her does things to me. My breathing increases as my heart thuds in my chest. Being this close to her makes my mind spin. My dick hardens to a painful degree. Putting myself above Kenzie's body sounds like the only plausible option. Widening my legs, I make room for her and lower my hips to hers. The heat radiating between us could start a five-alarm fire. My cock responds aggressively as I gently thrust against her. It twitches. Kenzie raises her hips, rubbing against me. *Damn, that feels incredible.* I'm already so close that I'm afraid I might embarrass myself. I've been celibate since the last time I was with

Kayla—the night she told me she lost the baby, and I had been tormented with feeling too much of everything and nothing all at once.

Not wanting to pressure Kenzie into anything, I try to slow things down with kissing. But before I know it, her hands weave into my hair, tugging at the strands. I pull on her bottom lip, giving it a nibble, and she opens her mouth and moans, setting things in motion.

My hips act on their own and grind down into her. When I lift myself up to reposition, she slides her legs apart and wraps them around me, pulling me in tight. "Ahhh. Babe." I groan. Fisting my cock over my pants, I'm sure I'm leaking into my boxers. Holding myself in a one-handed pushup, I squeeze my overzealous cock, reminding it I'm in charge. It throbs in my hand. *Bastard.* I clasp it tightly, again warning it if it doesn't behave, I'll leave, giving myself the worst case of blue balls I've ever had. My threat is serious until Kenzie continues rubbing and gyrating against me. I'm just a man. Powerless to her dry humping my cock like her life depends on it.

I pull my lips from hers, breaking the heated moment. It would be easy to jump back into it, but I want to make sure Kenzie is okay. Looking into her beautiful blue eyes, I ask, "Babe, if you want to stop, you're going to have to tell me. I don't want you to feel pressured to do anything you aren't ready for." *She's not just any woman to me.* She matters, and I don't want her uncomfortable.

Wiggling below me, she smiles and answers, "I'm all yours. I want this. Want *you*."

Stunned, I question, "Really?" She laughs and pulls me down for a knock-your-socks-off, heated kiss that leaves me with no more questions. Overheated, I throw off the covers while my mind spins with all the ideas of what I want to do to her.

"What are you doing?" she asks.

Scooting myself over her, I climb out of the bed before saying, "I'm getting things more comfortable." Then... I drop my pants and boxers. My hard cock bobs out in front of me and I grab it and give it a squeeze. Kenzie's eyes go wide, and she makes an O with her mouth. My pulse skyrockets in my veins. I lean over the bed and reach for the hem of her tank top. Just as I'm about to tug it up, her hand wraps around my cock. It feels divine. The ultimate pleasure. "Babe," I caution her. "If you do much more of that, we'll never get to the finale, and I have big plans."

"Oh." Her fingers loosen their hold on me and my cock throbs in protest. I suck in a deep breath, trying to keep myself under control. Once I've regained my composure, I open my eyes to see Kenzie completely naked before me. Her shirt gone in record time, replaced by a canvas of beautiful pale skin, laid bare just for me. A feast for the senses.

"Eager, aren't you?" The backs of my fingers glide along the silky-smooth skin of her collarbone, down over the hard peaks of her nipples.

"Well, you were naked, so I wanted to be naked with you."

My woman is a fucking goddess. Like a road map, she's covered with curves that scream fun and adventure. I don't know what I've done to deserve her, but I know I never want to take this moment, or her, for granted.

I stand and stare at her, not wanting to miss anything. "Kenzie, you are the most beautiful woman I have ever seen." She blushes and looks away. Crawling over her, I nudge her chin back so she's looking at me. "I'm serious. You're breathtaking." Then I lower and kiss her with all the passion coursing through my ravenous body.

Pulling away, she mewls at me until I string slow kisses down her body. Starting with her neck, I leave tender kisses and quick nibbles. When I get to her collarbones, I leisurely lick across them before working over to her sternum, kissing down until I'm level with her breasts. They may be on the smaller side, but I've got a handful to squeeze, twist and tug. Her nipples are rosy pink and incredibly reactive to my touch. As soon as I suckle at them, her hips begin to move and a moan falls from her perfect lips. My cock grows harder at her movement, and I'm afraid it's going to call it early. Figuring there will be more time to spend on her breasts later, I continue on down her body. I move off the bed and tug her to me. Lowering to my knees, I spread her legs wide, throwing a knee over each shoulder. My mouth waters, excited for my first taste of her. With one hand, I reach up and spread her, then I flatten my tongue and lick from back to front, paying extra attention to her clit.

"Josh," she squeals as her hips rise.

Using my hand, I apply enough pressure to keep her in place while I lick, suck, and nip at her. It doesn't take long before she's writhing below me. A hand goes to my hair, tugging on it, as moans fall from her lips.

Suspecting she's close, I insert one finger and curl it toward me. After a few strums, I rub up against her G-spot and she lifts off the bed, taking me with her. "Holy shit. Do that again." *Yes, ma'am.* I insert another finger and follow orders like the good soldier I am. Only two strokes later and her muscles are squeezing my fingers while she screams out my name.

Slipping my fingers from her, I lick them clean before I pull a condom from my wallet. I quickly sheath myself and tease her hole with the head of my cock. A deep moan fills the otherwise quiet room, and I take it as my invitation to keep going. Slowly, I push into her, grunting as I go. When I bottom out, I can't help but moan my pleasure. "That feels so good." To which Kenzie replies with an "mmm" of her own.

Moving slowly, I pull out almost the entire way before I piston back in. After only a few strokes, we're in sync. Using the leverage of the floor, I can angle myself so the position we're in mimics the cowgirl and I easily slide in and out of her hot, needy channel.

"Right there," she orders. I feel the tentative squeeze of another orgasm building inside her, and I swivel my hips when I reach her clit. She arches her back, pressing her breasts into my face. I swirl my tongue around one pert nipple before her body shakes. Her muscles squeeze my cock and it feels amazing. I continue to thrust into her as she rides the waves of her orgasm. When she relaxes, I pull out and turn her on her stomach. Pulling her butt up, I don't give her any warning before I push back into her.

"Josh," she sobs into the bed. Just as I'm about to check and see if she's okay, she pants, "More." It doesn't take but a few strokes to feel her tighten around me.

"Fuck," I grit through my teeth as my orgasm explodes out of me. We collapse on the bed, sated.

Chapter 16

Kenzie

Until Josh, sex had always been like baking. In order to get the result you want, you must precisely follow a recipe of sorts. And that's how I've looked at my relationships too, but I found it left me unsatisfied. I needed more oomph or pizazz to uncover that thing that really sparkled, that diamond in the rough. Which is why I remained single and opened my shop.

Standard baking is fine. When done right, it yields items that are perfectly similar in appearance and taste. You get what you expected. But I want more. I long for something new and different. For me, baking is about following the recipe, but it's also about making art. To me, art can be something more than what you see. It's a full-body experience. And I strive to do that in everything I make.

Unfortunately, over the last few years, I've found

myself pulled in far too many directions. My creativity stifled because of my responsibility to make sure Cake-Stop succeeds. But it's finally doing just that, and I've been able to get back to the heart of it. Making edible art that not only pleases the tastebuds but the eyes as well. And just like the bakery is coming around, I am too.

When Josh and I finally had sex, it rocked my world. I can't imagine anyone sweeter or more thoughtful. And can I mention the orgasms? Unless we count self-administered by my B.O.B., I've never had one. They're absolutely amazing, but the best part was being cuddled in Josh's muscular arms as I drifted off to sleep. In fact, now that I've experienced that, I find it incredibly hard to sleep when he isn't there. Which makes for some cranky mornings when he's on the road. Thankfully, I usually get my attitude in check before my employees show up for their shifts. Usually.

"Good morning, Kenz," Toby cheerfully sings, entering the kitchen as I'm prepping another set of muffins for the oven. *Was it really a good morning?*

Josh has been gone for an entire week. I've survived because of texts and FaceTime calls, but it's been tough. When I can finally fall asleep, I only get an average of four hours a night. Instead of replying to Toby, I just grunt.

Stepping farther into the kitchen, Toby asks in alarm, "What was that sound?"

"What sound?" I question as I set the timer on the oven.

He looks at me and puts his hands on his hips. "You didn't hear it? It sounded like a bear trying to cough up a hairball."

I scowl at him. *I did not sound like that.* "First off, bears don't get hairballs, at least I don't think they do."

"And second?" he asks with a smirk.

"Huh?"

Shaking his head, he says, "You were giving me a list, but you stopped at one."

I tilt my head to the side. "I was?"

Coming up to stand next to me, he wraps his arm around my shoulders. "Kenz, how much sleep did you get last night? You have dark bags under your eyes. Josh must be out of town again, huh?"

I nod my head, exhaustion making it feel heavier than normal. "I only got a few hours."

My mood is off-kilter, and I'm irritable and sensitive.

I'm dealing with bone-deep tiredness, caused by a lack of sleep because Josh isn't sleeping next to me. I'm not feeling myself. I miss his scent and his soft snores. I miss his warmth curled up behind me. I miss his presence. And my body seems to notice he left a Josh-shaped hole in my heart. And my sleep cycle.

"Let me go make you a coffee. I'll help you prep your last things this morning and then, when they're all baked, you can go home and sleep."

With my head buried in my arms, I flash him a thumbs-up. My eyes feel so heavy. *I'll just close them for a bit while Toby makes me a cup of coffee.*

I feel a gentle rubbing on my back, and I don't want to move and risk having it stop. "Kenz, wake up." *Is that Toby?* I slowly blink my eyes open and recognize my surroundings. *Why am I sleeping in the kitchen of my shop?* Looking toward Toby, he's standing there holding a coffee and wearing a sweet smile.

"Hi," I say, a little embarrassed.

"Okay, let's get baking so we can get you home." I nod while reaching for the coffee. The first sip explodes on my tongue and I wonder what he did to it. I take another sip, trying to figure out what's different. It's silkier and richer than normal. I side-eye him and he laughs. "What?" he questions.

I hold the coffee up. "What's different about the coffee?"

"It's called Bulletproof coffee, and it's supposed to fuel your day... or that's what Greg, my friend, doing Keto, preaches."

I take another sip. "It's delicious."

"Good. Now, let's get you moving. The sooner you finish, the sooner you can go home." *So bossy.*

"Yes, sir," I mumble as I climb off the stool.

Toby isn't able to stay in the kitchen with me as I finish the last few items, but he pops his head in frequently to ensure I'm staying on task. Then he ushers me out the door at noon so I can head home to sleep. It's nice to know my shop is in excellent hands. I trust my staff and I know they'll make sure they handle everything. Even though sleep has been elusive for the past few days, it comes easily when I get home, and I sleep until my alarm the next morning.

The next day goes by quickly, and I'm in much better spirits. The fact that Josh is back today may have something to do with that. In such a short time, he's become my person, and every time he travels, I feel like a part of me is missing. I know I'll have to figure out how to deal with it because he isn't planning to retire anytime soon.

At three, as I'm prepping for the next day, a familiar voice I've been craving carries through the shop. In mere moments, the kitchen doors are flapping and I'm being lifted off my feet. "Hi," I squeal excitedly while wiggling in his hold.

Strong arms tighten around me, and a gravelly voice rasps, "I missed you so much, baby."

"Then set me down and show me," I tease. He laughs and sets me on my feet. With the flick of his wrist on my hip, he spins me and then lays the most incredible kiss on my lips. I rise on my toes and wrap my arms around his neck, threading my fingers through his hair. He dips and lifts me again, and I wrap my legs around his waist. While continuing to ravage my mouth, he walks toward the counter I'd just been working at and presses my ass into it. He pushes his erection against my center, and through my thin leggings I can feel everything. He's hot and hard. For me. I flex my hips forward and he groans into my ear. "You're dangerous."

"No," I say before I do it again. *I'm playing with fire and I don't care.*

His growl registers deep, heating my core, before he speaks again. "Do you want me to take you right here? Let all your customers and employees hear you scream my name?" I suck in a sharp breath. *Let's do that.* Or maybe not. My lust-soaked brain finally sobers and I decide that probably isn't a good idea.

"I'm almost ready, and then we can go home." *Home?* We don't live together, officially. Sure, when he's in town, he sleeps over most nights. I've been to his place too, but mine is closer to the shop, so we usually end up at my apartment. It isn't much, but it's enough. Josh's house is absolutely incredible. But I wouldn't feel right about being there without him, so for now, my place has become home base.

Josh heads out front to grab a coffee and a cookie while I finish up. When it's almost closing time, Josh and I box up the items for donation. The bell above the door chimes, letting me know a customer has come in. I turn around, giving her a smile. "Welcome to Cake-Stop. What can I get you?" She's familiar looking, but I can't place her. *Where do I know her from?* When she orders a skinny iced latte, I see Josh's shoulders go tight. He's turned away, so I can't see his expression, but based on his body language, he's uncomfortable. I ring up the order as my barista, Jen, makes the woman her drink. Watching as Josh slowly turns around, I'm surprised by his reaction. When his eyes land on her, his frown morphs into a snarl. *Who is she?*

The woman's eyes go wide and bright. Then she gets a sultry look on her plump red lips. She licks them and then purrs, "Hi, Josh. It's so great to see you." Jen hands over the woman's drink and she doesn't even acknowledge her or thank her. *Rude.* Instead, her eyes are laser-focused on Josh. She moves closer to him, and I stand back, watching their interaction. It's like a car wreck. You can't look away.

Dread swirls in my stomach.

"It's so weird running into you here," she chirps while dramatically flinging her hand around.

Josh grinds his molars and bites out, "What are you doing here, Kayla?" I freeze and my eyes go wide. *It's her. Live and in living color.*

The woman fake laughs, touches her visible cleavage, and answers, "I needed an afternoon pick-me-up. The real question is, why are you here? This isn't exactly on your *special diet*." Her syrupy-sweet voice goes acidic on her last comment.

Josh tightens his hands into fists. "It's none of your business why I'm here. Now, if you got what you needed, you can leave."

She smiles lecherously and counters, "If you're here, maybe that's for a reason. Maybe I should try something?" She turns and struts back to the counter. The air in the shop feels frigid.

Forcing myself to move, I meet her at the counter and ask as nicely as I can, "What can I get for you?"

Looking at Josh, then at me, she asks, "What does he order? I want to try whatever brings him in." I don't miss the snobby, judgmental dig she layers in her comments.

Unsure what to do, I answer truthfully, "He's tried everything on the menu."

She gasps. "That's not possible. He doesn't eat this... stuff," she scoffs while pointing at the items still on display. *She thinks she knows Josh, and yes, when we first met, he didn't eat sweets often. But things have changed. Now he just eats them in moderation.*

Annoyed at her blasé diss, I straighten my spine. Speaking clearly, I answer, "I assure you, he has."

I feel Josh move closer and place a possessive hand on my lower back. The woman sees and her eyes go wide. Then he speaks up. "Not that it's any of your business, Kayla, but this is Kenzie, my girlfriend. She's an incredible baker, and she owns this shop." Then he adds, dropping his voice, "And I eat everything she offers." *Is he suggesting what I think he is?* At the thought of him pleasuring me, I look up at him. He looks down at me and smiles before dropping a tender kiss on my lips. Lost in him, I barely register the click of her heels as she leaves.

"Damn, that was intense," Jen mutters as she goes back to cleaning the coffee machine.

"I'm going to lock the front door. We don't need to let any more crazy in here." Josh forces a laugh. I hear the tension in it and I'm worried about him. I don't think he's seen her since their breakup. She was just awful afterward, dragging him and his reputation through the mud. I hope he's okay after today's uncomfortable encounter.

Chapter 17

Josh

This season has drug on painfully slow. Now that Kenzie is in my life, I don't want to be away so often. Before now, I never understood why those guys in relationships were eager to get home. Honestly, when Kayla was around, I was in no rush. But maybe that's because I wasn't fully committed to her. Seeing Kayla in Kenzie's shop a month ago really solidified things for me. I never felt for Kayla the way I feel about Kenzie. I'm totally falling for her.

Every time she's near, my heart pounds in my chest. She's gotten under my skin. I crave her when we're apart; it feels like a part of me is missing. Until her, I didn't know being in a relationship could be so amazing. But what I truly miss are the little things. The sweet sigh she makes when she's in my arms. Her shy smile that is both flirty and mischievous. The flutter of my pulse when she looks at me and licks her lips. The love notes she hides in my wallet that I find when I'm away. My favorite thing about her is the way she hugs me. Just like her bakery items, she fills them with love. Kenzie is one in a million, and I'm so lucky she's mine. She's everything to me.

"Hey, Josh, what are you doing for Kenzie for Valentine's Day?" Lucas asks while we sit on the tarmac waiting for our return flight to Chicago.

"I don't really know. It's the first one I've really wanted to celebrate. I want to make it special, but I'm not coming up with any good ideas. What are you doing for Samantha?"

Smugly, he grins. "I've got it all planned. Since we're gone on the actual day, pampering will take place over several days. I'm flying my mom in so the day before we get back, Samantha can go to the spa and have a massage, manicure, and pedicure. Then the next night, I'm taking her on a romantic date night."

"Damn, brother. Put the rest of us to shame," Mika hollers from across the aisle.

Lucas grins. "What are you doing for Shiloh?"

Mika sits taller. "She's getting her gift early. I'm giving her a weekend away."

"Y-you're sending her away?" I clear my throat. "Aren't you supposed to be together to celebrate romantic holidays, eating lavish food and having kinky sex?"

Mika's eyes go wide. "Dude. I don't need to know

about your sex life." He laughs, then adds, "I don't need a holiday to do that stuff. But to answer your question, yes, I'm sending her away. She and Monica are going on a girls' weekend."

"Oh, that's smart. I wish I could do something like a couple's getaway, but with the bakery, that is impossible."

Just as the plane taxis, Lucas leans over to me and asks, "So, what are you going to do?"

"I don't know, man, but I need to figure it out," I tell him before I pull my noise canceling headphones over my ears. Chris Young's "She's Got a Way" comes on, and when his soulful voice delivers the lyrics, they register deep and I swallow hard. *Am I in love with her?*

Leaning back with my eyes closed, I consider that. I've never said those words to anyone other than my family, and at times I'm not even sure I meant it. No woman has ever made me feel that way. Until now. Every moment we're apart, I can't wait to see her. She invades all my thoughts and dreams. I want her next to me, experiencing everything with me. I want to make her happy, help her dreams come true. Learn with her, laugh with her. Realization strikes me like a hit against the boards, fast and jarring. My eyes fly open. *I love Kenzie.* Overwhelmed by the truth of that, I need to get home to let her know just how I feel.

Lucas pats my arm from the next seat. I remove my headphones. "You okay, man?" he asks.

I nod. "Yeah. I'm good. Just realized there's something I need to do."

He tilts his head at me suspiciously and asks, "Now?"

I laugh. "No, when we get back to Chicago."

"Okay," he says before he returns to the magazine he'd been reading.

The flight home takes forever. Okay, I might not be the most patient person. But as soon as I feel the wheels touch down, my legs bounce. Apparently, it's my attempt to free myself from the extra nervous energy coursing through my body. Looking at my watch, I see it's four in the afternoon.

The team bus hauls us back to the arena to retrieve our vehicles from the player parking. I wave at my teammates as I power walk to my white Tesla. Kenzie should be home by the time I get there. I stop by a florist on my way and grab her a bouquet of pink sunflowers. They catch my eye as soon as I enter the shop. They're unique and special, just like Kenzie and, just like their yellow cousin, they're happy, just like my girl.

Pulling up to her apartment building, my heart skips a beat. I see Kenzie walking down the sidewalk. She's bundled up in her bright pink winter jacket, matching stocking cap, and fuzzy mittens. She looks absolutely adorable. *Here we go.* Climbing from my car, I lock eyes with the woman of my dreams. "Kenzie," I call out.

A radiant smile breaks out on her gorgeous face. "You're home," she squeals before running over to me and jumping in my arms. Hugging her tight, I realize there is no other place I'd rather be.

Nuzzled into her neck, I place soft kisses on her heated skin. "I missed you so much," I rasp, suddenly overcome with emotion.

With concern in her voice, Kenzie asks, "Are you okay?"

I just nod and squeeze her tighter.

"Want to go inside? It's cold here today."

Setting her back on the sidewalk, I see the tip of her nose is red, and I bop it.

"These are for you," I say, handing her the flowers. She grins up at me and grabs my hand, leading me to her building. When we finally get inside her apartment, we eagerly rid ourselves of our winter gear and head to her couch. "Eep," she says as I pull her down onto my lap.

Holding her close, I look into her blue eyes and say, "Hi."

"Hi," she parrots back before snuggling into me. Having her this close is the best thing in the world. I wouldn't trade it for anything. "I missed you," she confesses against my chest. Resting my chin on her head, I echo her words. I'm noticing each time I'm away from her, it gets harder and harder for me.

Her stomach growls. I poke it and laugh. "How

about we get dinner delivered from Mateo's and spend the evening snuggled up together?" I suggest.

"That sounds perfect."

Pulling out my phone, we browse the menu before I order. I always get their lasagna, and Kenzie can't decide between that and the spinach manicotti. I offer to share, then I order breadsticks, salad, and tiramisu to share as well. After we gorge ourselves on the best Italian food in the city, we snuggle back on the couch while watching a random Netflix show.

Kenzie is a creature of habit. At eight every night, she begins her nightly routine by stretching. Of course, I sit back and watch because I love to stare at her luscious curves as they twist and lengthen in front of me. My fingers itch to touch her, to run the tips up and down her heavenly lines. But I remain still, nervous about what I need to do. Once she's done, she stands and snags my hand, pulling me to my feet.

"Ready for bed?" I ask.

She sighs. "Yes, I don't sleep so well when you aren't next to me."

We head to her bedroom after we make sure everything is off or put away for the evening. While she's in the bathroom, I undress, leaving me in just my black boxer briefs. When she emerges from the bathroom, her face is freshly clean and glowing, making her look ethereal. I give her a quick peck on the lips and she tastes minty. "Be right back," I say on my way to brush my teeth. I don't have much here except my toothbrush and a few changes of gym clothes in case I have an early practice. Usually when I sleep over, I go back to my place after she heads to the bakery. Yes, I'm wearing the same clothes as the day before, but there is no shame in my game. Instead of it being the walk of shame, I call it a strut.

I turn the light off before I crawl into bed, then I pull Kenzie to me and wrap my arms around her. With her near, my body responds like it has all evening. My erection's hard and I poke her in the back. She circles her hips and nudges my cock with her butt. A tingle shoots through me, lighting me up and making my whole body buzz. I pull her in tighter, thrusting my hips forward, rubbing my cock against her. She arches her head back and whimpers. "Josh, please. I've missed you so much." I pull back and she lies flat. In seconds, I'm hovering over her. Her expressive eyes beg me for more. I lower down, fitting myself in the cradle of her thighs, and position my cock against her hot center, the material of our underwear the only barrier between us. The desire to thrust is intense, but I force myself to focus on Kenzie.

"You are so beautiful," I tell her before I devour her lips. When my tongue enters her mouth to tangle with hers, she nips it, making me groan. *What is this woman doing to me? Anything she wants.*

When we finally part, we're both panting, but I drop my head to leave a line of kisses down her sexy as fuck neck. I trace the slope with my tongue and inhale the scent that can only be named chef's kiss. Why, you ask? Because it's a perfect mix of sugar and spice. I want to eat her. Baring my teeth, I nibble across one collarbone and then the other. Her sighs keep me focused and moving forward on my exploration of her body, feathering kisses down her sternum. *I need to see her.*

Pulling her tank top over her head, her perfect breasts before me. My mouth waters and I lick my lips. Taking one in my hand, I give it a rough squeeze. She moans and I flick her dusky-pink nipple. Kenzie pushes her chest toward me, and I understand exactly what she wants. *More.* I suck one nipple into my mouth while I continue to squeeze the other. While it's in my mouth, I bite it and she moans my name. *She's so responsive.*

Letting go of her breast, I trail my fingertips down to her waist and under her thin cotton panties. *Have mercy.* Releasing a throaty growl against her breast causes her to shiver. Eager to know how wet she is, I trace my fingers through her small patch of hair and to her silky lower lips. Gliding through them with ease gives me the answer I want. She's hot, wet, and ready for me. But I don't want to be selfish. My rule is she always comes first. I plunge my first finger into her needy center and she lets out a contented sigh. It's like I've scratched an itch she hasn't been able to reach, making her desperate for relief. Inserting another finger makes her hips flex. Her muscles squeeze around my digits, alerting me to her impending orgasm. Thrusting back and forward only makes her wetter.

"Josh, I'm so close," she pants. I release the suction on the nipple I'd been savoring, and pinch it. Her muscles tighten and her body rolls. "Yes!" she screams. I continue to play with her nipple, pinching and twisting it until I'm confident she's coming down from the pleasure her body just succumbed to. Removing my fingers, I bring them to my lips. When her eyes are on me, I lick off the evidence of her pleasure.

"You taste like sin... and I need more."

Kenzie gives me a shy smile, nodding her head while I remove her panties. She reaches forward and palms my cock through my briefs. "Fuck." *That feels good.* I'm so close to coming. I know I have to stop her when she squeezes me. "Damn, baby. That feels incredible, but you have to stop, or I'll come before I want to." She teases me with another squeeze and then releases me.

I lick my lips at the sight of the wetness between her thighs. Scooting down, I get into position. Opening her, I see silky pink skin waiting for me. Lowering my lips, I swipe my tongue through her folds once, then again. Then I pull her clit into my mouth and suck on it, varying my pressure to see what she responds to best. While doing that, I trace her entrance with my finger. She circles her hips as if she's chasing it. I insert my finger and curl it in a come-hither motion, rubbing up against a soft, spongy section. I know I've found the spot that drives her wild.

Thrusting another finger into her tight channel earns me the noise I crave. Kenzie lets a hum from her lips that turns me into a desperate fool. I will do anything to make her happy and keep her pleased and sated. Swiping my fingertips against her G-spot, I feel the exact moment when her orgasm crashes into her. Her body tightens and her internal muscles squeeze. Her hips rock and she fists my hair. I resume licking and nipping at her pussy until her body slumps back against the bed. Her eyes are closed and her breathing is labored. Slipping my fingers from her, I remove my underwear and move back above her.

Kenzie's eyes flick open when my cock nuzzles up against her. Pulling back a little, I ask, "Are you sensitive?"

She nods, but then says, "In a good way, though." Returning her smile, I stare at her. Reaching over, I push back some stray hairs that have worked their way across her face.

"Kenzie... there's something I need to tell you." Her body goes rigid beneath me and her eyes are wild with fear. *Shit.* "Sorry, I didn't mean that to come across so gruff." She somewhat relaxes below me. *It's now or never. Don't blow this.* "What I wanted to say is... I love you!" Shock spreads across her face. *Fuck.* I didn't know what to expect, but it wasn't that. Rambling, I try to backpedal. "I'm sorry. I'm doing this all wrong. I've never told a woman that before, and I screwed it up." Pushing up, I'm embarrassed, and I question whether I should leave. *What if she doesn't feel the same? Did I just ruin things? I've never been in love before. Maybe I'm wrong.*

Kenzie places a hand on my forearm, pulling me out of the chaos in my head. "Josh, you didn't screw it up. You just caught me off guard." She smiles at me hopefully. I force one in return, but she knows it is fake. "Hey. Talk to me."

I'm quiet for a moment. I've always been able to talk to Kenzie about everything, so why am I struggling right now? *Because you think she doesn't love you.* The thought of that sits in my gut like a fifty-pound boulder. *What am I going to do if it's true?*

"Josh, please," she begs.

What have I got to lose? Everything. Feeling unsettled, I divert my gaze and mumble my response. "I just confessed my feelings, and I think I scared you because you don't feel the same." I chance a glance at her and see a soft expression on her face. Kenzie runs her finger down my jawline, forcing my chin up and my eyes to her. Focusing, I notice they're not only brilliant, but they sparkle with happiness. Her pink lips curve up, gifting me the smile that's just for me. It's chock-full of love.

"It's true you surprised me. But I love you too. I've been scared to say it because I didn't know if it was too soon." At her words, euphoria floods my brain. *She loves me too.* I lower myself to her and kiss her passionately. *She loves me too.* My heart thumps wildly in my chest, making me feel somewhat lightheaded. My cock reminds me he's still in play. Reaching for it, I run it through her moist folds, circling her entrance. "Don't tease me," she warns.

"Never," I say with a smirk. I push into her, her body accepting mine, like we've both come home. It feels different this time. More intense. More pleasurable. Just *more.* Is that what love does? This time is special, and it's a moment in time I'll never forget.

Chapter 18

Kenzie

Waking up next to him this morning is surreal. Last night was pivotal for our relationship. My heart is still giddy with excitement. *He loves me.* The man who was so sure he would never have a relationship, who seemed so far out of my league, loves me.

Sinking back into the covers, the knowledge of his love warms me. I've never been happier. Josh sleeps peacefully beside me, and I should be tired, considering we only got a few hours of sleep, but I'm not. I close my eyes, remembering all the ways he made me feel beautiful and sensual last night. Sex between us has always been hot and explosive, but last night was different. We connected in another way that was more akin to making love than having sex. It was slow, tender, and intentional. And it was divine. I've never felt more connected to anyone.

Being a professional athlete, it seems he's out of town more than he's home. *Home.* That's what it is now. Before, it was a tiny space that fit in my price range. It was where I could sleep when I wasn't at the shop. Now it was something I craved. Since Josh, it's become my fortress of happiness.

Because of my early hours at the bakery, I hadn't made it to any of his games yet and I feel like a terrible girlfriend. Josh says it doesn't matter. He knows I watch them from our bed until I pass out.

The next time he's in town for a series, I arrange a surprise for him with a little help from Stephanie and Tristan. Because he's the coach, Tristan hooks me up with some incredible seats. And now, here I sit in the front row, directly across from their team bench. Stephanie sits with me, trying to calm me as nerves riddle my anxious body. Dressed in a Logan jersey, and armed with a handmade sign that reads "I'm in love with the captain," I wait for Josh to notice me.

As he skates circles around the ice to warm up, his level of focus impresses me. Most of his teammates have seen me, and they all watch for the moment he does. With a fist bump, Ace says something to him. His expression goes from happy-go-lucky to intense in seconds. He runs his gaze over the stands, looking for something. *Did Ace tell him I'm here? Yes, he did.*

When his eyes land on me, a giant smile spreads across his gorgeous face. I push the sign forward and his smile grows wider. He skates over and I stand up and go to him. He removes his glove and spreads his palm out on the Plexiglass. I place mine against his. I can feel the heat radiating through the barrier.

"I love you, Kenz," he mouths.

Overcome with the emotion of it, I laugh and mouth back, *"I love you too."*

He looks over at Stephanie and thanks her.

"Coach," she hollers back. His bright baby blues settle on me again and he winks. Putting his glove back on, he skates over to the bench and fist bumps Tristan.

Watching his game is absolutely incredible. The excitement of the fans, the speed of their play. The horns that blast when they score. It's all so intense. At the end of the game, which they win 4-1, my body buzzes with energy. Stephanie takes me down to the players' tunnel to wait for Josh and Tristan, and the excitement over the win saturates the air.

As the captain, Josh is the last to leave the locker room. But when he does, he's never looked more handsome. His blond hair is still damp and tousled. Dressed in a suit, he looks like he's ready for the catwalk. *Damn, he's sexy.* With his chest puffed out, he strides out with confidence. Without missing a beat, he pulls me into his arms. My legs wrap around him as we cling to each other. He buries his head in my neck and says, "Kenz, I love you." He pulls back and his eyes are filled with emotion.

"I love you too." I smile, happier than I've ever been.

The excitement of that night carries us through the next few away series. Recently, I've become more comfortable when he's away. Do I miss him? Terribly. But the excitement that lights his eyes when he returns makes it bearable. And I've gotten back into reading, so during the time he's gone, I bury my head in the latest steamy romances. The only drawback is the feverish dreams I have and not having any way to curb my overactive libido. Josh supports my reading habit fully, especially after the favorable reception home he receives.

As March turns to April and then to May, Stephanie and I finalize the plans for the dessert tables for the upcoming Steel You Heart gala.

Steph had quickly become one of my best friends. When time permits, we hang out, share a meal, catch a movie, or go for a late pedicure. She's amazing, and I'm a very lucky woman to be included in her inner circle. Like me, Steph is a private person. But she's also one of the kindest, most sincere and loving women in my life.

Steph walks around the counter to me and gives me a big hug. Dressed in a black power suit with a sheer royal-blue lace top, she looks like she should be running a high-stakes meeting, not slumming it in my shop.

"How are you?" I ask.

"I'm better now," she answers with a wide smile. Squeezing her tight, I notice her zippered binder.

Tapping it, I question, "Got the final numbers and dessert approval?"

"Sure do." She smiles.

We move to a table, and Toby brings us both a warm drink—coffee for her and peppermint tea for me. When they're set on the table, she looks at the beverages. "You're having tea?"

I nod, then answer, "My stomach's been upset the past few days, and peppermint tea and saltines are the only thing that seem to temper it."

"I'm sorry to hear that. What do you think it is?" Steph leans in to make our conversation more private.

"Honestly, I'm hoping it's just nerves. I want this gala to top last year's." As we're reviewing the list of desserts, Steph gasps. "Are you okay?" I ask. She swallows hard and her eyes go wide. "What?" I'm desperate to know what has her so spooked.

Looking around, she leans in and whispers, "Kenz... could you be pregnant?"

Stunned by her question, I sit back. "No. There is no way."

"Okay, that's probably good. Maybe it's something viral?" Then, without a second thought, she's off to another talking point. As she confirms using the same venue and layout, I ruminate on her pregnancy suspicion. *Could I be pregnant?* No, we always use protection, and I've had a period each month. Thinking back, though, those last few were different. They were more spotting than anything. Then, as if a lightning bolt strikes me, I flash back to that February night when we confessed our love for each other. Josh hadn't used a condom, had he? Realization sets in. He'd gone bare. At first it surprised me, and right when I was about to say something, my third orgasm for the night ripped through me, washing it from my brain. *Maybe I am pregnant? I can't be. This is too soon.* Suddenly I'm way too hot. Touching my brow, I feel it's damp. My stomach churns like it's trying to turn buttermilk into butter. *What am I going to do?* Thoughts of what my reality could be in just under seven months slam into me like a semi.

"Uh, Steph," I mumble in a shaky voice.

Her gaze flicks to mine and a worried look stretches across her face. "What is it, Kenz?"

"I could be pregnant. We didn't use a condom once, a little over two months ago."

Steph reaches out and pats my arm. She smiles and tells me it'll be okay. I try to believe her, but my thoughts are chaotic, and I'm pulled into a spiral of worry. "Kenz, you should take a test and find out." I nod my head, but I can't force myself to speak. Noticing my panic, she says. "Okay, I'll text work and tell them I'm out for the rest of the day for personal reasons, then I'll run to the store up the street and grab one. Will you be okay for five minutes?" Again, I nod without speaking. "Oh, honey. It'll be okay. We'll get answers first and then go from there."

Twenty minutes later, both huddled together in the bakery's tiny bathroom, I'm staring down at two pink lines. My mouth drops open in disbelief and shock, and I start to sob. I don't know what to feel. Elated? Scared? Steph wraps her arms around me, my hands clutching the back of her shirt like she's my only life raft in all of this. *This isn't the right time. Josh just told me he loved me. He doesn't want a baby already.*

"Steph," I mumble. Pulling back, she tucks a stray hair behind my ear and dabs at my tears with a tissue. "How am I going to tell Josh?"

Steph looks straight into my eyes and says confidently, "You just tell him, and he either steps up or doesn't." My heart cracks at the thought of him leaving me. *Would he?* Thoughts of Kayla pop into my head. He's been here before and he stepped up for Kayla and he didn't even love her. He has to do the same for me, right?

Feeling more confident, I say, "You're right. I need to tell him. It'll all be okay. He loves me. Maybe it's not the best time, but babies are happy blessings." Steph smiles at me.

"You are so right," she agrees.

For the next few days, I waffle between confidence about telling him and fear of how he'll handle it. I know telling him will be a challenge, based on what Kayla did to him and how hurt he still seems about their fictional baby. From what he says, I believe he was invested one hundred percent in making things work for his baby. I know he'll be an excellent father. But right now, I'm riding the fence in guessing how he'll react. When he's home next week, I'll tell him. I want to do it in person, not while he's in another city vying for a position in the Stanley Cup playoffs.

Two days later, early in the morning, my phone rings. Seeing that it's Steph, I answer right away.

"Hello."

"Hey, Kenz, did you hear from Josh?" Panic registers. *Why?*

"Not today. We talked last night. What's up?" I ask.

"I talked to Tristan this morning. It looks like half the team contracted Norovirus, so they're out for the rest of the playoffs. The entire team is planning to stay in Colorado for a few days until they're all healthy enough to travel home. As far as I know, Josh hasn't become ill."

I'm relieved, except now I have to wait longer to tell Josh he's going to be a dad.

My phone rings several times while I'm at the bakery, and every time I see that it's Josh calling, I let it go to voicemail. I know avoiding him isn't the answer, but I'm too chicken to talk to him. *What if I blurt out I'm pregnant?* Determined that isn't how I want to tell him, I decide the safer approach is to ignore his calls.

About an hour before we close, while I'm elbow-deep in bread dough, Toby pops his head back and hollers at me. "Kenz, Josh is on the phone. He said he's tried calling you several times today, but you haven't answered. He sounds worried."

Looking up from my sticky dough, I blow the stray hairs out of my face. "Toby, can you tell him I'm fine and I'll talk to him later when I'm not in the middle of something?"

Seeing that I'm busy, he smiles, turns on his heel, and heads back up front, presumably to tell Josh what I just said.

Five minutes later, he's back with a stern look on his face. Before he even begins, he crosses his arms and scowls. "Kenz, what is going on? Why haven't you answered your phone today? You always answer his calls."

Afraid if I speak, I'll confess my pregnancy to Toby, I attempt to remain guarded and say little. "I'm just tired, Toby. That's all. I haven't slept well the last few weeks, and it's finally caught up to me and I'm grouchy."

He shrugs. "That's understandable. But I don't think he'd mind if you were grumpy, hangry, or PMSing. He's crazy about you." Then he pauses, squints his eyes, and studies me. "But I don't think that's what it is. Something else is going on. I can feel it. And you aren't ready to tell me."

I frown. Usually I tell Toby everything, but I can't tell him I'm pregnant before I tell Josh. Frustrated and overwhelmed, I squeeze my eyes closed and a single tear rolls down my cheek.

Toby rushes to me and wraps his arms around me. "It's okay, Kenz. You can tell me when you're ready. I love you and I'm here for you, no matter what." Nodding, I let out the breath I'd sucked in when I'd been trying to stop myself from crying. Relief that I didn't upset my friend gives me a minimal escape from my worries. Toby squeezes me and then steps back. "I'm going to give you some space. If you need me, just holler. I'll close up the front and deliver the donations."

"Thanks, Toby," I say with a shaky voice. Another squeeze and he disappears, leaving me alone with nothing but my worries.

Chapter 19

Josh

"**M**an, it's good to be home," I tell myself as I walk to my car after the team bus delivers us to the arena following the world's longest away trip. For the past week and a half, we were in Colorado. When we arrived, we were scheduled to play two playoff games against the Mountaineers. We played the first, losing in OT, but more than half our team came down with Norovirus before we could play the second. We had to forfeit, and with our previous losses, we were out of the series and the playoffs. As one player who thankfully remained healthy, I had ample time to mull over everything, and I'd be lying if I said it didn't make me rather grumpy.

We hadn't won the Cup last year after two consecutive dominations, and I thought this was our turn to show the hockey community we were back. Making me further grumpy was my inability to talk to Kenzie. I wasn't sure, but it felt like she was avoiding me and I couldn't figure out why. All I know is it made me uneasy. I was glad I was finally home so I could check on her. I'd talked to Toby yesterday when I called CakeStop after my calls to her had gone unanswered. He said she was fine, just really busy.

Now I'm on my way to her apartment to see her. I need to make sure. Normally, I'm a pretty relaxed guy, but the closer I get to her apartment, the more anxious and troubled I become. My stomach rocks. "I better not have the shits like the guys," I mumble to myself as I pull up to her building.

Waiting for her to answer is agony. I just want to pull her into my arms. To know everything is okay and get rid of this icky uneasy feeling I have.

The door opens slowly, and the woman I love stands there looking... haggard. *What is going on?* Kenzie's hair is going in every direction possible. She has dark circles under her eyes. She's pale and looks utterly exhausted. I won't even go into her outfit, a statement piece for sure. It screams *I've not been feeling well and I'm stained with vomit*. My heart drops. "Baby. Are you okay?"

She nods and opens the door wider to allow me access before shuffling away. She groans as she settles on the couch. There are sleeves of opened saltine crackers and half-empty bottles of water scattered over her coffee table. Used tissues cover the couch and floor. Lowering into a chair nearby, I look at her and my heart squeezes. "Kenzie, do you need me to take you to the doctor? You don't look like you feel too good."

She looks at me with sad eyes and shakes her head. "No, I'm fine. It'll pass. It usually doesn't last all day," she croaks.

"Is it stomach flu? That's usually twenty-four hours, right? Hopefully, it isn't Norovirus like most of the team had."

Kenzie shakes her head again, but she won't make eye contact. Alarm bells go off in my mind. My tone drops as I question, "What do you mean, no? Do you know what's wrong with you?"

Her head whips up defiantly. "Nothing is wrong with me. I'm perfectly fine."

Okay. "Perfectly fine?" I skeptically ask, my tone probably making me sound like a dick. "So then, what's with all this?" I motion to the state of the living room and her appearance.

Grabbing a half-empty bottle of water off the couch, she sips at it while rubbing at her stomach.

"Are you sure you are okay? There's nothing I can get you? Ginger ale, Gatorade, chicken noodle soup?"

Taking another sip of water, she lowers the bottle and says, "See, I'm fine. Looks like the worst of it has passed."

What is she talking about? I'm so confused. Before I have time to ask what she means, she bolts off the couch and sprints to the bathroom like she's training for the Olympics. In her mad dash, she doesn't get the door shut, and the sound of her vomiting fills the small space. When I think she's done, I rise and head down the hallway to check on her. "Baby, you don't sound fine." I move into the bathroom and flip on the fan to get some ventilation in there. I pull a washcloth from under the counter and soak it in cold water while she rests her head on the toilet seat. Squatting, I place the cooled cloth on the back of her neck and she hums. "Kenz, I'm really worried about you."

She lifts her head up, wipes away the wetness on her lips, and says, "I appreciate that, but I'm okay. This will pass. At least I hope." Then she's lost in thought and mumbles, "That's what the books say."

"What books?"

She startles, like she forgot I'm here. "Huh?"

"The books?" I drawl. Her eyes go wide and she looks panicky. I'm dreading the next moment. *What is she going to say?* My body tenses up like I'm going to be slammed against the boards, and my heart thumps in my chest. Preparing for the unknown, I set my hand on the sink to steady myself.

"Books?" she asks. I nod, needing an explanation. Worry is running rampant through my body, and I feel like I'm preparing for an attack. I don't want to say anything in case it comes off growly and wrong. I'm not angry right now; I'm scared.

Turning herself away from the toilet, she looks into my eyes. "I don't know how to say what I need to say. I'm afraid you'll be mad at me." *Shit. What is she going to say?* Right now, I'd like to leave this bathroom, rewind the last day, and pretend everything's normal.

With my emotions a complete wreck, I rasp, "Just tell me." Lowering my head, hoping it will soften the blow, I try to prepare for something that might destroy me. I don't know what she's going to say, but I feel her slipping away, and the truth of that cuts just like a knife.

Kenzie sniffles, and with tear-filled eyes, she drops a bomb on me. "I'm... pregnant, Josh."

My head snaps up. "You're what?" I whisper. In the bathroom's silence, the words echo off the tiles, resonating deep. She startles at my response. Terror flashes in her eyes and she moves back as if she's afraid I'm going to attack. *I might.* The only probable explanation pops into my head. "You've been cheating on me?" I rasp.

Kenzie stills and horror fills her face. "What?" she screeches. "No, it's yours."

That's not right. We always used a condom. "That's bullshit. I've always used a condom. I can't believe you. It's some other fucker's baby, and you're trying to pass it off as mine. You... you're worse than Kayla." As I rant, I see Kenzie close in on herself. She wraps her arms around herself as tears flow down her cheeks. *Good God, give this girl an Emmy. Then it hits me.* "Maybe you aren't even pregnant. Guess everyone will have to see," I seethe at her. *Hell knows, I'm not sticking around to find out.* Bile rises in my throat. She disgusts me. My chest heaves and my breathing is labored as I stand up on shaky legs. Her words have rocked me to the core. *I need to get out of here. Now.* I take a step back and growl, "I never want to see you again. You and me, we are through." Then I stomp out of her life, slamming the door on the way out.

Chapter 20

Kenzie

He not only doesn't believe it's his baby, but he's comparing me to Kayla. How could this have gone any worse? Replaying the words Josh spewed at me, my heart shatters. *He didn't believe me and he walked away.* Cognitively, I get it. What Kayla did to him was reprehensible. And my heart screams in protest. I am not her. *How could he even think I am?* Apparently, he doesn't think much of me. Did he even love me? How could he if he never really trusted me? Was he always waiting for the opportunity to pull away? Was anything we had, real? I'm kicking myself now. I knew it was a mistake to get involved with him, but he wore me down. Was it all an act?

Crushed, my weary body shakes as shock sets in. How am I going to do this, raise a baby by myself while running a bakery? Fear licks at my heart and my skin prickles with goose bumps. Tears saturate my vomit-stained shirt. Never could I imagine Josh would react like he did. Yes, I assumed he might be shocked, but once it sank in, I figured he'd be excited like I've become. True, I've had days to wrap my head around our news because of the all-day sickness and the occasional vomiting. Despite that, I'm thrilled. I just wish Josh felt the same.

My heart cracked when he accused me of cheating or trying to trap him like Kayla. In those moments, he was so angry, and I saw a new side of him. His voice was full of spite and nothing like the man I love—deliberate wounds left stamped on my heart as he stomped away.

My stomach churns and, for the first time in a week, I don't blame the little bean in my uterus. Curling into a protective ball on my bathroom floor, I consider my options. There is no way I'm going to get rid of it. I'm not religious, but it just doesn't feel right. I could have the baby and give it up for adoption, but that doesn't sit well either. This is the last piece of Josh I will have and I can't send it away. The only option that makes sense is to have the baby on my own.

More tears fall as I imagine raising our child without its father. I'm close with my parents, and I never doubted their love and support, but they live across the country. Our child... would only have me. The thought of that destroys me. My heart aches for my baby. I lay my hand on my abdomen, thinking about how a life was just beginning. *And he just walked away. Hadn't I proved I was nothing like his ex?* I want to be strong and cling to the saying "his loss," but it feels like more. It isn't true. Both our child and I will suffer now that Josh isn't going to be part of our lives.

I don't know how long I stay curled up on the floor, but my cell phone rings incessantly. *Go away.* I don't want to talk to anyone, but whoever it is keeps calling. I'm not planning to answer it, just shut it off.

Sitting up, I stretch out my legs. They're stiff and achy. I rub at my puffy eyes, wincing at their tenderness. Pushing up to standing, my body feels heavy, like I'm carrying an extra twenty pounds. Slowly, I trudge out to the couch where I left my phone. Lifting the blankets, I can't see it. Following the ringing, I discover it has slipped between the cushions, so I dig it out. There are quite a few missed calls and texts from Steph. *What is so urgent?* All I want to do is crawl into my blanket on the couch and forget about everything, but I have a nagging feeling I should find out why she's been calling. Lowering myself to the couch, I select her contact and wait for her to answer.

"Kenz, are you okay?" Steph asks in a panicky voice when she answers.

Swallowing past the bolder in my throat, I do my best to hide any emotion in my voice when I answer, "I'm fine, why?" *Liar.*

Lowering her voice, she asks, "Because you don't

sound right and Tristan just got a really strange text from Josh. What is going on? Did you tell him about the baby?"

Grimacing, I recall my last few hours. "Why are you whispering?"

A few seconds go by before she answers. "I'm whispering because I didn't tell Tristan you're pregnant. I didn't figure you wanted me to tell anyone. Was I right?"

How thoughtful. Fresh tears fall and I sniffle. "Yeah, you were right. I wanted to tell Josh first, but now that he knows, I definitely don't want to tell anyone else," I whimper.

"What? Why?" she squeaks.

I grab a tissue from my coffee table and wipe at my nose. "Well... he didn't handle it well. He said some terrible things, proclaimed we were through, and stormed out." It hurts to admit it, even to one of my best friends.

She huffs. "What did he say, Kenz?"

"I don't want to tell you. I don't want you to think poorly of him. He's furious and said some things that he normally wouldn't."

Pausing for a moment, she hums to herself.

"What?" I ask.

"Did it have to do with Kayla, that awful puck bunny he used to date?"

My stomach sinks. "No. Why would you ask about her?"

"Hold on a sec," she orders, and dread covers my body. "Tristan, can I see the text from Josh again? I have Kenzie on the phone and I want to tell her what it says."

A deep voice answers, "Are you sure about this, Steph?"

"Yes, she needs to know." Her answer makes my stomach churn, and I break out in a cold sweat.

"Steph, what does it say?" I beg.

"I'm sorry, Kenz," she says before she murmurs the text. And the rest of my world crashes down around me.

> Coach, I won't be attending the Steel Your Heart gala in a few weeks because Kenzie and I are no longer together. I need some space from her. I discovered she was worse than Kayla, and I don't want to make a scene at such an important event. Management can fine me any amount or come up with another punishment, but I won't be there.

"I need to go," I say before hanging up. *Josh will never believe me.* How, in a matter of weeks, has my life gone from perfect to ruined?

Chapter 21

Josh

It's been one week since Kenzie told me she was pregnant with "my baby." But it isn't my baby. The pain of her deception is so intense. I can't seem to accept her words. *Why would she insist it's mine?*

For a moment, I allow myself to think about Kenzie and me having a baby, and I've never been happier. But then I remember it wasn't possible. I never had sex without a condom, and my anger crashes in and destroys that happy fantasy. As the good feelings are replaced with tension and anger, I think about her insistence. Were condoms one hundred percent? No. I'd learned that lesson with Kayla, even though everything had been a lie. The message stuck. My thoughts and emotions swirl chaotically in my mind. This feels like history is repeating itself. *Is that possible?* There's no way that could happen to a guy twice. *I would have to have the worst luck.*

Shaking off my doubt, I know for a fact I always used a condom. I'd never deny it. If I was going to start a family, it would have been with Kenzie. But we aren't ready for that. We just declared our love for each other. The emotion of that night floods my mind. It had been so intense. I'd never said those three words to any woman, and I'd believed no woman who said them to me. Until Kenzie.

Unfortunately, I was dumb enough to believe that she differed from Kayla, but I was wrong. Like always, I had to learn the hard way that she was even worse because she made me fall in love with her. And getting over her seems impossible. I thought that yelling at her would make me feel better, and at the moment, it did. But when I slammed her front door, the fire shooting through my veins extinguished and I felt my knees grow weak and my chest tighten. I'd hobbled to my car and climbed in. Not feeling safe to drive, I set my head on my steering wheel and cried. *Why did this hurt so badly?* Because I loved her. But that's now in the past. I refuse to let myself feel anything but anger for her now. She lied and deceived me, and there is no way I'm moving past that. Forgiveness isn't something she deserves.

Another few weeks pass, and no matter what I do, Kenzie is always on my mind. And I hate that. She was the woman of my dreams and now she is the one of my nightmares. On the night of the gala, I'm true to my word and don't attend. Instead, I sit at home and disregard my strict diet by eating junk food. Really, it's depressing.

A loud pounding on my front door stirs me from sleep. *When did I fall asleep?* Looking at my watch, I see it's nine the next morning. *Why am I still on my couch?* Sitting up, I'm still exhausted. Dealing with a broken heart really takes a lot of energy. I rub my eyes as I try to wake up. Then... I hear chanting. Sitting back, I close my eyes, trying to concentrate on it, hoping to determine what's being shouted. It sounds a lot like "open up, open up." *Who the fuck is at my door?* Before I even pull up my front door camera, someone yells, "Josh, we know you're in there." Grumbling, I get up and move to the door. I let my anger free. Gripping the handle tight, I'm ready to yell at anyone who's willing to interrupt my solitude.

"What the fuck do you want?" I grind out through my clenched jaw as I rip open the door.

"Well, good morning to you too, Captain," Ace says with his always-present smile.

Rocco smirks. "Did we come at a bad time, Cap? Do you have someone over? Maybe Kenzie? Is that why you both weren't at the gala last night?" *She wasn't there either?* I don't care.

Growling, I lean forward and pop him in the chest. "Keep her name out of our conversations."

Ace elbows Rocco and side whispers, "That doesn't sound good."

Rocco, who's unafraid of anything, pushes me. "Why?" His eyes are full of questions.

"We all adore Kenzie and her baked confections. It's not like you two broke up or something," he says.

Pulling my hand through my hair, I shift my focus down. "Actually, we did a few weeks ago."

"What?" the entire group says in tandem.

"Yeah, things were great until I discovered she was worse than Kayla," I confess. Mika and Lucas stare at me in disbelief.

Ace pouts. "There is no way she is worse than the she-devil herself," he argues, while the rest of them nod like fucking bobbleheads. *I hate those things.*

I cross my arms while watching them. *It's because you never told them about what happened with Kayla.* "You guys don't know shit about what happened with Kayla, or Kenzie, so your opinion of the matter is point-less," I growl.

Mika steps forward. "So why don't you tell us the facts and then we can decide on our own." The fucking bobblehead gang is at it again, nodding and showing their approval. They don't realize they're asking me to reveal the two most painful things I've ever experienced. They're acting like it's nothing. But it is something. Something I'm not sure I'll ever get over. Do I want to open up my still oozing wounds or just tell them to fuck off and hope they leave me alone? I'm leaning toward the latter, telling them to get off my porch when Mika says, "Do you remember when I messed up with Shiloh and you guys all showed up... repeatedly?" I nod. He puts his arms out. "We're here now."

Shaking my head, because he doesn't understand, I growl, "But the difference is, I didn't mess up. She did, and she can't undo what she's done. It's forever."

Lucas steps closer. "I don't know if you're purposefully being vague, but I heard something at the gala that makes me think maybe you have some misinformation. Why don't you talk it out with us and maybe this group of assholes will see something you don't see? Eh?"

"Yeah, what's the harm? You're already a moody sonofabitch," Rocco chimes in.

This conversation has already exhausted me. "Fine," I grumble as I open my door wider.

As Ace walks through, he asks, "Are these long stories? Will we need snacks delivered?"

Rocco laughs, tapping on his phone. "Already on it. Wings will be here in twenty."

"You better have ordered the hickory smoked BBQ ones," I say, my stomach making its own request. He smiles widely. *Asshole.*

While waiting for the wings, we head into my living room. Guess at least I'll be comfortable while I'm reliving my worst moments. *Why am I doing this?* Looking at the group of guys here, I remind myself that these are my best friends and if anyone will have my back, they will. So, after a deep breath, I begin.

"Kayla was a liar. In fact, the entire time I knew her, we only fucked twice." Ace gasps and Rocco slugs him. Then they both look at me like they're waiting for what's next. Pausing for a moment, I finally admit, "I'm aware she was as awful as you all said she was, but because of what we'd gone through, I felt tied to her. To avoid drama, it was just easier to keep her around. At no point did I ever seriously consider marrying her."

Rocco leans forward and asks, "So then what happened?"

Taking a moment, I relive that night where I learned the truth. "Do you guys remember the series we arrived home from early in November of the year before last?" The group nods. Of course they remember. We never get home early. "When I came home that night, I found Kayla in the hot tub with her best friend, who was visiting. I was just about to say hey when I overheard their conversation."

"What were they talking about?" Ace asks, intrigued.

"Without rehashing all of it, basically Kayla admitted the pregnancy and miscarriage were fake." I take a deep breath, glad that story's over. Looking over at my guys, they're all shocked.

"That conniving bitch," Mika growls.

I laugh. "She was. She *is*. But Kenzie is even worse."

"No way," Ace defends. "If, at the end of your story, I agree with you, I'll buy everyone dinner at Mateo's."

"Deal," I agree with a smirk on my face. *They don't know what she's done. They only know the person she fooled us all into believing was real.*

"I don't believe it either," Lucas says. And there go the bobbleheads again. *Fuck me.*

Leaning back in my chair, I clear my throat. For some reason, I need my words to come out strong. Maybe then they'll be believable. As the days pass, and the further I am from her confession, the more my anger fades and I see glimpses of what transpired between us that afternoon. And despite all the anger, sadness, and disappointment I still hold on to, I question things. *Is she a cheater? Is she really like Kayla?* I don't let myself linger on those questions for too long because it's too painful. The only person I could talk to about it is the one who's ripped me to shreds. And that's not happening. Because of her betrayal, I've scrubbed her out of my life completely. Making it the most painful thing I've ever done.

"Kenzie is just like Kayla," I reaffirm. "Actually, I take that back. She's worse."

All the guys look at me as if I'm growing two heads. But I push forward.

"Kenzie told me she was pregnant and that it's mine. Unfortunately for her, I always used a condom, so I know it can't be mine. She's trying to trap me like Kayla was."

"I'm confused. How does that make her worse than Kayla?" Mika asks.

Hanging my head, I admit, "Because I loved her."

"Maybe you don't have all the facts, Josh," Mika says in a shaky voice. I wonder if he's remembering the scandal he went through with a New York paper suggesting he cheated on Shiloh. It was such a shit show. Before he could even defend himself, she'd already broken things off with him. But he was innocent. Some puck bunny looking for a payout didn't care who or how she ruined someone else's life. He moped for months until we forced them together to work out their shit.

"This isn't like you and Shiloh, man," I say.

Out of the corner of my eye, I see Lucas sit forward. "Josh, I heard something at the gala that I probably wasn't supposed to, but it might change things. It was about the condom."

I don't know what he's going to tell me. "I used protection every fucking time. How could she be pregnant?" *I used a condom every time, didn't I?* Maybe there's a sliver of hope inside me that's making me question everything now.

"They aren't one-hundred percent, dude. Didn't you learn that in eighth grade health class?" Ace laughs to himself. "Plus, Kenzie isn't like that." I glare at him, pissed at the truth of both his statements.

"And," Lucas adds, "I heard you didn't use a condom once." *What?*

Gritting my teeth together, I try to keep my cool. "Is that right? I'd like to know who holds that handy piece of information," I challenge.

Lucas holds up his hands. "Don't shoot the messenger. I overheard Stephanie and Toby talking at the gala. They were whispering about how Kenzie had remembered you didn't use a condom the night you two confessed your love for each other." Then the room goes silent. Familiarity buzzes through my veins. *Did she say something about that?* Then, as if a gong is struck next to me, her words resonate in perfect clarity. Instant regret fills me. My gut sinks and my mouth runs dry. My clammy hands shake as the realization of what I've done registers. *Fuck! I'd been so caught up in that night that I'd forgotten a condom.* But that's never happened before. *It's because she told you she loved you.*

Panicked, I lower my head between my knees. I tug my hands through my hair, disregarding the sting. *What have I done?* I ruined everything. A chance to be happy with the woman I love. All because of my past bullshit with Kayla. Kenzie will never forgive me, not that I deserve it. My mind flashes to the memory of those moments. Hunkered on the ground next to the toilet, she'd just been sick in. She'd looked exhausted and pale. Weak and fragile. And at the mention of the word pregnancy, I lost all control. Hurling the ugliest of words and accusations at her. I'd sabotaged us from becoming anything more than a chaotic wreck. *What am I going to do now? Can I fix this?*

Remembering my guys are over, I lift my head and look around my living room. Eyes filled with concern stare back at me, making my skin itch. I may be the captain, but I hate to have all eyes on me. Opening my mouth like a fish, I go to say something, anything, but nothing comes out. I'm terrified to admit that I was wrong. *But that's my baby.* Kenzie is honest to a fault, and I threw that in her face. How could I ever doubt her? Unable to stand all the attention, I cover my face with my hands and groan loudly. "What am I going to do?"

My stomach twists with guilt, and dread washes over me. *She'll never forgive me.* I majorly fucked up with the woman I love more than anything. And she's carrying our child. *How will I ever make this right?* Desperate to be part of what she's going through, I fly out of my chair.

"Whoa, Josh, where are you going?" Lucas calls out as he follows me. I race into my kitchen, looking around for something, but I don't know what.

"Dude, what are you doing?" Lucas asks, concern edging his voice.

I stop, stare at him, and answer, "I fucked up. She's right. I didn't use a condom." The truth finally sinks in. Shocked, I whisper, "That's our baby, and I was a complete asshole to her. She's never going to forgive me."

Mika joins us, along with the rest of the bobble-heads. "I'm sure you weren't that bad."

Letting a pained laugh out of my aching chest, I admit, "It was worse than you can imagine. I accused her of being a cheater and a liar, and then I told her she was worse than Kayla."

Ace and Rocco both mutter, "Oh shit."

I scowl. "As if that wasn't bad enough, I told her I never wanted to see her again." Hanging my head, I drop to my haunches. *What am I going to do?* Reaching into my pocket, I palm my phone. I can call her and apologize, beg her forgiveness. That'll work, right? *It has to work. I can't lose her. I can't lose* them.

"What are you doing, Josh? You look a little crazed," Mika asks as he drops to my level.

Staring at my phone, I answer, "I think I'm going to call her."

Lucas huffs. "That's a bad idea. I doubt she wants to talk to you if you truly did what you said."

"But I need to see if she's okay. What if I go into the shop? Then she'll have to see me."

Rocco laughs. "Dude, you sound like a creepy stalker. That'll just piss her off." *I don't want to do that.*

I snap my fingers. "I got it. I'll send her flowers."

Ace scoffs under his breath as he casually leans against the counter. In his slight southern drawl, he says, "I'm no expert, but I don't think flowers are going to help you."

"You guys are no help," I grumble as I lower to my butt. For what feels like the hundredth time this morning, I ask myself the same question. *What am I going to do?*

Chapter 22

Kenzie

It's been over a month since Josh decimated my heart. Tears spring up at the drop of a hat and I find it difficult to control. One moment I'm crying and the next I'm spitting mad. I'm sure the pregnancy hormones aren't helping at all, but there's nothing I can do about it. He said horrible things, but the worst was telling me he wanted nothing to do with me or the baby. *His baby.* Just thinking about that fills me with an anger so intense that my blood pressure spikes and I have to sit down. My heart thumps and my breathing is labored as I think of how much his words shredded me and destroyed our happiness. When he walked away, he shattered my heart. *How could he?* It devastates me that my little bean won't know his or her father. Frustration courses through my veins. *Maybe that's for the best. We don't need him.* I'm not going to force him to be part of our lives.

I've been having a rough time lately. When I'm not dealing with morning—or better yet, all-day—sickness, I'm trying to get enough sleep so I don't mess up anything at the shop. Looking back, I see how far I've come. Those first days, I was so distraught that I struggled to do basic things. If it weren't for Toby, I wouldn't have gotten all the desserts ready for the Steel Your Heart gala. Because the Chicago Steel cosponsored it, I decided not to attend. I was there for delivery and set up, but I slipped away, leaving Toby in charge shortly before the event began.

Steph told me the event ran smoothly and Toby did a fantastic job. I knew he would, and that makes my decision about the shop even easier. My plan is to make some changes before I get too close to my due date. I've already started gathering resumes for bakers so I can hire one to handle the early morning prep. This will help before and after the baby arrives. Once the little bean is here, it won't be smart to be at work at four a.m. I'm also going to promote Toby to the manager, so he'll be the one in charge while I'm on maternity leave. Despite the challenges of being a single parent, the pieces are falling into place. On those days I feel abandoned and incredibly broken, I try to remember to be thankful and grateful for that.

Later this week, I have my anatomy scan. I'm only eighteen weeks pregnant, but my provider says we'll see everything. I saw my little bean for the first time at my twelve-week appointment when they were doing some standard testing. Thankfully, nothing was detected. At this next appointment, where they'll check how everything is developing, I'll also learn if I'm having a boy or girl. I've been having dreams about having a son, but we shall see.

On the day of my appointment, I wake up late—my old friend, nausea, putting on a show, and the hot water in my apartment malfunctioning. I look like a hot mess. I pull my hair up into a wild top knot. Dressing quickly, my clothes are wrinkled because I passed out last night before the dryer finished. My skin is an array of colors. I have deep circles under my eyes and my face is ghostly pale. I kind of look like the walking dead, especially when you consider my outfit: slouchy sweatpants and a stained tank top. *I'm killing it today.* If I entered a fashion show, I'd for sure take top honors as the Queen of Grunge. I laugh at myself, running my tongue against my teeth. At least they're brushed. I remembered that after I'd gotten my third round of muffins in. This little bean is sucking all my energy and brain power out of my body. What will I be like by the end of the pregnancy? *That's a scary thought!*

I push through the double doors with my arms full of bakery boxes that are filled with a customer's order of specialty cookies. After I set them down, I spin around to check everything in the case is fine, and I freeze. Standing off to the side with an iced coffee in her hand is Kayla. I assumed after the last interaction she'd never be back, but apparently, I'm wrong about a lot of things lately.

"Kenzie," she says, waving her fingers at me. Concentrating hard, I don't roll my eyes.

"Kayla. Can I help you with something?" I ask in the nicest voice I can muster. She steps closer, eyeing me up and down. I can feel her judging me, and I find I don't have it in me to care. "Kayla," I say again.

"I'm here to check on Josh," she says with a smirk. *What is she playing at?*

"Why?" I ask, feigning confusion.

She rattles her iced coffee in her hand, mixing it before she takes a sip and smiles. "Because he looked distraught in some pictures the paparazzi got of him last week, and I was worried about him. Is he okay?" Again, she's full of fake concern.

Distraught? That doesn't make sense. He walked away and left me and our baby. I lay my hand on my abdomen protectively. *Why would he be upset?* I look at Kayla and notice she's staring at my hand with a look of disbelief in her eyes. Quickly, I move my hand, crossing my arms over my chest. "I don't know why he's upset. We're no longer together."

Kayla goes from shock to elation in a half-second,

happily asking, "You aren't?" Another smirk appears across her lips and my heart drops. *Is she going to worm her way back into his life?* I'm still pissed at him, but I should warn him. He doesn't deserve to deal with her again. Just as I decide to reach out, his horrible words flash in my mind, *"I don't want to ever see you again,"* and my heart sinks. I dismiss the urge to help him. He doesn't need me looking out for him. He made that pretty clear.

"Kayla, is there anything I can get you?" *Please say no.* I need to get away from her. She makes me want to rage.

Before I can do just that, she answers. "Nope. You've been more than helpful." Then she blows me an air kiss before sauntering away. *That's a lost hope if she thinks she has another chance with him.* After what she did to Josh, I can't believe he'd entertain that. But then again, I thought the way he treated me was out of character too. Maybe I don't know him at all.

Toby rushes up to me and says, "You're going to be late. You need to leave for your appointment *now*."

For my anatomy scan, I decide to take the train into town so I don't have to worry about parking. It feels so good to walk to the station, and it's such a nice day out. I arrive at my doctor's office right on time and am run through all the normal weight and blood pressure checks. The appointment goes really well. When I see the baby, I think my heart's going to explode with joy.

My favorite part is hearing my baby's heartbeat. It's surreal. The whooshing sound I hear in real time steals my breath. My heart fills with love for my little bean. I guess I shouldn't be referring it to as a bean anymore; the baby is now the size of a bell pepper, at least that's what my pregnancy app tells me. The sonographer measures and documents how my baby is growing and tells me everything looks right on track. Toward the end of the appointment, when I can't take the suspense anymore, I ask her to tell me if I'm having a girl or boy. Moving her transducer, she zeros in on the answer. I squint my eyes, trying to decipher what she sees, but obviously, my eye isn't as keen as hers.

"It's a boy," she declares, and I feel my heart skip a beat. *We're having a boy. Not* we... I'm *having a boy.* Butterflies take flight in my stomach, and my nerves fray. *I don't know anything about being a mom, much less a boy mom.*

"Congratulations," the sonographer says, breaking me from my worries. The sound of her cheerful voice gives me hope. *I'm tough. I can do this. I'll figure it out.* Feeling confident again, happy tears gather in my eyes.

"Thank you," I say, my voice thick with emotion. Wiping the gel off my stomach, I breathe a sigh of relief. *Our baby is perfect.* Josh's face appears in my mind and I quickly push it away. I can't say *ours.* He doesn't want us. *My* baby boy is perfect. I pull my shirt over my tiny bump, rubbing it and speaking softly. "It's you and me, buddy. I love you so much. I can't wait to meet you."

After my appointment, while riding the train, I text Steph and Toby to tell them they're going to have a nephew to spoil in a few months. Both reply to me with absolute excitement. Even though they aren't family, they're the next best thing.

Now that I know I'm having a boy, I should call my parents and share the news that I'm pregnant. I'm nervous because I'm not sure what their reaction will be. When I get home, I decide to FaceTime them instead of calling.

As the request rings, my heart pounds in my chest, my hands sweat, and my stomach flutters. Now that I think about it, maybe that last bit is the baby. My provider said his movements would feel like little bubbles. It's all still so new. I'm not sure if it's the baby or gas. Lately, I've been craving Mexican food, and sometimes it makes me gassy. You know, beans and all. Or maybe it's my little guy telling me to watch the spice. Setting my hand on my bump, I say, "It's okay, little man. Mom will remember to order mild next time."

My iPad screen flashes and soon I'm looking at my mom. Her long brown hair is swept up into a bun. Looking at the clock, I see she must be on her lunch break. My parents meet at home on most work days to have lunch together. It's adorable.

"Hi, Mom."

"Kenzie, darling, how are you?"

Smiling, I answer, "I'm good. How are you? How's Dad? Is he home too?"

After a moment, I hear the shuffle of my dad's footsteps on the vinyl kitchen flooring. Then he appears next to Mom. "Is that my Kenzie I hear?" Mom nods and I smile. I have the best parents.

"Hey, Dad. How are you?"

"Doing great, doll. How are you? How's the shop? Any new recipes for me to taste test?" I laugh while my mom tsks at him. When she's done, I answer his questions.

"I'm good and so is the shop. And yes, I have a few new recipes I think you'd very much like. You just need to visit."

"Your mom was just telling me that the other day. When would be best to come?"

"I'm in the process of hiring another baker and promoting Toby to manager, so I should have more freedom in the next few months."

I hear my mom clap her hands together and say, "I love Toby. I'm so glad you're promoting him. He is such a sweet boy. I always wondered why you two didn't go out."

I almost choke on my tongue.

"Mom, Toby is my best friend... and—" I start.

"And what?" she presses. *Just tell her.*

"Mom, Toby is gay. Plus, I was sort of seeing someone," I confess.

My dad's brow arches before he clears his throat. "Kenzie, what does that mean?" I wring my hands together. *How am I going to tell them this?*

"Well, we were seeing each other and now we aren't." I end that topic because I don't want to have this in-depth relationship talk with my parents.

"B-but..." I stutter. "That's why I'm calling. Mom, Dad, I'm pregnant. You're going to be grandparents. Congratulations!" My parents sit there silently. *Did I make a mistake in telling them?*

Another minute passes and my mom blinks several times before she begins with her questions. *This could go either way.* "Is the father the guy you were dating? Where is he? When are you due? How are you feeling? What can we do to help?" I breathe a sigh of relief. Only care and concern are in her voice. Now to answer her questions.

"I'm due in the middle of November with a little boy. He's growing like a champ and everything I've had done from bloodwork to ultrasounds, show he's healthy and perfect. I'm doing good too. The first trimester was tough. I had all-day sickness and was exhausted. But that's all seemed to have resolved and I am feeling so much better."

"Oh, that is so good to hear. And a little boy. How exciting!" *Now to the fun part.* Tears well up in my eyes as I think about Josh and how much I miss him and wish he were a part of this. Swiping at my nose, I look at the screen. *Go on, Kenzie. Tell them.*

"Y- you asked about the father. Yes, it was my boyfriend, and I'd rather not go into details about what happened between us. But I will tell you he's chosen to not be a part of our lives." I hear my mom gasp, and that is the trigger to make my tears finally fall.

Mom's sweet voice wobbles as she says, "I'm so sorry, Kenzie. What can I do?"

I force a smile and sniffle, knowing I have to be strong. "It's okay, Mom. I have a plan. My situation isn't ideal, but I'm not going to force someone to be in my life if they'd rather not be."

Dad weighs in next, his deep voice filling the line. "There's my girl. Strong as ever. You've never been afraid of hard work. You will succeed at becoming a mother just as you've succeeded at CakeStop. I love you and am so proud of you." *Strength be damned.* Still feeling broken over Josh's dismissal, tears cascade down my cheeks.

Mom pipes back in. "I love you, Kenzie, and I know this is going to be the luckiest little boy. He won the jackpot getting you as his mom."

It's official. I have the world's greatest parents. "I love you both," I cry.

My dad, who has never been comfortable with tears, clears his throat. "So, if I'm understanding correctly, it looks like before Thanksgiving is a good time to visit?"

Wiping away the tears, I answer, "That would be fantastic. Thank you."

"There's no place we'd rather be," Dad answers. Meanwhile, Mom is debating if she'll be called Grandma, Nana, Gigi, or Grammy. I see my dad's eyes roll, and I just laugh. It's nice to have some levity after the dark clouds that have been hanging overhead.

Chapter 23

Josh

Without the routine of hockey season, I find myself with a lot of extra time on my hands. And I don't like it. Too much time allows my mind to ruminate on how badly I fucked things up with Kenzie. You'd think with all that time to ponder, I'd come up with a solution to fix what I'd done, but you'd be wrong. I can't come up with dick. The guys have even helped by listening to many of my ideas, and so far, according to them, they're all pathetic. This is hopeless.

I want to be there for her and the baby, but I don't know how. She won't let me. I've tried everything shy of a carrier pigeon. And I've gotten no response. I'm going crazy, and I have to do something.

I start out small. For an entire week, I send flowers to the shop every day. But that doesn't seem like enough, so I place several large orders of cookies and cupcakes with CakeStop to be delivered to various hospitals and senior centers around town. Reading my pregnancy book, I learned about expectant mothers and their fatigue, so I send Kenzie gift cards for pregnancy massages and pedicures. When I was brainstorming with the guys, I didn't tell them I've also been by the bakery at closing several times, hoping to get a glance of her.

Last week, the gods showed me favor and gifted me a Kenzie sighting. Hidden in my Tesla, a few blocks down, I sat slumped in my seat, waiting for her to walk by. And she did just that. Dragging a collapsible bag on wheels, she must have been heading to the shelter. At five months along, she's fucking adorable. Dressed in tight black leggings that screamed comfort, and a magenta tank top that accentuated her baby bump, she was breathtaking. *That's my baby with my baby.* As she passed, I forced myself to remain in the car and out of sight. As soon as I saw her, my heart twisted. It ached, demanding I go make things right. *I wish I could.* Life without her is no life at all. Everything is gray and muted. I need her sunshine back in my life.

A few weeks ago, at the annual Steel Fourth of July party, Monica and Christian invited us all to the Fields' family farm for this weekend. I didn't really listen because I wasn't feeling up for some country event. Ace and Rocco insisted we all ride together. Since they'd both accused me of being a moody asshole lately, I go. Only I wasn't prepared for what was going to happen.

Rocco drives us to the working dairy farm that had been in Monica's family for decades. Her dad runs it now with the help of her three older brothers. I'd met Josiah, the youngest of the brothers, several times, as he visits his sister frequently. He's a standup guy, from what I could tell.

We all planned to stay in town at the local Super 8, so we meet there before the large group of us descend on the farm like a horde of locusts to a field. Within hours of arriving, we're given a tour, introduced to the calves, and then seated in a nice outdoor venue. *What is happening?*

When I see Samantha and Shiloh lower their heads together and start whispering and pointing, I know something's up. I look around, clueless. Then one of Monica's sisters-in-law hands me a piece of paper. *Holy shit. They're finally doing it.* Thirty minutes later, we're all seated in an elaborately deco-rated barn, waiting to congratulate the bride and groom. These two have been circling each other for years and avoiding the intense chemistry they share.

When it's time for their vows, I never expected words promised to another person to register so deep within me. My mind fills with chaos as I sit there alone in a wooden chair, surrounded by my best friends and the women they worship. I miss Kenzie even more. My heart aches knowing I forced our separation with the ugly accusations and words I hurled at her. I treated the woman I professed to love no better than the dirt I walked on. I ruined what we had because I reacted out of fear, anger, and past hurt. Even though my past had colored my response to what she said, it was still incredibly inappropriate and harsh. If I'd stopped myself and thought about the situation, I would have concluded a few things: Kenzie wasn't a liar, and she was nothing like Kayla. By saying she was worse, I know my words shredded her. I feel horribly sick whenever I think about it. And even now, I don't see a way to make things better. I want to, desperately, but nothing feels right. Just like Lucas had, I need some grand gesture to not only apologize but to promise I'll do better.

Lying in bed that night after we celebrated with our friends, an idea strikes me. I need to not only apologize to Kenzie and promise to do better; I need to show her how excited I am to be a father and how I want to travel this road with her. Considering all that happened, I understand that maybe that door is already shut and Kenzie won't let me back into her life, but I know she won't keep me from my child when she sees how excited I am about being a dad.

When I get back into town the next day, I put my plan into action. On the ride back to the city, I shared it with Ace and Rocco, and they were fully on board to help me. Rocco had even chimed in with, "I'll do anything to make you stop being a broody asshole." Ace just laughed, and that was that.

Sunday night I sit on my couch, ordering the items necessary for my surprise. I hope it'll be enough to convince Kenzie to let me at least be part of my baby's life. I also hope it will give me a chance to be in hers as well. Thanks to my large NHL salary, I can order and ship things quickly, and by the next weekend everything I need for project *bring my babies home* is piled high in my garage. The guys are coming over first thing Saturday morning to help paint, assemble, and organize. Everything is ready, but I'm a nervous wreck. There's just one more thing I need to take care of before I make my move.

"Toby. You got a minute?" I holler out as Kenzie's second in command and best friend exits CakeStop.

His eyes go wide. He scowls and spits, "Not for you, I don't."

Holding up my hands, I counter, "That's fair. I get it. I'm the enemy. But..." Pausing, I study his face, hoping for a little compassion. A flicker of interest appears and then vanishes in a heartbeat. "I'm here to make things right," I confess.

"Make things right?" he snarls, causing me to step

back. "So, you think you can come in and flash your sexy smile and Kenzie will melt at your feet? You don't get it!" Just when I think he's done, he steps up to me, posturing. To anyone watching, this might seem funny because of our size difference. I'm 6'3" and he is 5'10". He's probably barely 140 pounds, where I'm solid at 220. But I can't afford to underestimate the wrath and anger in his eyes. He pokes my chest as he begins his tirade. "You destroyed her. You broke her heart. You told her you didn't want her. You told her it wasn't your baby. You called her a liar. You said she was worse than Kayla. And I've met that bitch. They are nothing alike." Each accusation he hurls is true. I won't deny them. It stings having someone so close to Kenzie calling me out on my shit. But I refuse to deflect it. I was the asshole. I did those things. Knowing I broke her heart and hurt her so much is agonizing. But I need to own it and fix what I've done.

Stepping back, out of the direct line of fire, I say, "Toby, I'm not arguing at all. I did those things, and I don't expect Kenzie to come crawling back to me. I know I don't deserve her."

"You're right about that," he grumbles with his arms crossed over his chest.

I scratch at my head and confess, "I know I don't deserve her, but that doesn't stop me from wanting her. I was wrong. I know it now, and I want the chance to apologize. I'm begging you to help me do that. She deserves that and so much more. I want to be part of her and my baby's life. I love her, man. I know I fucked up and don't deserve a second chance, but I'll do whatever it takes to make things right."

Still scowling, he replies, "She's my best friend. I'm only listening because I saw how happy you made her. Unfortunately, I've also seen how unhappy you make her. Deep down, I know you're good for each other, and I want to see her and the baby happy and cared for. If you get a second chance, you better treat her like a queen. Kenzie is the best person I know, and she deserves nothing but goodness. Can you do that?"

He's right. Kenzie deserves someone much better than me. But no one can love her as well as I can. Sure, I stumbled a bit, but I'm not perfect. Hopefully, she'll forgive me in due time and we can get back what we had. The emotion of everything hits me. I nod my head and gasp, "Yes."

He smiles. "Good. What do you need?"

Now that Toby's temper is defused, I explain what I've been up to and what I have planned for the weekend. "That sounds incredible, Josh. I know Kenzie will love it. But how do you plan to get her there? She won't answer your calls and don't even think about coming into the shop and making a scene."

I laugh. "I would never." Toby just side-eyes me like he's not sure. Laughing again, I explain, "That's where you come in." As Sunday is her only day off, I need Toby to get her over to my house without raising suspicion. And then I'll take it from there. Piece of cake. *Right?*

Chapter 24

Kenzie

It's finally Sunday and my blessed day off. I slept in until seven and I feel like a new woman. I indulge in an extra-long shower. I use the new lotion my mom sent me—it promises to reduce stretch marks if used regularly during pregnancy. *We shall see.*

Never being around a lot of pregnant women, I wasn't sure how my body would change. Obviously, I realized my belly would grow, but I was unprepared for how pregnancy would make me feel. From the heaviness to my now tear-shaped breasts to the ever-growing curve of my stomach. My hair is thicker and my face has gotten fuller. I even notice a sprinkling of freckles have popped up on my cheeks. It's hard to describe, but I feel more feminine than I ever have in my life.

My primary focus is on my baby and my bakery. Even though I'm doing it alone, I still count myself blessed. I'm feeling calm as I find my way back to my happiness. Toby and I are planning to go to the market today to pick up some fresh vegetables for the week ahead. Stepping to my closet, I pull out a pair of well-worn denim overalls. "These will be great as my belly gets bigger," I tell myself as I rub my stomach.

A short while later, there's a knock at my front door, and I finish tying my hair up in a paisley-patterned bandana before I answer.

"Toby," I say as I answer.

He cackles. "Dressed for the farmer's market, I see."

"Hilarious." Sticking out my tongue, I rub my belly. "I wanted to be comfortable, and other than the leggings I wear every single day, none of my other pants fit."

"Do we need to go shopping? I mean, you look adorable. But I'm always down for clothes shopping. You say the word, and I'm your man." I can't help but laugh. Toby is my favorite. He has been such a source of strength these past few months. I wouldn't have made it without him.

Pulling him into a hug, I say, "I know. You are the best, but it's not in my budget."

"If you change your mind, let me know. In the meantime, are you ready to go to the market? I'm driving, right?"

Before we've even left the parking lot, we're rocking out to Toby's amazing playlist. After about twenty minutes of driving, right when we should arrive, I look out the window and realize this isn't the way to the market. "Toby, where are we going? Is there a new market out this way?" He shakes his head but doesn't say anything else. My stomach turns. The only times I've ever been out here were when Josh brought me to his house. While we were dating, it was more practical to stay at my place, but occasionally, we ventured out into the suburbs and headed this same way. *We can't be going to Josh's, right?*

"Toby," I fret, the panic rising in my voice as I clutch the door, willing the car to stop.

"Kenz," he answers, as if nothing is wrong.

Something is definitely wrong if he's taking me to Josh's house. My mind spins. Maybe we're going somewhere else. I mean, it's not like they're friends and are arranging some sort of meet up. No. Toby knows how badly Josh hurt me, and there is no way he would force me to see him. That assurance melts away the closer and closer we get. *I need to get out of here now. I'm not ready to see him. I'm still hurt.*

Running my fingertips along the door handle, I question whether I could jump from the car safely when he turns at a stop sign. *I'm pregnant. Scratch that.* Feeling desperate, I shout, "Stop the car!"

Startled, Toby slams on the brakes and we both get a kiss of whiplash as the car fishtails. I'm glad we were only going twenty-fives miles an hour, or I'd probably be nursing a migraine along with my sudden-onset panic attack.

"Kenz, what's the matter? You don't look too good," Toby says. *No shit, Sherlock.*

"You, my best friend, are taking me to see the man who stomped on my heart and ordered me and our baby out of his life. Right?" I blow out an exasperated breath. "Of course I don't look good. I can't breathe, I'm sweating like a hog, and I think I'm going to hurl."

Moving the car over to the side of the road, he parks and switches the air conditioning to high. Soon, blessed cool air is power blasting me from his dashboard. After a few minutes, I feel better. That is until I remember where we are.

"Why are we here, Toby?" I growl.

Giving me a sheepish smile, he confesses how Josh caught him at the shop a few days ago and confessed everything. *What?* I don't understand. He didn't want to be a part of our lives. He accused me of cheating. Those were his words. He yelled them at me right before he stormed off. Now I'm supposed to forget that and pretend that everything is forgotten? Oh, hell no. His words devastated me then, and they still sting now. I've moved on. I am committed to raising my son by myself. I don't need anything from him. Wait, why is this even an issue? He was adamant the baby wasn't his. Chaotic feelings and thoughts invade every part of my brain, tormenting me. Josh admitted to Toby that he knew my baby was his.

"He acknowledges the baby is his?" I ask, shocked, unsure what to do with that information.

Toby nods his head. "He desperately wants to be part of his life." I wince. Josh has flipped Toby. *That hurts, but not as much as thinking Josh only wants to be a part of the baby's life.*

"He wants to be part of our child's life, but not mine?" I question on a sob.

Toby shakes his head. "No, he wants both of you. But he doesn't think you'll ever forgive him. I'm screwing this all up. Can't I just take you there and let him explain?" *I don't know if I can do this.*

Nervously, I twist my hands together in my lap. As if Toby can read my mind, he reaches over, settles them and says, "Kenz, you are the strongest woman I know. You are full of love and compassion. You forgive and give others a second chance. Josh sees that, and he knows he hurt you beyond belief. He just wants a chance to apologize. Will you give him that?" I look at Toby with tears in my eyes. *Can I do that?* Fear and worry swirl in my mind. "If you say so, I'll take you home right now and Josh can figure out another way. That's on him. I want you to be ready." He squeezes my hand, and a single tear falls down my cheek. I swipe it away.

"I'm ready. Let's get this over with."

Chapter 25

Josh

The guys and I finished everything late last night. Toby told me he'll get Kenzie and have her to my house around ten o'clock this morning. So for the past few hours, I've paced, done laundry, and rearranged almost every room of my house. At a quarter to ten, the anticipation is pumping through my veins. It's a combination of excitement and anxiety. Unable to stand still, I stalk to my front door and pull it open to sit vigil on the porch stairs until Toby and Kenzie arrive.

A few minutes later, I see an unknown car approaching, and I pray it's them. Turning slowly into my driveway, I see Toby wearing a grimace. *Oh shit.* I stand up and debate whether to approach the car or let them come to me on their own terms. Toby exits his vehicle and strolls over to the passenger door. Pulling it open, his voice drops to a whisper and I think I make out, "I'll stay with you the entire time." He steps back and Kenzie exits the car, sucking all the air from my lungs. I haven't seen her face-to-face in so long. My eyes roam all over her, noting all the changes to her body. Had I forgotten how fucking beautiful she was? Temporarily stunned, my gaze remains fixed on her and I catch a blush spread across her cheeks. She is undeniably the most gorgeous woman I have ever seen. They say pregnant woman glow, and she certainly does. I want to fall at her feet and not only beg her forgiveness, but worship the ground she walks on. Toby grabs her hand, leading her toward me. She's yet to make eye contact, and I find myself disappointed. *Look at me, Kenz, please.* Despite my silent pleas, her eyes remain fixed on the concrete walkway.

Toby gives a little wave with his free hand. "Hey, Josh."

My heart hurts. *I made the mistake, and it's time I fix it. Or try.* "Hi, Toby. Hi, Kenzie. Thanks for coming."

"I didn't have a choice," Kenz mumbles.

Toby squeezes her hand and whispers, "We talked about this. We can leave anytime you want."

My heart continues to tumble. She doesn't want to be here, be near me. I'm itching to even share the same space as her, and she hates me. How the hell am I going to convince her to forgive me? Before I let that thought drive me deeper into despair, Toby breaks the silence. "You both need a chance to talk this out. Otherwise, you'll never be able to move on." *Move on. Is that what she wants?* I don't want to move on from her. I want her back. Kenzie finally lifts her gaze to me, and all I see is sadness. My heart stutters. I did that to her.

Keeping my eyes focused on her, I whisper, "Thanks for coming. Do you want to come inside?" Her eyes go wide and she looks to Toby. "I have something I want to show you. Please?" I beg.

Time passes slowly as she considers my request. Seconds feel like hours. "Okay." Pulling on Toby's hand, she informs him, "You're coming too." *Threes a crowd.* I want to apologize to her. I didn't expect she'd need support. But beggars can't be choosers.

After they follow me inside, I stop before I take them upstairs. I need to say something. Turning quickly, I have half a second before they bump into me. "Oof," Toby says. Since he hasn't been in my house before, he's distractedly staring at everything with his mouth open wide. Kenzie has returned to staring at the floor. It's like the blind leading the blind.

Running my hand through my hair, I breathe out slowly before I begin to talk. "I have a surprise to show you, Kenzie, but first I need to say something." She peeks up at me through her thick eyelashes. "I am so sorry about what happened. I fucked up. I was a complete asshole to you, and I wish I could undo that, but I can't. After I stopped insisting I was right, I realized it was you who had it right. I hadn't used a condom. There's no denying it. You're pregnant with my baby." I feel tears forming and I close my eyes, pushing them away.

"I understand if you hate me. I reacted poorly, and instead of being mature about it, I withdrew into the residual pain from what Kayla did and accused you of being worse than her. I am so sorry. I know you're nothing like her, which is why I fell in love with you. You are a breath of fresh air. The sunshine on a cloudy day. The good in everything, and the woman I still love. I understand you may not forgive me, but from the moment I realized this child was mine, I've wanted nothing more than to be a father. Please let me be that?"

Through everything I've said, my eyes have remained locked on hers. I've noticed her lower lip wobble and her button nose scrunch, so I know her tears are close. "Can I show you something?" I ask.

She doesn't say anything but nods and follows me up the stairs. She makes a sound, and I turn back. Toby's dropped her hand and is encouraging her to go alone. "You'll be fine, Kenz. You need to do this with Josh." His eyes connect with mine, and I mouth *thank you.* He gives me a head nod. Kenzie watches our interaction.

"Okay," she whispers.

Leading her down the hallway, I stop in front of a closed door. "Go ahead, open it." She does, and once she's inside, she stops and gasps. Following her in, I stand back and watch her. She twists back and forth, and for the first time, I see her small baby bump clearly. My heart warms. I want to pull her in and hold them both. *My babies.*

"Josh, this is amazing," she gushes as she turns toward me, her eyes bright. The room is the perfect shade of gray. It'll work for a boy or girl. The crib I selected is white, matching the changing table, dresser, bookshelf, and doors. The wall behind the crib is darker gray, and it's accented with stars. Samantha and Shiloh told me I needed to get Kenzie the Cadillac of rocking chairs, and I did. I didn't want to decorate the entire room without Kenzie's input, so I stopped after I bought the softest elephant-covered sheet for the crib. There was a matching rug I bought too. I haven't put it out because I didn't want to overwhelm her.

She's right, this is amazing. It's perfect, really. We may not be perfect, but having her in this space is all I dreamed about while I was envisioning this surprise. "I'm so glad you like it."

"I love the gray," she says as she walks closer to the furniture.

Joining her at the crib, I admit, "I didn't know if we were having a boy or girl, so I went neutral."

She laughs. "That was smart." The smile on her face melts away some of the chill I've sensed between us since she arrived.

Nervously, I step closer. "So can I ask?"

"Huh?" she answers while turning the elephant mobile with her fingers.

"Do you know if we're having a boy or girl? I've read some books this last week, and if I understand everything, you're far enough along to tell, right?" I guess I'm the typical guy. I want a son so I can teach him how to play the world's best sport: hockey. My palms sweat as I wait for her response. Maybe it's a girl? I don't really know much about girls, but I'm willing to learn. No matter what, I plan to be there for my child. *Holy shit.* My nerves are frazzled.

Turning to me, she answers, "I'm far enough along, yes." And then she pauses and smirks. I'm not above begging, so I do.

"Please tell me if you know." She smiles and I mirror it. My anticipation is hammering through my veins, demanding an answer. Instead of replying, she prolongs my suffering and walks over to the glider. She settles into and pats her belly.

"This is really comfortable." She sighs.

Smirking, I say, "I'm glad you like it. The reviews said it's perfect for nursing and rocking."

Kenzie kicks her feet up on the footstool. "I can see that. And this little table is so cute."

Walking over to her, I explain, "That's for your water. The books said that nursing moms need to drink a lot of water."

"You're just assuming I plan on nursing? Or that I'll be living here?" she questions. The air in the room shifts. Her tone isn't angry, but it isn't sweet either. I don't know if I've made her upset or if she's just having a conversation with me.

Holding my hands up, I confess, "At this point, I'm assuming a lot. I know so much can change between today and tomorrow. I'm just filled with hope and waiting to see what shakes out."

She rises from the chair and moves to the half-opened closet where a few generic baby clothes hang. "What are your hopes, Josh?" With her still turned away, I feel less vulnerable and freer to share what I'm feeling. Pulling a onesie that says "Milk Drunk" on it down, I lay all my cards on the table.

"My biggest hope is that you'll come back to me and we'll raise our child here together." I see her fingers falter as she hangs the item back up. "But if that's not in the cards, I want to share custody of our baby and co-parent." Just saying those words is like ripping my tattered heart out of my chest. It feels like all the air has been sucked out of the room, and I bend over and rest my hands on my knees, forcing myself to breathe.

Chapter 26

Kenzie

Standing in this gorgeous room, it's the first taste of happiness I felt regarding Josh in weeks. Since he stomped all over my heart, I've had to come to terms with raising our baby on my own. However, he's promising everything I want. I'm still hurt over what happened and not ready to jump back into things with him, yet. Sure, I think this nursery is an amazing gesture, but I'm not making any promises. I owe that much to myself. Turning around slowly, I see him hunkered over, and my heart beats wildly in my chest.

"Are you okay?" I ask, concerned.

He looks up, sweat doting his brow. "Yeah, I'm fine. Just trying to remember that I pushed you away and I can't force you to come back. This isn't about me, it's about you and our child."

He's right. "Yeah, but I get how all this is overwhelming. A lot has changed in a short amount of time, and sometimes it's a struggle to get your mind around it all."

Josh stands up and runs his hands through his hair. He is so handsome, and I've missed him so much. It would be so easy to walk over to him and straight into his arms. I know by the way he's staring at me, he wants that and so much more. But despite my libido cheering for that option, my mind and heart remind me I'm not ready for that.

"Kenz." His voice, full of gravel, sends chills down my body. "I know it isn't fair of me to ask, but I have to. What do you want?"

My eyes dart around the room. "If I'm honest, I don't know. When I found out I was pregnant, I knew it wasn't the perfect timing. Hell, we hadn't talked about long-term commitment, marriage, or children. But I never could have imagined your reaction to my announcement. It crushed me. *You* crushed me. And I don't need to relive that ever again. I need to move on. But I'm not sure what that looks like." Looking up, I see his shoulders are slumped in defeat. My heart flinches. I don't want to hurt him. I take a moment to breathe before I further explain.

"Yes, I want you to be part of our son's life, and that will also keep you involved in mine. However, I haven't decided how involved I want you to be. I still love you, but I'm hurt, and I want to make sure I don't get hurt again."

"Son?" he rasps. I nod. Stepping over to the closet, he pushes the semi-closed section and reaches for something. Tucking it behind his back, he turns to me. "Close your eyes." I look at him, unsure. "Please Kenz, for me?" he begs. I do.

A few seconds later, I hear him say, "Open them." He's standing holding an infant-sized Chicago Steel onesie. Cue the waterworks. Stupid pregnancy hormones. Quickly, he turns it around, and across the back is Logan, his last name. I can't hold back a happy sigh. *This is the sweetest thing anyone has ever done for me.*

"It's so cute!" He lets out a chuckle, and I feel some more of the tension between us drift away.

A knocking at the doorway startles us, breaking the moment. "I'm sorry I interrupted, but the suspense was killing me. I had to come see what was up here. This is incredible. Did you do this, or did you hire a decorator?" Toby asks from the doorway.

Josh puffs out his chest and challenges. "What do you think?"

"Decorator?" Toby laughs. And Josh shakes his head.

"Nope. The guys and I did it all this weekend."

Toby's mouth drops open. "No! Please tell me at least some of their wives helped you pick out the linens and accessories."

Putting his hands on his hips, he matter-of-factly says, "Not a single one. I picked out everything."

Toby walks farther into the nursery and laughs. "If hockey doesn't work out for you, maybe you have another career option." I laugh too. For sure, Josh would be in demand because he'd be the sexiest decorator out there.

Toby leans his hip on the crib and says, "So, it looks like you two are doing this."

I go to reply, and Josh jumps in before I can. "Yes, we're having a baby together, but nothing else has been decided." I smile at him, bridging another fissure between us. For the next hour, Toby and I ooh and ahh over all the adorable baby items Josh found for the nursery. As I'm holding the tiny clothes and the soft stuffed animals, it's hard not to imagine myself spending lots of time in here with my growing belly as we prepare to bring our son home. I refuse to let myself get too carried away. I don't know what the future holds. Just like Josh, I hope we'll be together raising our son, but I'm not planning to rush into anything. I need a guarantee that he won't hurt me again. Because this time, I have to consider someone else's feelings too.

My stomach growls, reminding me I'm now eating for two. "Do you want to stay and have lunch? We can order in and have it on the patio," Josh asks excitedly.

Toby and I look at each other, having a silent conversation with our eyes. While still looking at me, he answers, "Actually, I have to get going. Kenz can stay if you can give her a ride home after."

I put my hand on my hips, demanding, "Where are you going?"

He smirks at me, knowing I still have feelings for Josh. He's trying to be my fairy godmother. It's annoying. "I have a date to get ready for. You should totally stay. Have lunch with Josh. I mean, you have to work out all those co-parenting things. And I bet he'd love to hear about how your pregnancy has gone so far. Show him your ultrasound pictures. I know you have those saved in your cloud."

"Thanks, Toby," I mutter.

"You don't have to stay, Kenzie. But he's right. I'd love to hear how everything's going so far and to see pictures. I can take you home whenever you want to go," Josh interjects.

Catching his eyes, I see they're filled with hope. "Okay, I'll stay for lunch. Thank you."

We walk Toby to the door, and before he leaves, he turns to Josh. "She can't have raw fish, soft cheese, lunch meat, alcohol, herbal tea, or too much caffeine." I laugh while pushing him out the door.

"We'll be just fine, Toby. Let's not overwhelm him yet, okay?" After Toby drives away, I turn back and look at Josh. He's frozen. Waving my hand in front of him, I wonder, *Did Toby's list break him?* "Josh." Registering my voice, he blinks rapidly. "Are you okay?"

He laughs as he spears his hand through his hair. "Yeah. I just realized there is so much I don't know about pregnancy or being a parent."

I smile at him, offering an olive branch. "We can learn together."

He knocks my shoulder with his. "I'd like that." We share a smile that makes me crave so much more, but my stomach growls again, ending the moment. Josh claps his hands together. "But first... let's get you fed. Does Mateo's sound good?"

"Always," I practically moan.

After he places the order, we stare at each other awkwardly. Shifting from side to side, I wonder what to say. *This is new.* Everything between us has always been so easy, but this... this isn't.

"It's a nice day. Do you want to go sit out on the deck until the food gets here?" he offers, seeming just as uncomfortable as I am.

"Sure," I answer, hoping a change of scenery is just what we need to break the tension strung between us. Settling into a lounge chair, I close my eyes and let the warm sun dance across my face. *This is nice.* Rolling my shoulders, I let myself relax. When I started the day, this impromptu visit with Josh hadn't been on the agenda, and as we neared his house, I felt my body tense up. Now I'm dealing with tight shoulders that will most likely result in a headache if I don't do something about them. I focus on my breaths and visualize the muscles loosening slowly.

"Uh, Kenzie, are you okay?" Josh questions. I open my eyes and see he's turned sideways on the chair next to me and leaning toward me, concern etched on his face.

Waving him off, I answer, "I'm fine, just a little tense. I was trying to relax some and ward off the headache I fear is imminent."

His light blue eyes have darkened. "Can I do anything? Maybe give you a shoulder massage? Would that help?"

Pausing a moment, I consider his offer. What will it mean? Am I ready to feel his touch again? Picturing his large hands, my heart thumps harder in my chest. Considering it for a moment, my mind wanders and my entire body grows warm. *I still want him. I miss his touch.* Concerns plague me. I'm hesitating to say yes.

Worry flashes in his eyes and he softly says, "I just want to help."

Chapter 27

Josh

Does she hear the desperation in my voice? I need to make things right between us. Being away from her was torture. What's worse is that I'm responsible for it. There's only one answer: I need her back in my life. Looking at her, I can't help but trace over the curves of her body. Some are old, and some are new, but they're all heavenly. Every one acted like a beacon, calling me home. I just need her forgiveness before I can make that journey. I won't be a headstrong conqueror, plowing through walls and demanding things. I'm determined to give her the time and space to decide on whether I'm worth another chance. Waiting for her answer, my fingers flex. I want to touch her, but more than that, I want to take away her pain.

"Okay," she whispers, like she isn't sure she wants me to hear. But I do, and I jump to my feet.

"Can you scoot forward and I can slide in behind you?" Anticipation of our first touch buzzes through my body. *Keep it together.* When I'm settled behind her, I lock my knees possessively around her hips. Being this close to her again feels amazing. The heat radiating between us is familiar and comforting.

Tentatively, I touch her by running a finger over her collarbone, and she shivers. Moving her hair out of the way, I'm dying to kiss her neck. *You can't.* I shake my head and move on to massage her instead. Her head dips forward, and she releases a groan. Her muscles are tight, but after a few minutes of focused rubbing, she's starting to relax.

"Does that feel better?" I ask when she's gone limp and silent. Her bright eyes peer over her shoulder at me.

"It was incredible. Thank you so much. I could fall asleep."

Just as I'm finishing up, my phone alerts me to a message. "Lunch is here. I'll go get it. You want to eat out here?" She smiles and nods.

Slowly, I make my way to the front door. I need a minute. Being that close to Kenzie put me in a tailspin. My body is lit up like the Fourth of July, and I'm trying to control myself. Focusing on my breathing, I walk back into my kitchen to plate up the food when my world stops. Standing there, lifting on her toes, is Kenzie reaching into the cupboard for plates. After grabbing them, she lowers and spins around. My eye catches on the smile stretched across her gorgeous face. Just that simple gesture gives me more hope than I've had in the past few weeks. I'm about to stride over and wrap my arms around her when my brain reminds me she's not ready for that. Instead, I move to the other side of the kitchen and begin unpacking the food. Once our plates are piled high, we head back out to the deck to enjoy lunch.

"This is so good." Kenzie moans from across the table, and I shift in my chair. If she keeps moaning, it's going to make things even harder, literally and figuratively.

Smiling, I catch her eye and lick my lips. "I'm glad you're enjoying it." I'm not trying to play with fire, but sitting across from me is the most irresistible woman I have ever met, and I want her to be mine again.

Her eyes dance and her cheeks turn pink. I remember the last time I saw this same expression grace her beautiful face. It was the night before I left for the series of games in the playoffs that we lost because of Norovirus. Kenzie had been complaining all week long that she'd been exhausted. Wanting her to get a good night's rest, I devised a plan. I spent the evening alternating between giving her a full body massage and delivering orgasms until she drifted off to sleep completely sated. Little did I know it would be the last thing I'd do before I destroyed us.

Looking at her now, I wonder what would have been if I hadn't been so quick to rush to judgment. *I've missed so much.* Determined not to miss anymore, I do the only thing I can—I ask about it. "Can you tell me about the pregnancy so far?" Hanging on every word, I learn that my little boy is six months along. He is growing like a champ. He moves more every day, and his favorite thing to do is tap dance on Kenzie's bladder. Her laugh when she tells me all that warms my heart.

"When are you due?" I ask. I ordered some pregnancy books, but I haven't read too much yet because I was busy setting up the nursery.

Kenzie wipes her mouth. "I'm due November 10th."

Consulting my mental calendar, I wonder if I'll even be in town for the birth or if I'll be on the road. I don't want to miss it, but from what she says, babies come on their own schedules. "You said he moves a lot. Do you just feel that or can others?"

Her eyes sparkle and she smiles as she answers, "Until recently, it's only been something I can feel, but in the last two weeks, I've felt him move on the outside." Excitement builds up within me. *I want to feel him.*

"I hadn't told anyone yet because I wasn't quite ready to be accosted by everyone who wants to feel the baby move."

I want to feel my son move, but I'm not going to force it.

"What's with the frown?" she asks.

I reach up and touch my lips, confirming her accusation. "I want to feel him move, but I don't want to make you uncomfortable."

Kenzie smiles at me. "Josh, you've never made me uncomfortable. If you want to feel him, you'll need to come over here and put your hand where I tell you."

Jumping out of my chair, I rush over to her side and sit next to her. Again, our bodies come into contact. My need to touch her makes me edgy. I feel like I want to crawl out of my skin.

Reaching for my hand, she instructs, "Lay your hand right here." I'm sure my son will kick me hard, especially after the way I've treated his mother. Lord knows, I certainly deserve it.

Her hand rests on top of mine and presses down. "Did you feel that?" she asks. I shake my head no. She taps our hands against her tiny bump and we wait. A short while later, I feel a flutter below our interlocked fingers.

"Wow," I gasp in amazement. Staring down at our fingers, I wonder when that happened. It feels so good. I don't want this moment to end.

Kenzie laughs. "I'm so glad you felt that because I have to pee again. As soon as I'm done, could you drive me home? Both the baby and I need a nap after that delicious meal."

I nod my reply because I don't want to actually say it. I want Kenzie to stay and nap here with me. But I can't force this. I know it's the right thing to bring her home, even though it's killing me inside.

On the way back to her place, I feel like I'm floating. Shortly after getting in the car, she takes my hand in hers. It's a struggle to focus on the road, especially while she's tracing her fingertips across my skin. Her delicate touch sends warmth throughout my body. As I pull up to her apartment complex, I wish for five more minutes. Being in Kenzie's space again is better than winning the Cup. I've never felt luckier. She's it for me, and I'm desperate for another chance.

Unbuckling her seat belt, she shifts toward me. Her eyes dance as they watch me adore her. *She is so beautiful.* "Thanks for the nursery tour, lunch, and the ride home."

"It was absolutely my pleasure. I've missed you, and it was so good to see you," I confess.

Her cheeks pinken and she admits, "It was good to see you too. I have a doctor's appointment in a few weeks if you want to come."

My heart practically leaps out of my chest, and I stutter. "A-are you s-serious?" She smiles and nods. "Yes. I will definitely be there. Thank you for inviting me." I grin like I've won the Mega Millions jackpot.

Feeling extra lucky, I figure I'll take my shot. "Could I maybe bring dinner over tomorrow?" Her smile morphs into surprise. *Uh-oh.* Backpedaling, I say, "I know I've hurt you, but I want us to at least be friends. Our little man deserves to have parents who like each other." Dropping my head, I can't make eye contact with her. I want to confess that I want so much more than friendship, but now isn't the time. Not knowing if she wants more has been a struggle. Coming to terms with that has been hard. In fact, in all honesty, I'm not sure I have. My brain refuses to accept it. I don't want to just be friends with Kenzie. I want everything. And I know it's selfish of me to want it, but I can't help it. She's the only woman I've ever wanted and ever will.

Clearing her throat, she squeaks out a timid "oh." The air in my Tesla shifts, and suddenly I'm freezing. Kenzie's silent for another few minutes before she whispers, "I think we can be friends. That would be better for everyone." A shiver runs through my body. Her words sound so empty and devoid of any feeling. Before I can ask, she unlaces our hands and exits my car without another word. *What just happened?* Resting my head on the steering wheel, I replay the conversation over and over, looking for the moment things went sideways.

Chapter 28

Kenzie

Everything had been going so well... until Josh mentioned us being friends. I try the word on my tongue. *Friends*. Not only does it sound wrong, but it feels wrong too. To him, a friendship isn't bad, we're having a child together. But until I heard him say it, I didn't realize how much more I wanted. I miss being loved by him so much. Sometimes it actually hurts to breathe. I don't want to just be friends. *I need more.* Feeling cast aside, I knew I needed to leave before my overly hormonal, emotional self lost it. I didn't need to cry in front of him. He didn't need to know I still wanted him. Especially since he didn't want me anymore. Getting over him was already proving difficult, but now that he was asking to be part of our lives, it was going to be impossible.

Walking into my apartment, my body slumps as the emotion of the past fifteen minutes sinks in. I'm glad the upcoming doctor appointment I invited Josh to is still a few weeks away. I'll have some time to construct a Josh-proof box I can stuff my still-raw feelings into.

The next morning, bright and early, I'm at the shop making cookies, bread, and cupcakes when I hear a familiar rap on the back door. I quickly dust off my hands. "It must be Toby," I tell myself as I walk to the door. Pushing it open, I expect my best friend with his arms full or some other excuse for needing help, but it isn't Toby. Surprised, all I say is, "It's you."

Josh gives me a killer smile, which makes my heart flutter. "Can I come in? I'd offer to make you a coffee, but last night I did some reading and found out you aren't supposed to have too much caffeine." *Why is he here?* We hadn't discussed this. Looking at the clock, it reads six a.m. *Friends don't show up at six in the freaking morning.* Confused, I look at him and ask, "Why are you here, Josh?"

He averts his eyes while he confesses, "I missed you, Kenz. I wasn't sure yesterday would ever happen, and now that it has, I want more. Before everything went to shit, you were my best friend and I want you back." Okay. His explanation doesn't clarify anything for me. If anything, it makes it all much more confusing. Does he want me back as his girlfriend, or does he just want my friendship?

The timer on the oven goes off, and I shuffle past him to pull loaves of freshly baked bread out. As soon as they come into contact with the cooler air in the kitchen, they hiss and crackle. Setting them on the cooling racks before sliding the next set in, I feel eyes on me, tracking my every movement.

When Josh steps up next to me, my knees buckle. Locking them, I force myself to remain upright. "What can I help with?" he offers in his sexy, deep baritone, sending shivers across my body. I love and hate that voice. In my sleep, it taunts me, turning dreams into nightmares as I relive the horrible accusations he lobbed at me. But now, when he's offering help, or before when he'd tease me in the bedroom, it's positively decadent and sinful.

"Are you sure?" I ask.

He smiles. "Toby told me you're hiring a morning baker to do all this, but until you do, you're it. So, I'm here to help. Is that okay?" *Really?*

"Okay. If you're sure?"

His smile eases my worries. "I am. The only thing I ask is that you let me have a death by chocolate cupcake and you agree to dinner with me this week."

I duck my head, hiding myself from him. "The cupcake I can do. Dinner... is that a good idea?"

He replies in a gruff tone, "Yes, I think it's a good idea. I've told you I missed you. I want to spend time with you. Is that okay?"

What he's saying is making this even harder for me. I'm trying to maintain my boundaries and protect myself, but he's charging through them as if they aren't there. Why can't we just decide to co-parent without being overly friendly? In order to be successful parents, we don't need to spend a ton of time together, we just need to get along. A flood of confusion and emotion washes over me and I feel my eyes grow wet. I sniffle once and try to muffle it by clearing my throat. I don't want to answer him because I know my voice will be a dead giveaway.

Overwhelmed, a tear rolls down my cheek and I try to swipe it away before another slips out. Turning away from him, I try to gain my composure. I blink my eyes rapidly, trying to push back the heavy tears. But nothing I do helps, and soon I'm sniffling again. Warm arms encircle me, pulling me against a hard, muscled body. "I'm so sorry I hurt you, Kenzie. Please tell me what I can do to fix it," he pleads against my ear, his voice thick with emotion too. I drop my head and he turns me around in his arms until I'm tucked tightly against his chest. "Kenz, babe, tell me what I can do."

Chapter 29

Josh

My heart is breaking. I'd do anything right now to make things better for Kenzie. Before our breakup, I can't remember the last time I experienced anything this emotional. It was probably the miscarriage. But considering that it was fabricated, losing my grandparents registers as the saddest. Their loss was traumatic for me, as I was closer to them than my actual parents. I never felt love from my parents, but my grandparents made sure I knew they loved me. They would have adored Kenzie, and they both would have openly berated me for how I treated her when she told me she was pregnant. As I hold her tight, I give thanks that I'm able to be here now.

Kenzie stiffens in my arms when I call her babe, and I reprimand myself for moving too fast. I couldn't help it. I want to do right by her. Fight her battles. Slay her dragons. Protect her... even if it's from me. Pulling back, I nudge her chin up so she'll make eye contact with me. "Am I making things worse?" That question pulls at my gut. It was tough to get past my lips. I don't want to believe that I'm doing more harm than good.

She nods. "I'm just so confused, Josh. I don't know what you want from me. Can you tell me?"

My mind warns me this is a trap, but Kenzie has never been one to play games. She has always been straightforward and upfront about things. So do I tell her bits of how I'm feeling or just rip the Band-Aid off and bare my soul? Looking into her sad eyes, I know the answer immediately. *Tell her the truth and hope for the best.*

Blowing out a deep breath, I pray she feels the same as I do. *Only one way to find out.* "Kenz, the time apart from you has been unbearable. Knowing what I've done to you. The ways I've hurt you. I'm not sure you'll ever forgive me. But I'm here to fight for you. For another chance. I want you. I want our baby. I want to see where this could go."

He waits a minute before saying more. "I know we've danced around the idea of friendship, but I don't want just that. Yes, I want my best friend back, but I want the love of my life back too. I will say I'm sorry for the rest of our lives, if that's what it takes. Not trusting and pushing you away were the worst mistakes I ever made, and I'm begging for your forgiveness."

Kenzie sets her head on my chest and says nothing.

I'm not sure how to interpret it. My nerves are shot. I know I have to accept whatever answer she gives me. I just hope it's one that ends with us together, raising our son.

Seconds, minutes, and hours pass. Maybe even days. Not really, but it feels like that. She pushes off my chest while wiping tears from her red-rimmed eyes. "You're right. You've hurt me worse than anyone ever has. I'll never forget the anger and judgment you spewed at me. Instead of responding like someone who claimed to love me, you called me names. You hurled accusations at me without giving me an opportunity to defend myself. You refused to believe me, choosing instead to lump me in with your spiteful, ladder-climbing ex who only used you." Kenzie pulls away more, creating a noticeable distance between us, making my body shudder.

"I've missed you too, but I refuse to be treated like that ever again. If you want another chance with me, earn it. I won't deny you your right to know your son, but the relationship we have is on shaky ground." Wiping her still wet eyes, she steps away from me, returning to what she'd been doing before I arrived. The kitchen is silent as I consider her words. My shoulders drop and my stomach tightens as it all sinks in. I know I'd hurt her, but until I heard it from her lips, I didn't realize just how badly. Will I ever be able to make it up to her? Do I even deserve a second chance? *Probably not.*

I see how exhausted she is and I decide there's something I can do about that right now. I slap my hands together, and she startles. "Shit. Sorry," I apologize. "Okay, I'm done making loud, startling noises. What can I do to help?"

Kenzie turns around with her splotchy face and I give her my best smile. She returns it and asks, "Do you mind starting a batch of your favorites?"

My smile grows wider. "Only if I can have one... maybe two."

"Deal." She laughs, easing some of my concerns.

For the next two hours, we bake, frost, and share laughter and secret smiles. It turns into the best morning. Toby pops in and, after a quick hello, I know it's time for me to go.

Kenzie's leaning against the counter. She's flour-dusted, her hair tied up in a bandana, and she's wearing a raggedy, stained apron. She has never looked more breathtaking. The sun streams through a window near her, making her look ethereal. She's an angel. My angel.

As I approach her, her eyes flick to mine and a sweet smile pulls at her soft, pink lips. "I'm going to get out of here. The offer of dinner tonight still stands if you're interested. No pressure."

She lays a hand on my chest, and the heat it carries radiates through my body. I want to cover it, but my hands are occupied, each holding a death by chocolate cupcake. They'll be my reward after I work out.

"Okay, we can do dinner. Can we eat in? After a full day on my feet, I need to elevate them so I don't end up with cankles."

"Cankles? Is that really a thing?" I ask.

She nods and grimaces. "From the pictures I've seen, it isn't pretty."

Stepping closer, I move both cupcakes to one hand before I push an errant strand of hair behind her ear, allowing my thumb to trace the delicate curve of her cheek. Her eyes soften and my heart thumps. She has such an effect on me. Lowering my voice, I murmur. "Hey, beautiful. Is there anything you're craving?"

Her face lights up and she says, "Tacos." Her voice sounds breathy.

A warmth fills my chest and I answer, "That I can do." Holding a cupcake in each hand again, I head for the door. She shuffles in front of me to open it. *Thank goodness. That would have been tough with my hands full.* "Thank you. See you tonight at about five."

"Sounds good. Thanks for your help this morning, Josh."

That afternoon, I punish my body with an intense workout. When I get home, I savor my reward— Kenzie's cupcakes.

Dinner goes great and we talk for hours until she's nodding off. I help clean up before leaving at eight. When I get home, before I go to bed, I squeeze in a five-mile run on my treadmill and a quick soak in my hot tub.

As I lie in bed and drift off to sleep, I relive the feeling of being around Kenzie again. I don't want to force things between us, but I know she needs help in the morning getting everything ready for the day. Since it's the offseason, I figure I can do that at least until she tells me to go away or she hires someone. I'm hoping for the latter.

Chapter 30

Kenzie

I'm officially into my third trimester, and the exhaustion I'm experiencing is nothing like what I expected. At times, I feel like I could simply fall asleep where I'm standing. My body aches everywhere and my son has decided he loves to practice Parkour right about the time I enter my REM cycle. And I have to pee every fifteen minutes.

Josh has been a godsend. For the past few weeks, every day I open the shop, he is there with me, ready to bake, frost, or do whatever my heart desires. Honestly, I couldn't have survived without him. On top of that, he brings me dinner every night, gives me foot and back rubs, and does chores around my apartment. He started back to practices last week, and I can tell he's exhausted, but he still shows up for me. I can't even describe how much that means to me. No one has ever done that for me before.

I have a new baker starting next week, who will take over my early morning shift. Instead of getting to the shop at four, I'll arrive between nine and ten to make sure everything is going well, supplies are stocked or ordered, and to check schedules and payroll. I trained Toby on all of it so that when the baby comes, I won't have to worry those first few weeks as I adjust to motherhood.

Josh and I have been spending a lot of time together. We've eased into a very comfortable place. A place where we hold hands and snuggle. Last week, he even kissed me again after he treated me to an amazing foot and calf rub while we watched a movie.

As we sat on my couch, my feet in his lap, our gazes met, and we exchanged a thousand unspoken words in that moment. Josh slowly leaned in and placed a soft, tender kiss on my lips, then pulled away with a smile. As innocent as it was, it lit my entire body up.

My pregnancy hormones and my near-constant desire to mount him have made it uncomfortable a time or two. My libido is off the charts, and no matter how many conversations I have with myself, I'm still not ready to charge through the sex boundary. Considering everything that's been happening, I guess you could say we're dating again. However, I should probably check to see if he's on the same page. We haven't made an official proclamation or anything.

osh only has a few days before he leaves for his first road trip of the season. It was hard when he traveled last season, but with a baby on the way and our relationship status in limbo, I'm more stressed than usual. Snuggled together on my couch sharing a bowl of popcorn, I realize how easy it was to drift back into us. "Josh," I begin. He turns to me and as soon as his blue-eyed gaze lands on me, my body heats up.

"Yeah, babe?" *Babe. I guess that's me.*

Picking up another piece of popcorn, I toss it at him, hitting him on the forehead. He smiles at me. "You know, if I'd known you were going to throw that, I would have tried to catch it. In my mouth," he says, accentuating the last part.

"I have a question," I tell him, my voice trailing off.

He drops the smile and stares at me. A look of uncertainty flashes across his face. "Okay," he says in a super serious tone that makes me rethink my question.

Pulling my lower lip in between my teeth, I nervously nibble at it while I figure out how best to ask my question. A moment passes, then two.

"Kenz, you're killing me. What's your question?"

Fumbling, I say,. "Uh. Um. Well... you see. Ugh." Frustrated, I hang my head.

Josh pushes my chin up and looks into my eyes. "Babe, what are you scared to ask me?" *How did he know I was scared?*

"We've been spending a lot of time together lately and we've gotten closer." He nods his agreement. "So if someone were to ask what I am to you, what would you tell them?"

He pushes a stray hair behind my ear and then cups my jaw. "I'd tell them you are very special to me. You are carrying my baby and you are my best friend." Swallowing hard, my feelings ball up in my throat. His words are pleasant, but they aren't what I want to hear. What my heart desperately needs.

Once again, I lower my head, crushed, and I whisper, "I see."

Josh lifts my face to him again and growls, "I don't think you do. I wasn't done. I would also tell them you are my everything. The one and only woman I will ever love. My future."

His words are like a balm to my weary heart. "Really?" I ask.

Josh lowers his forehead to mine. "Really," he confirms, and my heart rejoices.

Setting the popcorn bowl on the floor, he pulls me onto his lap so I'm straddling him. My pregnant belly fills the space between us, but he pulls me closer. I cherish the closeness we've gone without for months. The moment our lips touch, sparks crackle around us, reinforcing the undeniable chemistry we've always had.

I lay my hand on his chest to see if his heart is beating as fast as mine. It is. In fact, we're in perfect rhythm together. He takes his large hand and wraps it around my neck, pulling me deeper into the kiss. I gasp, opening my mouth, and he swipes his tongue inside, stealing my breath. I pull back, panting. Our baby somersaults in between us and I feel something, probably an elbow, poke out. His eyes go wide. "Was that...?"

All I have to do is smile before he pulls me into another soul-stealing kiss. His hands trace down my sides and grab my hips, anchoring me in place as he thrusts upward. *That feels incredible.* Moaning into his mouth, I pray he'll do it again. My prayers are answered when he again thrusts up, snapping his hips. Wanting so much more, I grind down on him, creating an absolutely delicious, hot friction between us. I circle my hips at a feverish pace, chasing the orgasm I feel building.

Josh tucks my shirt over my belly and runs his finger over the front clasp of my bra. Before flicking it open, he pulls his lips from mine. "Is this okay?" he pants. Excitedly, I nod. Within seconds, he's released my much larger breasts, and he growls at the sight of them. "You are beautiful," he says before pulling a nipple into his mouth. The suction sends me over the edge, and I throw my head back, moaning out my plea-sure. As I'm coming down from the high, his hands skate up my back, supporting me, and I allow myself to relax back. The lost weight provides a reprieve from the constant strain of carrying fifteen extra pounds on my frame.

"That feels amazing." I groan.

"Lean back and enjoy it, babe," he croons, his deep, sexy voice further relaxing me.

"I'm not too heavy?" I murmur.

"Not at all. Besides, I have the most incredible view of the most gorgeous body I've ever seen." He takes his tongue and traces it over my baby bump and up my sternum between my breasts. He chases the trail with his hot breath, and goose bumps break out over my body. I have never felt more desired in my life. I close my eyes, savoring the moment, and when I'm about to fall asleep, I feel him pull me up. He scooches forward on the couch, wrapping my legs around him, and picks me up. *Thank goodness for muscles.* He walks to my room and lays me down on the bed. I open my eyes, the shift in position pressing on my bladder.

"I need to go to the bathroom," I tell him.

As I disappear to take care of business, Josh sits down on my bed. Feeling bold after what we've just shared, I strip off my clothes, leaving them in a pile on the floor. I brush my teeth and exit the bathroom. Hungry eyes track me across the room as I get closer to the only man I've ever loved.

"Kenzie," he whispers, reverence laced in his voice.

This moment, right now, is a turning point for us. When I reach him, I step between his legs. His eyes are full of love and he places a tender kiss on my growing belly.

"Will you please stay the night with me?" I step back and he stands up. He pulls his shirt over his head and I slide my fingertips down his perfect abs to his belt. I tap it. He takes the hint. After undoing the buckle and the button on his jeans, he slowly slides the zipper down. *Tease.* Dropping them to the floor, he looks at me. I drop my eyes and focus on the outline of his hard cock while licking my lips. Next go his sexy black boxer briefs, and I have to remind myself to breathe. Anticipation charges through me. Every touch from him electrifies my body. His cock proudly bobs between us and he wraps his hand around it, giving it a slow pump.

My tongue darts out, licking my lips as he growls, "Lie back. Let me make you feel good." I nervously scoot back. *It's been a while.*

I can feel his eyes on me and he mutters, "Damn, you're gorgeous." When he gets to my eyes, he stops. "What's wrong?"

Whispering, I answer, "This will be the first time since we learned I was pregnant."

Josh sits back and sets his hands on my knees. He traces lazy circles with his finger and says, "I won't hurt you."

Shaking my head, I pull at his arms, and he crawls over me willingly. "You can't hurt us. Just certain positions may be more comfortable." A stern look spreads across his face.

"Tell me if I'm hurting you." I nod and he lowers himself into a plank pose where he's hovering above me. I reach up with my hand and pull his head down to mine. In mere moments, I'm lost in his kiss. With our tongues dueling, I let my hands explore. Tracing over the ridges of his pecs and down his abs, he sucks in a breath when I circle out to his sides. To his perfectly sculpted Adonis belt. *Sexiest man alive.*

Chapter 31

Josh

With Kenzie's hands running over me and our mouths locked together in a heated kiss, I feel electrified. My body is buzzing with the need to be inside her again; it's been so long.

She breaks our kiss and smiles at me just before she asks, "Will you make love to me now?"

Sex during pregnancy. I still have concerns, even though Kenzie has already said I won't hurt her or the baby. Having sex with a pregnant woman has to be about logistics, so I try to determine the best positions possible.

Since it's been so long, I want to see Kenzie's face when she comes. Reaching down, I run my fingers through her folds. "Oh, Josh," she says with a moan. Already soaking, she bucks her hips forward, grinding against the heel of my hand. *She's close.* Excitement builds within me as I back off the bed.

"Scoot this way," I tell her, directing her to the edge of the bed. Once she's situated, I tap her knees and direct, "Open for me, babe." I lower my head and leisurely drag my tongue back to front. When I get to her clit, I suck it into my mouth, giving it rhythmic flicks.

"Mmmm. That feels so good," she whimpers as she arches off the bed.

I trace my hand down her sternum, over her belly, and to her thigh. I squeeze it possessively and growl "mine" against her center. Her whole-body shivers from what I'm doing with my tongue or from my possessiveness, I'm not sure. Giving long, unhurried licks, I bring her to the edge of an orgasm time and time again. After the third time, she frowns and I insert two fingers, pumping them into her. I curl my digits toward me, hunting out the prize inside. When I finally brush against the promised land, she lets out a toe-curling moan that rattles me to the core. It makes me want to beat my chest. *I did that to her.*

Finally, when she comes down from the high of her orgasm, she pants my name.

"Yeah, babe? What do you need?" I ask.

Her sensual blue eyes flick open and she gives me a one-word answer. "You."

I drop my voice, quietly telling her, "Roll onto your side." I move in front of her and pull her in close.

Lifting one leg up, I run my cock through her wet heat. *Damn, that feels so good.* I know it'll be even better once I'm inside her. She nudges her hips forward, and I don't need any further encouragement before I line myself up and slide into her. Thoughts of poking my son with the head of my cock invade my mind for a moment before disappearing entirely. The tight squeeze she has on me blanking my mind.

She grips my biceps as she murmurs, "That feels so good." *I second that.* Slowly, I turn her to me and thrust in and out. Because she's still sensitive from her orgasms, the next one comes on quickly, and her muscles squeeze me as I continue pumping into her. I'm so close, but I'm not ready yet. I reach between us and make circles on her clit. At first, she pulls away with an "oh," but within seconds that moan turns pleasurable and she wraps her leg around me tighter, pulling me deeper. I pull one of her full breasts into my mouth and suck the hardened nipple. Every pull I take brings her closer and closer. She arches her back and her belly pushes into mine, reminding me of the life we made growing inside of her. Thoughts of that unravel me, revealing a primal hunger for her. I pump into her with a feverish pace while teasing her clit and breast. "Please, right there," she begs, and I can't help but deliver. Three pumps later, my orgasm rips through me like a bolt of lightning. It leaves parts of me singed, never to be the same again. We lie there together, panting, staring into each other's eyes.

"I love you, Kenzie." It probably isn't the right time to say it, but I couldn't hold it back any longer.

"Love you too, Josh," she replies before falling asleep. My heart hammers in my chest, threatening to break free. *She fucking loves me.* I'm on top of the world.

After cleaning us both up, I crawl into bed and Kenzie immediately cuddles up next to me, her head on my chest and her leg slung over my thigh. I pull her in close as I lie there, and just stare at her as she drifts back to sleep.

Ever since the first time I laid eyes on Kenzie, I've been drawn to her. In fact, she is the only woman I have ever pursued. She is utter perfection. From her radiant smile to the twinkle in her eyes, she captivates me completely. When I got to know her, my attraction for her grew tenfold. She is the most amazing person I have ever met. I still don't understand how I doubted her when she told me she was pregnant. Kenzie's nothing like Kayla, and she never would have lied or tried to trick me. I was an idiot for even thinking it.

Speaking of the she-devil, Kayla tried to weasel her way back into my life when Kenzie and I were broken up. Thinking about it now, my stomach cramps in disgust. She must have learned that we weren't together. Because she started trying to insert herself back into my life. She showed up at the rink or harassed my assistant when I refused to call her back. She didn't take too kindly to my attempts to ignore her, and she showed up at the arena one day. Stan recognized her and gave me a heads-up, and I let my boys know to be ready with their cameras.

When Ace, Rocco, and I came out of practice, she tried to get my attention by puffing out her chest and waving dramatically. I made her wait, signing autographs for a few fans before I made my way to her. I'm actually surprised she didn't burst into flames with the glare I directed at her. As soon as I got within a foot of her, she started with all the "baby, I've missed you" garbage. I actually snarled at her and said, "Why are you here, Kayla? After everything you did to me. All the lies you told." I didn't need to air the dirty laundry, expose what she'd done to me. I just needed her to admit she'd lied about me. About us. I planned to share that shit all over the web. Pay her back for a fraction of what she did to me.

"Joshy-baby. I am so sorry. You're right. I was horrible, but I've missed you so much. I'm here begging for another chance."

Crossing my arms, my snarky response came out just as I intended it. "Why the fuck would I give you a second chance?"

She pouted her lips and whispered, "Because I know you and that baker chick aren't together anymore."

I reared back as if I'd been punched hard. My breath caught in my throat. "What did you say?"

"She wasn't good enough for you, Josh. I'm who

you need to be with. We're the perfect match and you know it. Give me another chance to show you how good I can be for you."

Anger coursed through my veins. *How dare she.* Shaking, I sputtered, "Y-you're wrong. I'm not good enough for Kenzie. She deserves so much more than I can ever give her. She is the best there is, and I fucked up. I love her and will for the rest of my life. You, on the other hand, I never want to see again." Her mouth dropped open in surprise and I turned around and walked away.

"That was fucking awesome, Josh." Rocco hooted as he slapped my back. He turned to Ace and asked, "You got it all right?"

Ace grinned. "Sure did, and it's already been loaded onto all the major social platforms."

Not even thirty seconds passed before I heard Kayla scream like the banshee she is. Apparently, she'd already seen a replay of our conversation.

"She doesn't sound happy. I must not have used the right filter or my lighting was shoddy," Ace said with a laugh. Rocco laughed too, but I couldn't seem to find any humor in the situation.

I'd been completely truthful with Kayla; I'd fucked things up with Kenzie. But thankfully, Kenzie has given me a second chance. There is no way in hell I'm going to screw it up.

ockey has always been my first love, but the longer we're together, the more I realize that Kenzie and our son have taken the top spot. The next few weeks pass quickly. I'm on the road a lot, and unfortunately, I miss most of Kenzie's OB checks. We always make sure to FaceTime afterward so I can hear how she and the baby are doing.

Last week, when I was home, we made it to a birthing class and infant care, and both were eye-opening. I realized I know nothing, and I'm not sure the hospital should let me go home with a baby. During the birthing class, the instructor showed us a video of a baby being born. And since then, I can definitely say I don't look at sausage the same way. Other than trying to distract Kenzie from making fun of me and my aversion to blood, it went okay. Since I wasn't sure about the birth, I figured I'd pay close attention to the infant care class so I'd be ready. Unfortunately, it didn't go as planned, and when we were practicing diaper changes, I unintentionally removed our practice baby's leg. I'm not sure what happened, but thankfully, Kenzie fixed the doll before the class ended. Otherwise, that might have proved embarrassing.

We haven't chosen his name yet, but we have a few favorites. We're keeping them quiet until our little man arrives.

The last concern I have before she delivers—aside from me possibly not being here—is that I want Kenzie to move in with me, but I never seem to find the right time to ask her.

My FaceTime rings.

"Hey, babe," I say as I answer the call.

Her glowing face appears on my iPad, and my fingers flinch because they long to touch her.

"Hey," she answers in her sweet tone.

"How are you feeling? How was your appointment?"

Setting up the iPad, I see she's surrounded by lots of things.

"I'm good, but tired."

"Yeah? Are you packing?"

She nods. "Dr. Cruise said it was time to pack the hospital bag if I hadn't done it yet."

Nerves and excitement roll through me.

"Really?" Panic sets in. I'm going to an away series this week and next. "But you have a few weeks left, right?"

Interrupting my musings, she replies, "Technically, I can deliver after thirty-seven weeks. Since it's my first pregnancy, Dr. Cruise expects I won't deliver before forty weeks. But she wants me to be ready. I spoke with Stephanie today, too, just to make sure she's still willing to be my backup if you aren't here, and she couldn't be more excited."

"I'm so glad you have her, because if I can't be there, I'd want either Stephanic or Toby there with you."

Kenzie laughs. "Toby?"

I smirk. "Okay, okay. Scratch that. Toby would probably be a disaster. Plus, he needs to run CakeStop."

"I think that's safer. I don't need my labor coach passing out on me." As she's folding baby clothes for the hospital bag, I spot her holding something that doesn't look familiar. "What's that?"

She holds up a Chicago Steel onesie. "Samantha brought this into the bakery this week. She said our little man needs to go home in style. It even has matching baby joggers," she squeals as she holds up the entire outfit.

"He'll be styling, for sure," I confirm. "Is there anything you need done before our little man arrives?"

She looks around her small bedroom and frowns.

"What's wrong, babe?"

Shaking her head, she answers, "Nothing. I'm just trying to figure out how all the baby stuff is going to fit in here." *It's like she's reading my mind.*

"What if you didn't have to fit all in there?" I ask. The questioning look on her face tells me she's confused.

Before I speak, I pray she's receptive to my idea. "What if you moved into my house and we officially live together and raise our little guy there?"

"Really?" she questions, and I nod.

Her face lights up, and a smile spreads across my face. *I can't wait to see her in my place. To make it* our *place.* I've wanted no one in my space before. Kayla forced it and I was too broken to fight it. But I didn't want her there. I can't wait to share space with Kenzie.

"Okay," she murmurs. Then her face drops. "But when will I move?"

"I'll call the movers tomorrow and try to schedule it for this weekend. They do everything. You just have to point and direct."

She tries to disguise her excitement, asking, "Are you sure?"

"I couldn't be more sure about anything. I love you and I love the house. I've wanted you there for a long time. Plus, when your parents visit, they'll have a place to stay. So, what do you say?"

Pausing for a moment, she smiles and answers, "Okay, I'll move in with you." I wish I were there so I could pull her in for a hug.

Reading my thoughts, she says, "I wish you were here."

"Me too."

Months ago, when my world was in complete chaos, I wasn't sure I'd ever be happy again. But thanks to Kenzie, everything has changed and I couldn't ask for anything better.

Chapter 32

Kenzie

After the call where Josh invites me to move in with him, I know I need to call my parents. They know Josh and I are back together and he's the father of my baby. But now I've got to tell them we're moving in together.

After a few rings, my mom answers. "Hello."

"Mom," I excitedly say.

"Hi, sweetie. How are you? How is my little angel treating his mother?"

Rubbing my enormous belly, I laugh. "We're wonderful, Mom. It's hard to believe he'll be here soon."

"I know. I am so excited to see you and meet him. And Josh too."

There's some noise on the other end of the line. "Did I call at a bad time?" I ask. Glancing at the clock, I see it shouldn't be too late there.

"No, it's perfect timing. Your father was trying to get me to rearrange the pantry a certain way he saw on some infomercial." She laughs.

I chuckle and say, "I'm guessing you don't see the benefit, but Dad's working to show you?" She laughs again. I can picture her standing in their kitchen, surrounded by boxes and cans, while Dad explains how this new, easy organizational method will not only save them time but money.

"It sounds a little chaotic there. I was calling to share some good news."

"Go on," my dad encourages.

"Well, when you come to Chicago, you don't need to stay at a hotel for your visit."

All extra noise stops on their side of the line. "Kenzie, what do you mean?"

"Josh asked me to move in, and he has extra room for you to stay with us." I hesitate, wondering what they'll say.

My mom hums. "We won't be in the way?"

Thinking about how large Josh's house is, I laugh. "Heaven's no. Josh has a large house, and it would be more convenient for you to stay with us. We both want you to stay with us."

My dad answers, "If you're sure, we'll stay with you. Please tell Josh we said thank you."

The rest of our conversation is about the baby and how excited we are to see each other.

Hanging up, I fire off a quick text to Josh.

ME

Talked to my parents, and they said
thank you for the invitation to stay at
the house.

JOSH

It's no problem. It makes me feel so
much better knowing you'll have help
while I'm gone. I love you, babe. I
better go to sleep so I'm not dragging
at the game tomorrow.

ME

I love you too. Sleep well. I'll talk to
you tomorrow.

It's the first of November and I'm officially moved into Josh's house and mostly settled. True to his word, I didn't have to lift a finger. Which was amazing. By far, it was the easiest move I've ever made. And it happened just in time. Josh got home from his latest series yesterday and this morning I wake up early, feeling a tight cramping in my stomach. I sit in the nursery trying to rest, knowing I'll never be able to get back to sleep. With my feet propped up and my trusty water bottle at my side, I try to work through my discomfort. *Are these Braxton Hicks contractions?* But by the second hour of sitting in the world's comfiest rocking chair, I know something isn't right. My back hurts so much, I can barely keep still. The throbbing intensifies, pulsing down my spine and snaking all the way around to my stomach, stealing my breath. There isn't any doubt now—I'm in labor. My contractions aren't regular yet, but they're getting stronger. Three hours after I'd woken up, Josh comes looking for me.

"Kenzie, where are you?"

"I'm in here," I pant in a strained voice.

He enters the room, and as soon as his gaze lands on me, his eyes go wide and he looks concerned. "Babe, are you okay?"

I huff a laugh. "I'm great. But I... ahhh." He rushes to my side.

"What's wrong?"

Once the contraction subsides, I focus on him. "I think I'm in labor. My contractions have been getting stronger and more frequent over the past hour. I haven't been able to time them, but they feel like they're getting closer together."

Before he can say anything, another one strikes. "Ahhh." I moan through another one. It feels like my stomach is being squeezed by a vise.

Pulling his hands through his hair, he says what I'm thinking. "Holy shit. This is really happening." Again, I huff a humorless laugh. *No shit, Sherlock.*

"Josh, I hate to bug you, but I think I need to get to the hospital sooner rather than later."

He quickly stands and hurries to the door, forgetting me completely as he lists all the things we need to bring with us. When he's halfway down the hallway, I still hear him muttering, "Car seat, diaper bag, phone charger..."

"Josh," I holler.

Moments later, he's in the doorway, looking flustered. "Babe, I forgot you." Rushing to my side, he helps me to my feet and walks me to the door.

"Grab the diaper bag. It has everything in it," I remind him. A timid smile appears across his worried face.

"That's right, and the car seat is already in the car with the other bag you packed." He forces a laugh. "I don't know what I'd do if you weren't so prepared." *I don't either.*

We arrive safely at the hospital twenty minutes later, despite Josh's anxious state. Because I'm in active labor, I'm given a wheelchair ride to labor and delivery. Nurse Karen shows us to a room. Once I'm changed into the hospital gown, she returns to start an IV and hook me up to a machine that monitors the baby's heart rate and my contractions. Then she checks my cervix, and nothing could have prepared me for that—I practically shoot off the bed—and then she informs me I'm only dilated to a three. "You have a bit to go before we call Dr. Cruise in. Your water hasn't even broken, so she may want to do that to get things going," she says, then leaves.

"You're at a three. Remind me what you have to be at before you push," Josh says.

Before I can answer, another contraction overtakes

me, forcing me to silence. I try to remember what I learned in my birthing class, and no matter how hard I focus on my breathing, I'm still panting. A bead of sweat trickles down my back. "Breath babe," Josh calmly reminds me. When the worst of it has passed, I look at him and I feel my chin wobble. My emotions are raw. I'm a mess. A whirlwind of joy, fear, excitement, and pain overwhelms me. *This is the hardest thing I've ever done.*

As if he senses my unease, Josh strokes my hand. "Kenzie, babe. You've got this. You are the strongest and bravest woman I know." I nod as another contraction tears through my abdomen. Groaning because they feel stronger, I look at the man I love for strength. His smile is all I need to survive. "I love you," I whisper.

"I love you too," he says before lowering his forehead to mine. A moment is all we get before Dr. Cruise pops in. "I hear we're having a baby today."

"We hope so," Josh answers as I grimace through another contraction. She strolls over to check on my contractions.

"You are laboring beautifully, Kenzie. I'm going to check you." Dr. Cruise steps up to the side of the bed while pulling on her gloves. "Your nurses say you were a three when they last checked you about an hour ago. Let's see what progress you've made." As soon as she checks me, I feel a lot of pressure and then a large gush.

"Was that what I think it was?" I ask, worried.

She nods. "It was your water breaking, and it's perfectly normal. You're at a solid four. I'll get the nurses in here to switch your bedding and your gown. Prepare yourself, Kenzie, your labor is about to shift into high gear. I'll be back soon." Then she smiles and disappears out of my room.

Terrified, I look at Josh, but he looks as scared as I feel. *It's too late to go back.* Summoning courage from somewhere, I tell myself, *"You can do this."*

Within minutes, my room is busy with nurses changing my bedding. They leave a clean gown for me to change into before they file out the door. Josh helps me change, and before I even have the wet gown unsnapped, I double over in pain. It's sharper and more intense than it has been, and now it isn't just in my abdomen, but it has snaked to my lower back. I mindlessly rub just above my tailbone while praying for relief. White hot pain shoots around my back, stealing my breath and making me weak. When it passes, Josh and I work quickly to get the dry gown on and secured before anyone else interrupts. I climb back into my hospital bed and groan at the discomfort my body is enduring. *Why can't men carry the babies? I mean, they're the ones always telling women how much stronger they are.* Before I can consider that, Nurse Karen is back. "Let's check you." Now that she mentions it, the contractions feel stronger. "You're at five, halfway there. I'll update Dr. Cruise. I bet in a few hours you'll be holding a baby."

Once she leaves the room, Josh and I stare at each other in disbelief. Finally, he breaks the silence. "This is really happening. We're about to be parents."

I whisper, "Are we ready?" He shrugs and laughs.

"Guess we'll find out the hard way." I laugh, but it turns into a groan when pain wraps around me like a boa constrictor. "Breathe, Kenz," he says, reminding me of the syncopated pattern they taught us.

"Hee, hee, hoo. Hee, hee, hoo." We get into a rhythm of breathing as soon as I feel my stomach tighten. Over the next hour, I breathe as Josh rubs a tennis ball on my lower back. He's trying to ease some aches I have there, but when my doctor comes in to check on me, she tells him I'm suffering from back labor. I'm moaning, covered in sweat, and slightly winded. I grimace through her examination.

"Your labor seems to have stalled. And I see how hard you're working, but at the rate you're going, you are going to be exhausted by the time you have to push."

"Okay, what do you suggest?" I pant, knowing that I'm not confident in my ability to do this naturally. Hell, I wrote epidural as a possibility in my labor plan.

"You are almost at a six, and an anesthesiologist can come give you an epidural. It will relax your body enough to allow you to continue laboring without so much discomfort."

Decided, I turn to Dr. Cruise. "Please," I answer. Before I know it, my room is filled with more medical personnel and I'm hunched over a pillow, trying to remain as still as possible while shivering through contractions. Once the epidural is placed, I'm able to rest, and two hours later, I'm fully dilated.

Because of the epidural, I can't feel anything below my waist and both Josh and a nurse have to assist me in holding my legs back as Dr. Cruise directs my pushing. Our little man must like his home because it takes over an hour and a half of pushing before he's delivered.

His cry is the best sound I've ever heard, and I openly weep over his safe arrival. Josh cuts the cord as Dr. Cruise finishes up with me. The baby scores great on his Apgar tests and soon he is swaddled and handed to me. My heart feels like it's going to leap out of my chest. I'm overjoyed, relieved, and content. My son is here. Wiping tears from my eyes, I tuck him securely against my chest and whisper, "I love you." And I could swear he smiles up at me. Unlikely, I know, but that's what I'm telling myself.

Looking up, I see Josh staring at us, an expression of wonderment on his face. "Isn't he amazing?" I ask.

He nods. "You both are. I love you both so much." Smiling widely, I am so grateful for our little family. At one point, it felt like an impossibility, but now, seeing how far we've come, I don't doubt what we have will last forever.

A nurse approaches. "I'm sorry for interrupting, but we need to give your son a bath before we take you over to the mother-baby unit. Do you know what this handsome little man's name will be?"

Josh and I exchange a look before he speaks. "We're naming him Issac after his great-grandpa."

The nurse hums. "That is just so special." I hand her Issac and she whisks him across the room for his first official bath. Josh, the dutiful father he is, follows close behind with his cell phone out to capture everything. I take a moment to breathe. Dr. Cruise slips back in the room and walks over to my bed.

"I'm so proud of you, Kenzie. You did a fantastic job. Take care of yourself and Issac, and I will see you in a few weeks. Call my office if you need us sooner. Congratulations, Momma." She gives me a hug before she leaves.

The next forty-eight hours are a cluster. Between our friends' visits, breastfeeding attempts, and diaper changes, it is chaos trying to figure everything out. When we're finally discharged, we can't believe it. They're letting us take Issac home and we don't even have an instruction manual.

The drive home is agonizingly slow, as Josh travels with extreme caution. Once we get there, all I want is a hot shower and some comfy pajamas. I would also kill for some decent food. However, as if Issac senses we're no longer in the hospital and surrounded by a flock of nurses, he shakes things up. He starts with a meconium-filled diaper that has us trying to carefully scrape a tar-like substance off his tiny bottom. Then he wants to nurse but doesn't want to latch. Every time I think I have him on, he arches his back, pulls off, then whimpers because he's hungry. All his crying leads to him being extra gassy, which makes him cry even more. Let's just say the first half day home is trying. Add in my hormones and emotions, and there are no good words to describe it.

On day number two, Samantha and Shiloh come over and check on us. They bring dinners for the freezer. Josh disappeared upstairs a few hours ago, and if I were a betting woman, I'd guess he went to get some sleep. That's critical right now. We need sleep to survive, and in a few weeks, he'll be back on the road and I'll be left alone. Kind of. My parents are visiting from Seattle when Josh is back in town a few days before Thanksgiving. Because I'm still learning what it's like to have a newborn, Josh planned with Mateo's on a non-traditional Thanksgiving dinner. I'm so thankful I don't have to cook. I didn't think it could be this possible to be so tired and still function. Exhausted, hormonal, and anxious, but so damn happy. This isn't the life I thought I would be living, and I'm thankful for that too, because sometimes the unplanned moments are the best.

Chapter 33

Josh

ince Kenzie has been in my life, I've been eager to get home from road trips, but now with Issac, I'm desperate. Being away from them is the hardest thing I've ever done. Because he's so young, I know he'll never remember it, but Kenzie and I will. It's hard not to feel guilty, especially the first few times.

Playing for the NHL definitely has some perks, like my paycheck and the offseason, but other things are a definite burden. Before Issac arrived, I learned from other players that the NHL doesn't offer a standardized paternity leave. I met with Trey McConnell, the owner of the Steel, and he granted me two weeks. I only missed one away series, but I know that was enough. As the captain, my presence has a large effect on player morale.

Thanksgiving is next week, and along with the

holiday, Kenzie's parents will arrive to meet their grandson and lend help while I'm on the road. I'll only be home for a few days while they're visiting. And to say I'm anxious is an understatement. I only have a few days to win them over.

On my way home from this latest trip, I text Kenzie.

ME

Hey, babe, we just landed. Do you need me to stop at the store for anything?

KENZIE

I'm so glad you're back. I need a shower, like yesterday. But we need a few things from the store. Can you also grab something for dinner?

ME

Do you want anything in particular?

KENZIE

Something yummy.

ME

I've got you. Can you send me your grocery list?

KENZIE

Will do. Thank you, babe.

ME

No problem. I'll see you soon. I love you.

KENZIE

Love you too.

Before I leave the arena, I call in an order to Mateo's for dinner. I know some comfort foods like lasagna, garlic bread, and tiramisu will go a long way to helping Kenzie feel better. Stopping by the grocery store is quick and easy since we don't need much.

"I'm home," I call out as I push through the front door. Kenzie walks around the corner holding Issac close.

"Hi," she whispers.

Setting down my bags, I rush toward them and wrap them in my arms. "I missed you two so much," I say against her head. Her shoulders shake, and I pull back. Her blue eyes are misty with unshed tears. "Kenz, babe. Give me Issac and then you go hop in the shower while I get dinner out. Then once you're full, you can get to bed early."

"Are you sure?" Her voice is soft and weary.

Smiling, I nod. "I need some Issac snuggles." Kenz gives me a weak smile. "I love you. Now, hand over my son and go take a moment for yourself." Once she's passed over my little man, I go back to the bags I left near the front door. "Let's get the groceries put away before we get dinner ready for your mommy, okay?" His big blue eyes stare up at me, and I feel on top of the world. Smiling, I bop his nose as I lower him into the bouncy chair before I tackle the groceries. "I hear you've been giving Mom a hard time while I was away. I thought we had a deal. While I'm away, you're the man of the house, and it's your job to take care of your mom." Moving around the kitchen, I grab everything we'll need for dinner. Hearing Kenzie come down the stairs, I check on my little man and see he's fallen asleep.

"Is that Mateo's I smell?" she gushes as she enters the kitchen.

Laughing, I answer, "Of course. I figured a delicious, hearty meal would be just what you needed, along with a lot of sleep."

Freshly showered with semi-damp hair pulled into a messy bun on the top of her head, she looks refreshed and gorgeous. She gifts me a smile before she lifts on her toes and brushes her lips across mine. It's a taste of the divine, and I want more. I go to pull her in for another, when her stomach ruins the moment by growling loudly. I groan and she laughs. "Apparently, I'm hungry."

We sit down to dinner, and Kenzie moans her delight. I'm glad she's enjoying the meal. Too often she forgets her own needs, only worrying about Issac. I see all she does, and it blows my mind that she handles it all with grace and a smile.

"Josh." Kenzie says my name as she places her hand on my arm.

I look at her and smile.

She smiles back, lighting up the room. Looking

deeper, I see the weariness playing peek-a-boo in her eyes. "I was saying thank you for this." She points to dinner. "But you seemed lost in thought. Is everything okay?"

I force a smile. "Yeah. I was just thinking of how much our lives have changed recently."

She laughs. "Yes, things have definitely changed." She pauses for a moment, then adds. "For the better... right?" I don't miss the hesitation and worry in her voice.

Reaching for her hand, I confidently answer, "Definitely for the better." But then I lower my head and confess, "I just realized how much harder it is on you when I'm on the road."

Her eyes flick to Issac, who is happily vibrating away in his chair. "It is, but we'll make it work." Her confidence is impressive. I can only imagine what it's been like for her. Adjusting to motherhood with a partner who is gone so frequently has to be a struggle. I wish I could do more to help.

"We will," I agree. *What if...?* "Kenz, is there anything I can do to help you while I'm away? We could hire a nanny, a housekeeper, or have ready-made meals delivered."

She smiles at me. "I appreciate the offer, but I want to figure this out on my own. I know once I've got us on a schedule, things will be much easier." Then she let out a sigh.

"Tell me, how tough has it been? What can I do while I'm home for a few days?"

Sitting back in her chair, I notice her plate is empty. Man, she was starving. As I wait for her to answer, I scoop another slice of lasagna onto her plate. Her eyes sparkle. "Thank you." The way she looks at me makes me feel like I'm ten feet tall.

"Honestly, it hasn't been too bad. So far, it's been a guessing game as I try to understand all his different cries. I don't always interpret them correctly and that only leads to more crying."

I put my hand up like I'm in school, preparing to ask a question. "Wait. You're telling me he has distinct cries, and each one means something different?"

The smile on her nodding head says it all. *What have we gotten ourselves into?*

"I thought babies just cried and then you ran through a list of the major things they might need, hoping that one of them soothes them."

She laughs and questions, "Major things?"

Feeling stupid, I lower my head. "Josh. Tell me."

I look up and she offers me a sweet smile. "Kenz, I've never been around babies. I thought they just ate, slept, and pooped. You know, the major things."

"Babe, you're right. Those are the major things with babies, but they have distinct cries for each one. And learning those early on will help you soothe them quicker."

A distinct rumble comes from Issac's direction. "Was that—" is all I can get out before Kenzie laughs.

"Your son is a gassy dude, but I just fed him before you got home, so it could be something else. She smirks at me. Sure enough, the little man's face turns red and scrunches up tight right before a powerful explosive noise comes from him. Instinctively, I reach for him.

"Let's give him a minute to see if he's done, otherwise you might get an unpleasant surprise in the middle of a diaper change."

"My son wouldn't dare," I scoff. She waggles her eyebrows and snickers. "Would he?" I question. She shrugs her shoulders as a grin spreads across her beautiful face.

As if on cue, he let out another ripper, startling me. "How can something so small make such a disturbing noise?"

She laughs. "Just wait until you see what's in the diaper."

I motion to Issac. "You think he's done now? I hate to leave him sitting in that. It sounded messy."

"That's breast milk. Poop is looser. Want me to change him?"

Standing up from my chair, I confidently answer, "I've got this." *At least I hope I do.*

"We got this buddy. Right?" I whisper to Issac before pulling him from his bouncy chair. His butt is warm and squishy, and I wonder what I'm in for. Laying him on the changing table we have set up in our living room, I keep a hand on him while I grab a diaper and wipe. *This oughta do the trick.* "Let's see what we're working with." The smell of what he's done hits me first, and my stomach heaves. Once I peel back his sleeper, I know I'm in serious trouble. *I'm going to need many more wipes.*

"Dude. You are tiny. How the fuck did you make such a big mess?" Kenzie laughs from the other room. I holler to her, "Do I need a hazmat suit for this operation? This outfit's ruined and going straight to the trash. I've never seen such yellow poop. Why is it yellow?" Each comment I make comes out squeakier and squeakier, like I'm a teenage boy going through puberty. Kenzie keeps laughing. *At least someone is getting enjoyment out of this.*

Finally, when I have Issac completely disrobed, I attack the diaper. *Who designed this? I thought they were supposed to contain the poop. Maybe we got a flawed batch?* "Kenzie, remind me to go to the store tomorrow and pick up new diapers. I think this batch is flawed." Loud, unrestrained laughter is all I get from the next room. Carefully, I turn Issac over and see the problem, the poop, if we can call it that, hasn't been contained. It was so powerful it came up and over his diaper. I set him back down and slowly peel back the tabs, revealing the entire mess my son has made. "Shit," I mutter to myself.

A half-hour and a hundred wipes later, I've got it all handled. I dress my son in a fresh diaper and I'm about to put a new sleeper on when I hear another rumble. "Really, dude? You can't possibly have anything else in your system." Looking down at the butt of his diaper, I see it's still clean. I breathe out a sigh of relief when I hear Kenzie behind me.

"How are you doing?"

Ignoring the mess I made, I tuck Issac to my chest and turn around. "We're great. How are you?"

She pats her stomach. "I'm full. Thank you again."

I watch her eyes widen as they take in the changing table behind me. "If you take the little man and put him in his clean sleeper, I'll take care of that," I offer.

"Deal," she says while reaching for our son. He already recognizes his mom. It is a beautiful thing to see.

After I've cleaned up the remnants of the diaper change from hell, I wrap up the leftovers from dinner and clean up the kitchen. I run my bag upstairs and change into a pair of athletic shorts before I hunt out my family. Sitting snuggled on the couch are Kenzie and Issac, and I pause for a moment to take it all in. I couldn't be happier than I am right now. *What if she was your wife?* That isn't a new thought. Ever since we got back together, I've wanted more. I just don't want to push it. I already feel lucky to have her back in my life. I don't want to pressure her into something she isn't ready for. *But maybe she is ready.*

"When are your parents arriving?" I ask as I make my way over to the couch.

Turning her head to me, I see the weariness on her face, but it doesn't take away from the fact that she's the most beautiful woman in the world. "They get here the day after tomorrow and are staying for two weeks."

"And they're okay with our non-traditional Mateo's catered Thanksgiving dinner?" I question. I mean, I want to make a good impression on them. I hope to call them my in-laws soon.

She laughs, and Issac squirms on her chest. "They're actually looking forward to it. I've been raving about Mateo's since you first took me there."

Snuggling in next to them, I set my arm behind Kenzie, and she moves close to me. We both stare at our son with wonder and amazement. "He's so perfect. Thank you, Kenz, for the best gift ever."

Tipping her head to me, I can see unshed tears in her eyes. "I love you, Josh." Placing a tender kiss on her lips, a warmth radiates through my body, relaxing me entirely. *This is the life.*

Chapter 34

Kenzie

My parents are here, and they finally get to meet Josh and Issac. I have obviously introduced them over FaceTime many times, but it's different in person. Josh was here for the first few days, but he had to leave for another road trip. He's due back two days before Thanksgiving, and I couldn't be happier. The weekend following it is a home series, so he'll be here for a longer stretch of time. I've been planning some family activities, but because Issac is still so small, there isn't much to do. My parents watched him while I went to get my hair cut and had a massage. We've also taken field trips to CakeStop to check in with Toby and the rest of my staff. Toby is killing it in his new position as the manager.

Last night my dad mentioned he had a craving for a death by chocolate cupcake, so this morning I texted Toby and asked him to set a few aside for us.

Time gets easily skewed when you have a newborn. Leaving the house before noon is an honest-to-goodness miracle. At a quarter past one, we walk into my shop and the familiar buzz of the coffee machine and chattering customers permeate the air. My heart sings. This is what I imagined when I used to daydream about CakeStop before it was a reality.

"Kenz," Toby shouts from behind the register. Then he stops, whips his head back and forth, and questions in a growl, "Where's my nugget?" His reaction is adorable, and it causes me to smile.

"Chill, Toby. My parents have him. He's in the stroller and they're looking at something outside." Toby returns to smiling.

"Oh, good. I thought I was going to have to sell your cupcakes as punishment for no baby snuggles." I just roll my eyes and give him a hug.

The front door chimes and in comes Issac and his entourage. Toby's met my parents before and he gives them quick hellos before he descends on the baby with flair. "There's my squishy face. Uncle Toby is here. Did you miss me as much as I missed you? Who on earth dressed you today? Yikes. Too many colors and patterns."

Laughing, I answer, "I dressed him. Josh is coming home today and I have him in Steel colors since he doesn't quite fit into child-sized Steel gear."

Reaching into the stroller and unbuckling Issac like he's done it a million times, Toby pulls my grinning baby toward him. He baby talks to him, which is the cutest thing. Even though I don't have any siblings, Toby has filled that void for me. He is the best uncle ever. When Josh was out of town, he came over to hold Issac while I took a much-needed shower. He painted my toenails while I sipped on overpriced smoothies he brought me that were supposed to increase my milk supply. He is the best friend I've ever had.

"Hey, Toby. You're coming over for our non-traditional Thanksgiving dinner, right?" He's quick to answer yes, but he stops himself from saying more and turns away. "Toby?" I press.

He slowly turns back to me. "Yes."

I put my hands on my hips. "What aren't you saying?"

A nervous look appears and disappears in a flash, and I question whether I imagined it.

He grins. "It's nothing, really. I'm just dreaming about all those creamy carbs and having no dishes to wash."

Pursing my lips together, I let my inquisition go. "Since the shop is closed the next day, are you going to stay the night and go shopping with me in the morning?"

Toby looks at Issac, then at me and nods his head. "You, my dear, have yourself a date."

After Toby gets his fill of baby cuddles, we tuck Issac back in his stroller and grab the cupcakes. It'll be lunchtime for everyone when we get home. And a few hours after that, Josh will be home as well.

Later that night, after dinner and Issac's bath time, I'm in the nursery folding some clothes while my parents watch Issac before bed. Looking around the room, I can't help but notice all the special touches Josh put in. At the time, when he decorated the room with the guys, he only knew we were having a baby, not that I was carrying his son. Watching his face light up when he first saw the baby on ultrasound will forever be burned into my memory as one of my favorite days. He held my hand as the 4-D image appeared, squeezing it when he saw the flicker of our baby's heart. His excitement was palpable, making the room buzz with energy.

I don't hear Josh enter the nursery, as I'm busy folding and sorting. "Need any help?" he offers in his deep baritone voice.

"I'm good," I answer, recognizing it's the first time in weeks I've actually felt that way.

Today is Thanksgiving and we're having dinner with my parents and Toby. There isn't much to do other than tidy up. Having my mom and dad here with us has allowed me to keep up with most of my house chores.

As we gather around the table for an early dinner,

we share about what we're thankful for. Toby goes first, saying he's thankful for me making him the manager of the store. My parents, who've spent the entire meal passing Isaac back and forth, admit that they are most thankful for their first grandchild. My mom has tears in her eyes as she adds on her hope that there will be more.

When it's my turn, I look around the table, and my heart is bursting with love and happiness. "I'm so thankful for each of you. Toby, you are the best friend a girl could ever have. Since we met, you've supported and encouraged my dreams." Looking at my parents, my voice shakes. "Mom. Dad. You have always supported and loved me. You helped me dream and encouraged me to go after what I wanted. You are the best parents and grandparents, and I'm blessed to call you mine." My mom sniffles and we share a heart-warming smile. I squeeze Josh's hand. "You are the love of my life. You've given me the best gift I could ever ask for. Issac is so fortunate to call you Daddy, and I am lucky to call you mine." Josh leans over and kisses my cheek. Then he lowers himself to one knee.

"Kenzie, I am so undeserving of you." He grabs my hand and squeezes. Our eyes lock and everything around us disappears. "Over the last three months, you have made my dreams come true. All but one. And today, I'm rectifying that.

"You are an incredible woman, partner, daughter, friend, and mother. I am blessed to have you in my life.

I want to scream from the mountaintops that you're mine, but first I have to ask you one question." I stare at him, waiting. "Babe, will you marry me?" Opening the ring box, he shows me an incredible two-carat princess-cut diamond solitaire.

"That's stunning," I whisper.

He nods. "Yes, it is... And if you agree to marry me, it'll be all yours."

My hand flies up to my mouth. "I didn't answer you?"

Josh shakes his head no.

Then I laugh. "Yes, Josh. My answer is yes. I'll marry you."

He slides the ring on and tugs me into his arms for a passionate kiss. It almost drags me under when a thought strikes me. Pushing back, I ask, "You asked my dad?"

He laughs at me, looks over at my parents, who are all smiles, and answers, "Of course I asked your dad. In fact, both your parents gave me their blessing."

***

Over the next few months, life is busy. Toby is still managing CakeStop like a champ since I'm on maternity leave. The Steel is leading the division and is looking to add another Cup to their resume. When Issac is napping, I'm working with Stephanie on another Steel Your Heart gala. The past few have been a tremendous success in raising a lot of money for Embrace You. Their clients can focus on their breast cancer journey instead of worrying about some basic needs. I'm so grateful to be part of it. This year I'm revealing a handful of new desserts that we don't carry in CakeStop yet. After the gala we'll add them to the menu with a portion of the proceeds going to Embrace You for future clients' needs.

On top of all that, Josh and I are also planning our wedding. It's set to be a quiet affair with just our best friends and, of course, my parents. Considering all the drama that Josh has had with his parents—his father especially—he isn't inviting them, and after a long conversation, I understand. And then, after we tie the knot, we're jetting off to Kauai the following week for our first family vacation. I've never been to that Hawaiian island. I hear it's lush and magical, and I can't wait.

Most of all, I can't wait to be Josh's wife. In my heart, I'm already his, but it'll be nice to make it official. We're already a family. I still can't believe this is my life now. A business owner. A mother. Soon to be a wife. Sometimes I lie awake at night wondering if I'm dreaming. But then I'll feel Josh curl around me, pulling my body into his, and I'll hear those cute little baby snuffles from the monitor by the crib, and I know it's all real. I'm just so incredibly blessed to be living a life I never thought was possible.

Epilogue

Josh

Since joining the Steel, I have been fortunate to have my name added to the Stanley Cup twice. The playoffs are intense. Your feelings during it are a crapshoot. When you're winning, you're on top of the world. When you're knocked out, you feel down in the dumps. Mix in all the anxiety, stress, and excitement, and you never know how someone is going to respond. Advancement isn't guaranteed. You have to earn it through blood, sweat, and tears. Sometimes the team most predicted to lose surprises everyone, showing up determined and ready to battle.

This year, we easily took our side of the bracket. But the finals are going to be tough. The New York Chargers are always tough competitors, but ever since Lucas joined the Steel four years ago, the games between us have lacked in sportsmanship, and it's mostly on their side. Then when we acquired Jersey, their backup goalie, things went from bad to worse. It didn't matter that their former players were happier now. No, many of the players and half the fan base seemed to take their leaving as a personal offense. They hurled rumors and chanted negative slurs every time the Steel was in New York.

When the series begins between the Steel and the Chargers, broadcasters predict the teams will likely split the wins. According to them, either team could take the Cup. Really, it's anyone's guess.

As the captain of the Steel, I'm determined to keep my guys pumped and eager for the win. We worked hard over the past few years to become an unshakeable force in the league. Not only do we have an incredible group of skilled players, but we aren't just teammates, we're best friends. We don't just have each other's backs because we're getting a paycheck.

The teams split the series. On the night of the last game, the locker room is a chaotic mess of emotions. Some guys are anxious, others are edgy, and still others are nervous. We've been here before, the Cup within reach. *I need to pump these guys up.*

I whistle, calling attention to myself. "Guys, listen up. It's time to focus. Tonight is our chance to win the Cup. We need to go out there and do what we do. There shouldn't be any doubt about who is coming out victorious tonight, but there is. Now, we're going to show up, play hard, and win this thing." The guys grumble around me. "Right?" I bellow when I get a wishy-washy response. Their resounding yes gives the room just what we all need.

When I step on the ice, the feel of my skates on the surface is smooth and crisp. As I move around the rink, the breeze against my skin rejuvenates me, and my excitement for the game grows to impressive levels. *Let's do this.*

Coach Tristan calls us in to remind us of what he expects. He talks about what's on the line and that he knows what we're capable of. "Those guys are going to give you hell. They're going to do whatever they need to to get the W. They want the Cup too. Especially if it means beating us."

Rocco leans in. "Guys, we're doing this. We are superior on every level. Let's show everyone that." We exchange fist bumps as the starting line skates to their spots.

The game goes back and forth, each team bringing their A-game. The Chargers are less chippy than normal, but the attitude they carry hangs over the arena like a dark cloud waiting to unleash a storm. Between the second and third periods, with the teams tied at one, we sit quietly in our locker room, reflecting when Coach comes in with a smile on his face. *What the hell?* I look around and see that all my teammates wear the same confused look as me.

"Guys. First off, you should be proud of yourselves. You have played some damn good hockey tonight. For this last period, the only thing I'm asking of you is that you push through, giving one hundred and ten percent. You are already champions. Let's go get the Cup." The entire team breaks out in cheers.

With a minute and twenty seconds left, Lucas sends Ace a stretch pass, and he secures a breakaway against the goalie. Ace dekes him, sending a shot high on the goalie's stick side, securing the winning goal. Our team can barely contain their excitement for the rest of the game. And as soon as the clock runs out, the bench empties onto the ice amidst hoots and hollers from the crowd. Because we're in Chicago, I look up to the family box, hoping to see Kenzie, and it's a jumble of chaos.

<hr>

A month later, on a Sunday afternoon, while CakeStop was closed, Kenzie and I exchange our vows. It's only right seeing that her shop brought us together and where we fell in love.

As a favor to me, Coach Tristan took the online course to become ordained so he could perform the ceremony. Kenzie has both Toby and Stephanie as her attendants, while I have Rocco and Ace. Even though they're some of my younger teammates, and also the jokers of the team, our friendship had been instant. They're like the little brothers I never had.

Kenzie wanted everything simple, so she wears a

plain white dress that flows around her new, luscious curves from motherhood. My mouth waters when I see her, and my mind escapes to unspoken places where I dream of all I want to do to her.

Toby, the man of honor, wears a plum-colored suit that matches the matron of honor, Stephanie. Her dress incorporates all the colors we're wearing. It's similar to Kenzie's, but it's black on top and the skirt is covered in various shades of purple and gray flowers. It's a silent nod to her, being that she's the reason Kenzie and I are together. Rocco, Ace, and I are sporting gray suits with lilac-colored ties. Coach matches us in the tie department but opted to wear black so he'd match his wife. Issac steals the show wearing an all-gray knit outfit.

Two of my Steel teammates, Lucas and Mika, are also in attendance. Their wives befriended Kenzie early in our relationship and stood by her when I'd been an asshole about the baby. They forgave me, and so they're also here with their kids.

We have a quick ceremony and celebrate with a cake that Kenzie made and decorated herself. It's a vanilla cake with white buttercream frosting. And for me, she made death by chocolate cupcakes, although she did a different frosting. She made white chocolate buttercream and added a touch of blackberry so the colors would complement. Each one looks like a perfect rose. They're almost too perfect to eat. But I'll make a sacrifice and have one... or maybe two.

When the vow portion of the ceremony arrives, we opt to stick to simple.

Nervous, I repeat after Coach while Kenzie holds my hands and rubs circles on my skin.

"I, Josh, take you, Kenzie, to be my wedded spouse, and to live together in marriage."

I let out a breath before I continue. "I promise to love you, comfort you, honor and keep you for better or worse, for richer or poorer, in sickness and health, and forsaking all others, be faithful only to you, so long as we both shall live."

Now for her turn. She smiles at me and squeezes my hand in hers. In a soft voice, she speaks her vows to me. Her eyes twinkling the entire time.

Those words, those promises. They mean the world to me. Coming from a family where your parents are still married but probably shouldn't be, you wonder when they started slacking on the promises they'd made to each other.

As I swear my love and faithfulness to this woman in front of my best friends and God, I feel bad for my parents. They'd married young and then started a family shortly thereafter. It hadn't been an arranged marriage, but the higher-ups in their parents' social circles had encouraged their coupling. Honestly, I'm not even sure they really knew each other before they were pushed together. But if that was the case, why had they stayed together all these years? I've been gone for years and they remain unhappily married. Kenzie and I will never be like them. We have friendship and love, and our future together is so bright.

The following week, we jet off to Kauai.

Thank you for reading Slashed By You, the fifth book in the Chicago Steel series. If you'd like another peek into the Chicago Steel world, visit my website at https://907publishing.wixsite.com/my-site and sign up for my newsletter. While there, don't forget to snag the extended epilogue for Slashed By You and any extras for the rest of the series. Each book in the series is available on Kindle Unlimited. Happy reading.

Keep reading to check out the World of Chicago Steel.

World of Chicago Steel

Have you read Hooked By You, the first book of the Chicago Steel Series with Lucas and Samantha? If not, you can click on the link to start reading. The entire series is available with your Kindle Unlimited subscription. Here's a small taste of each to whet your palate.

Hooked By You–Chicago Steel Series Book One

Lucas

She's a goddess in heels. Absolute perfection. Well, almost. Samantha Fox is the heiress of Fox Sporting, my new management team. As one of the best wings in the NHL, I have never shied away from a challenge, and she is definitely a challenge. But if her company representing me doesn't stop me from wanting her, the fact she's engaged should, right? But the noticeably absent sparkle from her left ring finger makes me question. I vow to myself that I'll find out what that's all about. And if she's single, I plan to make her mine. Or at least, mine for the night. I just need one taste of the divine.

Samantha

Off-limits. That's what he is. Lucas Bouchard is the prestigious new client acquired by my family's company. From what I know, not only is he an amazing hockey player, he's a humble and generous philanthropist too. Also, he's a walking aphrodisiac. It doesn't matter that I've just broken off my engagement to a cheating, using loser. Every time our eyes lock, I find myself captivated. But he's not for me. No matter how many times I remind myself of this, though, it doesn't compute. Plain and simple, I want him. And keeping my distance might prove impossible.

Checked By You–Chicago Steel Series Book Two

Mika

She's the uber-sexy, single mother living next door. Everyone tells me to keep my distance. But there's something about her. Specifically, her eyes. They speak to me. Drawing me in like a siren. I want to know her, but she's more guarded than Buckingham Palace. However, after one afternoon in her presence, I find myself addicted and wanting more. Willing to do whatever I have to just to make it past her defenses.

Shiloh

My next-door neighbor is an insanely hot, single professional hockey player. As if that isn't bad enough, he's a nice guy too. After spending an afternoon where he showed my son how to skate and took us out to ice cream, I want to let him in. My past cautions me to put on the brakes, but I find myself going full steam ahead, ignoring all the red flags waving at me.

Clipped By You–Chicago Steel Series Book Three

Monica

She's his. Or she has been since her freshman year of college. According to Monica Fields, no man will ever hold a candle to Christian Fox. Too bad he's completely unaware. Or is he?

Christian

Since meeting her, a sweet dairy farm girl has captivated Christian entirely. But he's a guy. And he's the one who isn't quite ready to be done sowing his wild oats. Will he ever be? In this game called love, sometimes chasing after a woman is just the wake-up call you need. But what if chasing her to her family's farm and following her through a field scattered with cow patties in limited-edition white Nike Air Force 1s is the only way to catch her? And, when you finally do catch her, will she want you? Forever?

Speared By You-Chicago Steel Series Book Four

Tristan

Since he was little, Tristan's dream has been to play in the NHL. Then he falls in love with his soul mate in high school. A few years after being drafted, an injury cuts his professional career short. Devastated, he questions what is next for him. Instead of seeking solace from the woman who's remained faithfully by his side, he pushes her away.

Stephanie

Since high school, Stephanie's known she is going to do two things: marry Tristan Murphy and get a degree in business. Her plan is to work for a non-profit that focuses on breast cancer. Several years later, though, she finds herself recently divorced and in a new city with a new job. And she's learned a couple of major life lessons. 1. Life can be tricky. 2. We don't always get what we want.

What happens when their paths cross again?

Acknowledgments

It seems like sometimes words cannot do justice for what I'm feeling. No matter the occasion, I just don't feel that the emotions coursing through me can be accurately represented by a handful of letters. My appreciation is so much greater than just thanks. So, here's my humble attempt to thank those who've helped me along this path to becoming an author.

To Darren - From day one, when I came to you and told you I wanted to write a book, you offered me your unwavering support. You laughed with me, cheered with me, and reminded me of what truly matters. I am so thankful for you. Thank you for being my hockey hottie. I love you.

To my boys - Even though I won't let you read my books yet, I appreciate your interest, enthusiasm, and encouragement. Zach, from your TikTok suggestions to Kadin's ability to memorize all my characters and story-lines, you two are the most amazing cheerleaders. I'm so blessed to call you mine.

To Karen - You are simply the best. You aren't afraid to tell me like it is and let me know what to expect. You offer wisdom, encouragement, and best of all, laughter. No matter how busy you are, you make yourself available, no matter the request. Thank you for being you! You are a true gem.

To Shauna - Thank you for sticking with me. I know it was rough in the beginning, and hopefully it is getting better with each new book. I'll never be perfect at this writing thing and I appreciate your keen eye keeping me in check. Thank you for your listening ear, encouragement, and helpful suggestions. You are outstanding, and I am so grateful to have found you.

To Nicole - I am definitely not the most skilled author you work with, but you always offer one hundred percent of yourself to me and the story I'm trying to weave. You radiate encouragement and help me strive for better. I count it a blessing that our paths crossed.

To my friends, family, and readers - Thank you for the continued encouragement and support. Without it, this entire journey would be so different. I am so thankful that you've invested your valuable time in me and this series. From the deepest part of my heart, thank you so much.

Also by Jessica Buss
Chicago Steel Series

Chicago Steel Series

Hooked By You (Lucas & Samantha)

Checked By You (Mika & Shiloh)

Clipped By You (Christian & Monica)

Speared By You (Tristan & Stephanie)

Slashed By You (Josh & Kenzie)

Coming Soon

Delayed By You

Tripped By You

Blocked By You

Chicago Steel Series Novella

Happy Ho, Ho, Holidays (Trey & Nicole)

About the Author

Jessica Buss was born and raised in Anchorage, Alaska. She is married to her high school sweetheart and has two sons. Although she has both her bachelor's and master's degrees in Psychology, she stepped away from that field to be a stay-at-home mom. Now that her kids are growing up and she's getting more time to herself, she's giving this writing thing a chance.

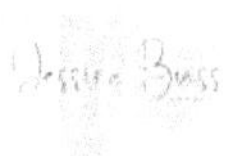

907publishing.wixsite.com/my-site